REPRISAL

PROJECT FALLEN ANGEL
BOOK 1

ANNA NOEL

"YOU SHOULD HAVE LET THE DEAD STAY DEAD"

REPRISAL
PROJECT FALLEN ANGEL

BOOK ONE

ANNA NOEL

Project Fallen Angel: Reprisal

For more information about the author and her books, visit her website —https://annanoelbooks.com/

Book design: Anna Noel

Formatter: Anna Noel

Editor: Marigold Edits//Alaina Morris

Proofreader: Amber Letto

Second edition August 3rd, 2023

www.annanoelbooks.com

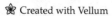 Created with Vellum

AUTHOR'S NOTE

I grew up with spy movies like Jason Bourne, Mission Impossible, and 007. I also grew up fascinated with the world of espionage. The real world.

That being said, I have the utmost respect for the real agents, and do want to acknowledge in my book that spy entertainment is nothing like the real world of espionage. Especially my book.

Reprisal is a work of fiction. Although there are historical elements, some have been altered to fit the story. These are not real events.

This book is set in a dark world with dark themes. Although the romance is lighter than most dark romances, subjects handled can be incredibly dark and graphic. This is strictly a work of fiction.

Reprisal may contain triggers for some. If you are not worried about this, you can absolutely go in blind. Please remember that dark romance is a work of fiction and that no actions or events are real.

If you do not have triggers, please feel free to skip this. If you do, please read below.

TRIGGER WARNINGS include: graphic violence, panic

attacks, suicide and suicidal ideation, death of a parent on and off page, death of a sibling mentioned, torture on and off page, child abuse mentioned, sexual as*ault mentioned, breath play, and light BDSM.

THINGS TO KNOW ABOUT REPRISAL

- Enemies to lovers
- Government Secrets
- Espionage
- Found family
- Hero MMC
- Morally gray FMC
- Stuck together
- Praise
- Tension/Steam

Reprisal belongs to the Project Fallen Angel series but can be read as a standalone.

PLAYLIST

"Gasoline" by Halsey
"Blood//Water" by grandson
"Die in This Town" by The Seige
"Until I Come Home" by Two Feet, grandson
"KILL YOUR CONSCIENCE" by Shinedown
"Ghost Town" by Layto, Neoni
"Just Pretend" by Bad Omens
"COPYCAT" by Billie Eilish
'Aint No Rest for the Wicked" by Cage the Elephant
"Bury Me Face Down" by grandson
"Death Valley" by Fall Out Boy
"Nowhere Generation" by Rise Against
"Dead Don't Die" by Shinedown
'THE DEATH OF PEACE OF MIND" by Bad Omens
"Born for This" by The Score
"Oh My Dear Lord" by The Unlikely Candidates
"Trouble" by Adam Jensen

For Alex, who doesn't even know how many times he's saved me.

I love you to the moon and to Saturn.

"What I'm not sure about, is if our lives have been so different from the lives of the people we save. We are all complete. Maybe none of us really understand what we've lived through, or feel we've had enough time."

Kazuo Ishiguro

ONE

DAMON

The woman in front of me was ruled dead in a triple homicide six years ago.

I watch her from under my cap through the haze of cigarette smoke in the air as she flips her long chocolate-brown hair over her shoulder. Batting her eyes at the biker before her, she places a delicate hand on his chest, shooting him a radiant smile. There's never been a single thing those beautiful brown eyes couldn't get her.

Ellie Huxley was twenty years old at the time of her death, home for the holidays, taken too young by her angry father, pushed over the edge by alcohol and a call from his secretary letting him know that the photos would hit the press the next day.

And yet here she is, six years later, toying with some biker at a dive bar in downtown Seattle, 2,860 miles from her past.

I know it's her.

I've been tracking her for the last couple of weeks.

Ellie Huxley was the daughter of Bernard Huxley, Senator

of Virginia for four years before the *accident* that left his wife, daughter, and son dead in their home on Thanksgiving morning.

Having gotten a full ride to Harvard University, Ellie was a brilliant, driven young woman with a promising future in politics. Wanting to improve the world, she was known for being generous with her time and allowance. In fact, no one has ever said a negative thing about her, despite her father's politics and morals. Not before her death, not after. But here she is, in front of me, alive and breathing.

For a shitty dive bar, Fredrick's is full to the brim with hippies and bikers alike, the smell of weed, cigarettes, and gasoline saturating the air. I wonder how many other bars around here are the exact same.

The large, tattooed man next to her beams, likely sure he's getting lucky tonight, and snakes his arm around her waist, his fingers breaching the bottom of her black leather jacket. He pulls her in and whispers something in her ear.

Ellie smiles coyly, pushing away from him just a touch.

My grip on my phone tightens as I snap a photo, hoping tonight is my night.

Ellie has evaded me for the last two weeks, ever since I caught wind that she's somehow alive, living in Seattle.

Unfortunately, I don't think I'm the first person who has caught wind of this.

Breathing deeply, I take a long sip of beer and attempt to look like I belong. I traveled a long way to get here and don't want to spook her.

I can see her through the large mass of people drunkenly walking about from the corner of my eye. She rakes a finger over the man's shoulder, fake laughing at his last poorly executed joke before looking up, her eyes meeting mine.

I look in the other direction quickly, lowering my cap in a feeble attempt to play it off.

The Ellie I knew was someone who wouldn't be caught

dead here. But that was a long time ago, before I thought she was dead for six years.

I sigh, thinking about my next move as I wait for the moment to pass. I'm not sure where to go from here. I'm not even sure what I'll say when I get to speak with her. I can tell this isn't the girl I knew all those years ago. What have I stumbled into?

You would think that someone who graduated from the FBI Academy would be able to come up with a better game plan. In almost any other situation, I would be able to. But this isn't any other situation. Not even close.

A hand slaps the table in front of me, snapping me out of my thoughts.

My head snaps up, only to be met by the most gorgeous, familiar brown eyes.

"Hi." She smiles at me, tilting her shoulder. Her coquettish verve along with my anxiety over being caught leaving me speechless.

"Hey," I reply, not knowing what else I can do.

"I haven't seen you around here." Something about the way she's looking at me, studying my every breath, makes my skin crawl. She's not here to flirt with me. She's here to gather information.

I nod. "I was traveling through and found that I really like this place. Wanted to stay here for a while." I don't take my eyes off her, hopeful she'll go with it.

She considers my words for a moment before pursing her lips. "What do you do for work?" she asks, her head tilting as her wavy hair falls over her shoulder.

"I never said I was traveling through for work," I smirk.

Her eyes narrow just slightly. "I figured it was the only reason anyone would come through here and stay." She shrugs.

We look at each other for several moments, sizing each other up. If I stand, I'll be about a foot taller than her. She's

3

not a large woman by any means, but something about her demeanor makes me think she'd surprise me if there were a fight.

I decide that now is my time. I have to take whatever opportunities are given to me, right?

"I'm actually here to find someone."

She looks me over curiously again, tapping her fingers on the table. "And who would that be?"

"Ellie Huxley."

There's silence as she processes. She keeps her eyes locked on mine, and for just a second, I think I may be wrong. Her response wouldn't be out of the ordinary to almost anyone else, but I see the ever so slight widening of her eyes, her shoulders setting back just so. She knows the name.

"I'm not sure who that is," she tells me, searching my face.

"Ellie…" I say carefully, unsure how she'll respond to me calling her out.

Her chest heaves slightly in her green t-shirt. Her reactions are so slight that anyone who isn't trained to watch for them would miss them.

"I told you I'm not sure who that is, but I'm sure you'll find her." She taps the table gently before turning away.

"Are you sure?" I ask cautiously, catching her wrist, the leather of her jacket cool to the touch.

She looks down to where my hand touches her as if burnt. I'm becoming more and more unsure of my information. She looks like her. Those eyes are far too familiar. Deep in my bones, I know it's her.

The last time I saw those eyes, I was shutting them, unable to look at the cadaverous stare any longer as she lay lifeless at my feet, right before being taken by an EMT in a desperate attempt to save her short life—a last-ditch effort to bring her back.

We were told it didn't work.

That was the very last time I saw her.

4

She looks around the bar, her hair blowing as the door barrels open, a couple of drunk bikers walking in, the smell of cigarette smoke more potent in their wake. They immediately yell, greeting their friends and calling out their beer order to the bartender.

"Who are you?" Ellie asks, her voice just above a whisper. I can see it in her eyes that she's trying to place me, and I try not to feel insulted. Maybe she meant way more to me than I did to her. I drop her wrist, and she immediately cradles it.

"My name is Damon," I tell her, raising my glass to my lips. I don't understand what's happening, but it's been six years. I'm here to save her, to warn her at the very least, and I need to remember that no matter how she's here today, she went through a trauma I've never known. After what happened to her, I don't want to spook her more than I must.

"Why are you here, Damon?" She meets my eyes again, and I can tell she's just as confused as I am. *What did I stumble into*, I wonder once more.

"You're asking a lot of questions," I smirk as I take a slow sip. A flash of fury flashes through her gorgeous eyes, which startles me.

"I can tell you don't belong here." She glances over me again, and I become even more unsettled, a cold settling into my bones.

For someone so pretty, her voice shoots fear through me, and I can't help but feel like someone dumped a bucket of ice water down my body. Something is wrong, and I don't know what.

"I'm here for you," I tell her simply, putting the glass back on the table with a thump, feigning confidence.

Her breathing speeds up as she takes another inconspicuous look around, ensuring no one is paying attention to our conversation. Or that I'm alone.

When she says nothing, I add, "I have things I have to tell you."

Looking down at her boots, her nose scrunches up. Her eyes are narrowed and angry when she meets my gaze again, her hands tightening into fists at her side. "Who sent you?" she asks finally, her voice firm.

"No one sent me," I assure her. "Look, Ellie; I'm not sure—"

Something changes then. A look of realization. Like she knows I don't belong here, she knows that something is going on that she can't control, and she doesn't trust me in the slightest. She doesn't care what I have to say.

The look on her face is something I've seen many times in my line of work. Survival.

The air shifts, and she smirks, her fingers wrapping around my glass before placing it to her lips. "I told you, stranger," she says, her voice now soft and flirty. "I don't know who that is. Maybe she'll be here another night."

She looks me up and down, winks, and walks off, leaving me more confused than ever.

I return to the small motel I've been staying at, strip off my flannel, toss my cap onto the chair beside the bed, and pull the gas station burrito out of the small refrigerator beside the TV. It hums softly in the silence. Not bothering to microwave it, I sit on the edge of the bed and take a bite before falling backward, sprawled out on the dusty comforter, trying my best to ignore the faint smell of ammonia wafting through the air.

I'm not someone who makes impulsive decisions. I swear, I'm not. But I knew I had to do something the second I saw her face cross my desk. Ellie caught the attention of someone powerful, and I need to help her.

Some may call it a hero complex. I'm not sure. Maybe it is. I just know I couldn't save her when she needed me the most, and I won't let that happen again.

Finding out that she was alive was a shock, that's for sure. But that doesn't matter to me. The why seems inconsequential to me for now. Eventually, I do want to know. But for now, I want nothing more than to save her.

The problem is, I don't even know from what. But something larger is happening, and it will happen soon. I can feel it.

I just need to figure out how I'm going to get through to her.

TWO

AMELIA

He called me Ellie.

I've heard that name before. I know that name. It's the only thing I know from my past.

It was my name before I was taken in.

I pull up to our large house, tucked into the trees outside the city. Opening the garage, I park my Ford Bronco in one of the many open spots, pleasantly surprised to see that both Lu and Amare are home.

I jump out, my keys jingling in my hand as I head for the door.

"Where have you been?" Luisa asks the second I step inside.

The two of them sit at the kitchen counter, the lights dimmed. Chinese containers line the surface in front of them, and I can't help but wonder why they order so much goddamn food every time.

"Fredrick's," I answer simply with a shrug. "Where's Coop?"

Luisa scrunches her nose, stabbing a piece of chicken with her fork. "I don't get why you like that place. And I think he's sleeping."

"Unless you're trying to find a 50-year-old biker to bang, I'm not sure why you go there, either," Amare chirps, and Luisa lets out a chuckle.

"You guys know I'm not," I sigh, settling into a stool at the island with them. "I just like getting out, and the people there are nice."

Amare observes me, reading me like a book. "So, what happened tonight that's made you upset?"

I roll my eyes. Ever since we got here, Amare has been like a protective big brother to the two of us. He cares too much. We were told not to form close relationships, but we all did anyway. We all care for each other like family. It's hard not to when you live with the same people for years, doing almost everything with them. Our job is to act. To pretend. Our lives depend on it. It's nice to have a few people to drop the mask around. People who make us feel almost normal.

"Someone I didn't recognize was there," I tell him with a shrug. "Well, I've seen him there a couple of times in the last couple of days. Always in the corner, his cap tipped down. I've been watching him warily. He just sits there with a beer every night and looks at me. But he does it the way someone trained would. I don't know; something about it just didn't feel right. I went up to him tonight, finally, and I feel like we were reading each other way too well."

Luisa lays her fork down, taking a sip of water. "I mean, there's agents everywhere, you know that."

"I know, but this man knew me, guys. As in, he knew my old name. He called me Ellie."

Amare smacks his beer on the table, and I flinch. "I feel like that's what you should have started with." His eyes roll back, used to my antics but annoyed all the same.

"I know; I was just giving some backstory," I smirk. "But

anyways, yeah. He called me Ellie and said that he had things that he needed to tell me."

"And you didn't bring him back here?" Lu asks.

"Why would I do that."

They look at me as if I said something so vapid, they can't possibly process it.

"Amelia, if he knows something about your past, then that means something has gone wrong. He's not supposed to be here. We need to find out why."

I wave my hand dismissively. "I don't think he's much of a threat. If we need to, I can bring him in. I think he'd come willingly."

"How do you know that?"

"It's just a feeling." I shrug, filling my plate with food. "What should I do?" I ask them, slumping back in the seat as I take a bite of Singapore Mei Fun. I look at Amare, taking in the look of disappointment in his dark eyes. A lump settles in the bottom of my stomach. I've seen that look before, and I don't like it.

"There shouldn't be anyone coming up to you like that," he says as if I don't know that.

"The name is dead, right? I would assume no one should be. I don't know what to do in this situation. I haven't had this issue before."

"None of us have," Luisa adds.

And it's true. I don't know much about who I was before I died, but I do know that I have to dye my hair every month to keep it the deep brown it is now, or my blonde roots will show.

I also know that I live far away from my old life. On paper, we all died years ago. None of us have a family. Well, none that would come looking for us, that is. We're ghosts, the perfect people to pull off top Secret missions without risking real assets. If one of us dies, it's not a big deal. No one will care. No one will come looking for answers.

We don't form relationships. We have people we speak to, and we do go out and socialize periodically, but no one comes to our house, and no one gets close to us.

Luisa is the only one who remembers her life before she died, and she wishes every single day that she didn't. As curious as I am, I believe her when she says that making us forget was a kindness granted to us.

"You should have killed him once he left," Luisa says, pushing away from the counter.

"I could have killed him then, but we wouldn't know why he knew my old name and why he's here," I tell her.

"But if he leaves, you won't know either," Amare retorts, leaning against the surface. "You have no idea if he's sticking around. I just don't know why you didn't bring him back."

I drop my fork, tossing my hands in the air in exasperation. "I don't know, okay? I panicked. I won't lie. You should have seen the guy. I don't know who he works for, but he was good."

My friends look at each other, and I can tell that they understand in a way. They may not have been in this exact situation before, but they get it. We may have undergone years of training, and we may be expected to separate ourselves from our feelings, but we're still living, breathing humans, no matter how the Agency looks at us.

"I think we should have a chat with him," Amare states finally, his large arms crossed over his broad chest, his umber skin shining under the light. When he sees my face, he adds, "It's just a chat. I'm not going to kill him, but if we bring him in, you have to realize that there's a strong possibility he'll die," he warns me, a thick brow quirked.

I nod, understanding. I have no loyalty to this man, so it doesn't matter. But I can't help my brain from stirring, trying to remember something it can't. I feel like it should matter.

"Yeah, that's fine," I wave him off, pulling my plate back to me.

"Do you think it's a bang and burn?" Luisa asks Amare.

It was, unfortunately, something we've asked each other many times. Since we're under non-official cover, we don't technically work for the Agency. There's nothing protecting us, and although there's only been one compound that the Agency has ever taken out, it's always a possibility. Something to fear. I think it's how they keep us in line.

Anytime anything suspicious has happened, we hold our breath until it's over. Until we're safe and we know we're not burned.

There's been more than a few times I've wished for it.

"I'm not going to say it's not, but I don't see why the Agency would blow up its own secret operation right now. We'd know if something went wrong," Amare tells her, raking his fingers through his thick, black hair. "If someone is onto them, though, it may do better for them just to burn the whole thing. If the project is found out—" he pauses, shivering, "I can't imagine the events that would follow."

All of us know that we're expendable. We can be taken out at any point and wouldn't be missed. That's the entire reason we were chosen and saved. We're throwaways. Every single one of us.

"I don't think there's any way we could be traced back to them," Luisa assures him. "I really don't think this is some kind of burner. This must be something else." She chews on her chopstick for a moment, staring into space. "I'll reach out to the handler," she announces finally, walking over to the sink to rinse her glass.

"Ehh, I'm not sure that's a good idea either," Amare says.

"Why not?" I ask, arching a brow.

"Because we don't know anything about this man; they could take him out themselves. Our lives don't matter in the grand scheme of things, but the Agency will do anything to keep this project from getting out. We know this. If that means us dying, that's what it means. If that man comes here and somehow gets out, that could mean this entire project crumbles. If we're nervous about a bang and burn, that's how you get a bang and burn."

I weigh his words in my mind. Of course, that makes sense, but if he's talking about the guy dying here, I'm not sure there's really that much of a worry. "Then why would we even bring him in?"

"If he says he has something to tell you and knows your old name, he knows who you are. He was able to pick you out in a crowded bar. He knows you, and what if others do, too?"

He's right.

We've come to realize that although the Agency saved us, they're not heroes. We're a means to an end for them—a way to ensure they don't lose their valuable assets. We mean less to them than pawns, yet we also mean everything.

No matter what we do, we're going to be doing something wrong. They want us locked up here, giving us more money than we know what to do with so we're happy to die for them.

But we've had this discussion more often than I can count. If something happened and we needed information, would we go against them?

The forest around us has plenty of places to bury bodies. They wouldn't have to know anything had happened at all. And what would they do, anyways?

They could kill us, that's true.

As if reading my mind, Luisa clears her throat. "Besides, when have we been known to follow the rules?" she adds with a smirk.

My lips turn up in a grin, and I can't help but chuckle. We're professional rule breakers. Our very existence breaks just about any law in the United States. What we do? Against every code in existence.

We shouldn't be here. But we are. Because we were given a second chance at life.

We're ghosts.

Fallen Angels.

Closing my book, I stand up, stretching my arms above my head and bending over.

Cooper lifts his head, letting out a lazy yawn. "I know, boy; we're going to bed in a minute," I tell him, scratching his furry head.

We live a lonely existence, and although we aren't technically supposed to have pets, I adopted Cooper from a local humane society three years ago. Dalmatians are constantly adopted by people who don't know about their quirks or think they're cool because of movies, and they frequently end up needing new homes, many times just to be adopted by terrible owners once more. That being said, at the time, I had needed him more than he needed me.

If there is one being on earth that I care about, it's Coop.

Grabbing pajamas from my closet, I blow out the lavender candle on my dresser and take a good look at myself in the mirror.

My usually wavy, long dark brown hair is a rat's nest. I run my fingers through the strands in an attempt to tame it, with no such luck. My large brown eyes have dark bags under them, making me feel human. My pouty lips are cracked, and the small cut I got on my nose on last week's job is finally growing lighter and lighter.

I don't mind looking like this. Like I'm not a robot, conditioned to look perfect and feel nothing. Fatigue is one of the few emotions you can wear physically, and it makes me feel so alive.

But that's why we don't remember. If we thought we had

something to live for, something tethering us here, we wouldn't be so willing to die if we needed to. We wouldn't be as eager to put our lives on the line so others can go home to their families every day.

"I need to refill my water bottle, Coop, but I'll be right back, and then we can go to bed," I assure him as if he understands as his big brown eyes stare into my soul, willing me to finally sleep. He snorts. "I swear!"

Heading into the hallway, I close my door so he can't leave. Occasionally, he'll decide he wants to go outside and play in the woods in the middle of the night, and it's nearly impossible to get him back into bed.

I step toward the kitchen, but a jolt of electricity down my spine stops me mid-step, a quiet creek following.

I take another step. Nope, it's not the floorboards.

Another creek.

Bristling at the noise, I turn around, attempting to figure out which direction it's coming from.

"Lu?" I whisper, hoping I'll hear her voice and not have to worry about anything else. I listen for a moment, and my heart speeds up when she doesn't answer.

Everything is quiet.

Thump.

Something hits the ground in the kitchen.

I take another step, hyper-aware of every particle in the air around me.

This house is relatively new. Well, it was new when I got here five years ago. I still remember the first time it came into view as I was dropped off for the first time. Sitting on top of a hill, the beautiful house sits deep in the woods toward the base of Mount Si. Tucked away from the busyness of Seattle but close enough that we can get there in under an hour.

A beautiful house, far too lavish for any of us.

The three of us have lived here since the beginning. The

first of the Seattle Fallen Angels, we were assigned here when the need arose.

Creeeek.

My hair stands on the back of my neck, my body stiffening. Something isn't right. Someone's here—someone who doesn't belong.

I spin on my heel, plastering myself against the wall. I stand there, toes pressed against the hardwood floor, listening intently for anything unusual.

But it's quiet.

I close my eyes, ready to act at a moment's notice.

Finally, another creek sounds from right around the corner, much too close for comfort.

Quick on my feet, I silently tiptoe to the door closest to me, wedging myself into the doorframe, attempting to make myself as invisible as possible. I get up on my tiptoes, my heels against the door so my toes don't peek out. I settle there just in time for someone to turn the corner, a small light shining down the hall.

My breath catches in my throat as my hand turns the knob, pushing the door open as slowly and silently as possible. Once it's open just enough to slip in, I silently fall back on my heels, ducking inside just in time for the light to pass.

I'm not foolish enough to attempt to close the door while whoever is here walks by. I know they've already seen it open. I just hope they didn't see me slip inside of it.

Holding my breath, I watch a large figure pass, an MK23 poised in his hand.

There is absolutely no reason anyone should be in the house. The intruder likely wants one of us dead. The only problem I can think of is if there are more. But if more of them are in the house, I'd have heard more noise. I don't think they would have sent only one of them in here alone, knowing what we are and what we can do.

The man was sent here alone.

I smirk. Whoever sent him has no idea who lives here and what we are. We can rule the bang and burn out.

I slip out of the room silently, gliding over the floor without a sound. We've trained for this.

Reaching another door behind the man, I whip it open, darting inside and slamming it shut. Plastering myself against the cold, smooth surface, I hear the man stop and see the light flicker under the door. The cold knob twists beneath my palm, and I let him open the door just a crack.

Squeezing my eyes shut, I count to three, letting my feet glide across the smooth, cool floor as he slowly pushes the door open. I hold my breath, waiting.

When his head is right between the door and the frame, I throw my full weight against it, slamming his head between them. He calls out but goes down like a sack of potatoes.

"What the—" he starts, but I grab his gun, the light pack attached shining in his dark eyes.

"Who are you?" I ask him, my knees pinning his arms.

The man looks up at me, fear in his eyes as he registers the shock of what just hit him.

"Who. Are. You?" I grit through my teeth, shoving the gun into his head harder.

He chokes, attempting to speak, so I pull back just a little. "I was sent here by my boss on orders from someone. I don't know who, I swear," he promises me, his eyes wide with trepidation.

He wasn't prepared for what was awaiting him. He definitely didn't know what we are.

For such a large man, he crumbled so easily.

"Why?" I ask.

"I don't know." He shakes his head. "I just do as I'm told."

For a second, I consider showing him mercy. Consider chaining him up in the basement, tormenting him until he spills everything he knows. But his resistance and words of denial make me think he'll never tell me. He's simply waiting until I let up to kill me.

"Were you sent to kill us?" I ask him, letting up the slightest bit.

The man is silent for a moment, his brown eyes meeting my own, his Adam's apple bobbing in a rough swallow as he pushes up in struggle.

"I was sent here to kill you," he informs me.

I take a second to think, and the man takes it as his opportunity to force me backward, throwing me against the wall. Gripping the gun, the man tears it away from me, pinning me there at the neck, the suppressor pressed into my temple.

"You know you stepped into a wolf's den, right?" I ask him, leering. I almost feel bad.

"All I know is what I was told to do, which is kill you," he grits, spit hitting my face.

I take a second to size him up better. I don't have the advantage I did moments ago.

The second his finger touches the trigger, I shove into him, knocking him back. The gun goes off, a bullet shooting through the wall. Whipping my leg around, I hit the firearm from his hand before punching him in the head, sending him to the ground.

The man gets up with a grunt, cursing as he lunges for the gun—but I'm faster.

Jumping to the ground, I grip the gun in my hands, whipping it around and shooting the man five times. He drops on top of me, knocking the wind from my lungs. I can feel his blood flowing over the thin fabric of my pajamas, and I shove him off me with a cough.

A moment later, Luisa runs from her room, and Amare barrels down the steps at the end of the hall, the small light from the gun highlighting his muscular, dark skin.

"What the *fuck* Amelia?" Amare asks, looking at the man next to me.

I stand up slowly, watching him the whole time to confirm he's dead.

I don't answer them. Instead, I kneel beside the man, searching his body for anything to help us understand why he wanted me dead.

Sliding my hand into a breast pocket, I take out a flip phone and open it. Staring back at me is a photo of myself, just blonde.

But it's me.

Ellie Huxley. It reads beneath it. *Bounty: $600,000.00.*

"Someone knows I'm here," I tell them finally. I try to get into the phone, but the rest of it is secured behind a code. I don't mess with it, understanding that it may be wiped. Instead, I pocket it.

"What do you mean someone knows you're here?" Lu asks, perplexed.

"I mean," I sigh, "someone knows I'm here. In this house. He said he was sent to kill me."

"That's impossible," Luisa states, clipping her hair back.

I shake my head. "Apparently, it's not. But what anyone wants with me, I'm not sure."

"Why did you shoot him then?" Amare asks, and I stare at him, my mouth agape. "Don't even look at me like that," he says, tossing his hands in the air. "You know damn well you could have taken him down without shooting him. I've seen you take down more men faster."

He has a point.

"I didn't want to risk him taking me out and going after you guys," I tell him, which is only a partial truth. He spooked me. I'll never admit it, but he did.

"We could have gotten more information from him," Amare responds with an incredulous look.

"We could have," I tell him with a nod. "But I think I can find someone who knows something way more willing to work with us."

We stand there in silence, looking down at the dead man at my feet.

I should feel something. I know I should.

But I don't, and I can't.

This is what we do. He's far from the first and far from the last.

THREE

DAMON

Do I want dairy milk or oat milk—that's the question.

I scowl at the oat milk in my hand as I weigh my options as if there aren't bigger things for me to worry about.

Ignore what the internet keeps telling you. Dairy milk is fine.

Grabbing milk from the shelf, I add it to my basket along with the other small things I've gotten to sustain myself at the motel. More precisely, the chips and multiple types of dip.

But I pause, my fingers hovering over the carton as I look back at the options. *Dairy milk hurts your stomach. Get the oat milk.*

I sigh, placing the carton back on the shelf and grabbing the oat milk. A teenager called me a pussy for buying it months ago, and I can't help but picture the look of raw disgust on his face every time I buy it now.

What do teenagers know, anyways?

To say I'm failing my mission would be a colossal understatement. Although it's only been two days since I spoke with her last, I know that if I can't get it done soon, it won't happen. There's been no sign of Ellie since that night. I knew I should have waited her out or followed her home.

That's so creepy. But if it may be a matter of life or death, it's fine, right?

Shaking my head, I walk through the aisles, looking for anything else I may want to snack on while feeling sorry for myself.

And that's when I see her.

A mess of long, chocolate-brown hair, she walks by the snack aisle with two others. But all I can see is her.

In just a pair of jeans and a long sleeve green shirt, she looks as beautiful as ever.

This is probably my last chance to talk to her this week, but I'm unsure how.

I take my basket to the front, ready to check out. Getting out of here early and waiting for her to come out seems like the best bet.

God, I do this for a living; you'd think I'd feel less creepy about it.

As the bagger hands me my items, Ellie rounds the corner, groceries in her arms as the others join her. I watch her for a moment too long, and her eyes land on mine. She smirks.

Unease spreads through my body at a rapid speed, my arms feeling like jelly all of a sudden.

I feel unsettled. It's a knowing smile, like she understands something I don't and I'm going to learn very soon.

I swallow my nerves and head out to my car, slipping into my Camaro, wishing for the first time that I brought my old beater I use for investigations.

It feels like an eternity before the three of them make their way out. I take a second to take the other two in.

The tall man takes bags from the cart and adds them to the back of a Bronco before running his hand through his hair. He places his hands on his hips as he examines something. As Ellie climbs in the front seat, the other woman rounds the back of the car, asking the man something. The cold Seattle air blows her blonde hair across her face, and she pushes it back as she squints up at the man in front of her, shielding her eyes with her hand.

Finally, the man climbs into the back of the truck while the blonde opens the passenger side door. Another moment later, the reverse lights come on, and they're pulling out of their spot.

I wait a second before turning my engine on, making sure they're several cars ahead of me.

I really, really wish I had brought the beater here with me.

The Bronco pulls out onto the street, and I curse as I watch the rapidly approaching cars. There's no way I'm going to be able to keep up with them.

But with massive luck on my side, one of the cars stop, allowing me to pull out in front of them. The Bronco is three cars ahead of me, stopped at the red light.

When the light turns green, we continue on, and I'm careful to stay a couple of cars behind, but no more than that. Every time a car looks suspiciously like it's about to merge into my lane, I speed up, not caring if they get pissed. There's no way I blow two opportunities to talk to Ellie. I need to warn her.

Suddenly, the car in front of me throws on its brakes as they all slow down, the Bronco signaling they are turning right. I take a moment to decide whether I should follow them onto the dirt road they're turning onto. They're definitely going to know I'm trailing them, but if I don't, I'll lose her for good.

I decide my only option is to follow and turn onto the road without signaling.

They drive for a few more minutes, dust kicking up behind them from the dirt and gravel road. I can barely see the back of their Bronco. All I can see is the endless sea of trees.

And then they stop, their brake lights shining through the haze of dirt and dust. My heart is caught in my chest as I freeze, unsure of what to do next. She's with people. Are they going to let us talk? Are they going to think I'm a stalker?

I mean, they wouldn't really be wrong. I did do a bit of light stalking to get here.

This is what you wanted, right? You wanted to talk to her!

I've been working as a detective for six years now, and although it's mostly inconsequential small-town problems like who's been tagging the school buses, I've never felt real fear during any investigation. Not even when we had a couple of girls go missing three years ago.

But something in my little pea brain is telling me I've stumbled into more than I've bargained for, and I suddenly wish I was back at the store debating types of milk.

A door opens, and Ellie jumps out, a glint in her eye as she ambles to my car, a small smile on her face.

I roll my window down and smile sheepishly at her. I feel like a small child caught with their hand in the cookie jar.

She looks around, bouncing on the balls of her feet before bending over, resting her crossed arms on the window. I lean back, all of a sudden feeling way too close.

Ellie bites her cheek, pursing her lips before bringing her eyes up to meet mine. My heart lurches.

"Why are you following us?" she demands softly, refusing to break eye contact.

"I told you. I need to tell you something," I tell her with a sigh, propping one hand on the wheel, hoping she'll listen to me this time.

She looks around for a moment, peering down the road as if making sure we weren't followed before leveling me with a stare.

"Okay, well," she starts, reaching for the front of her jeans.

I put my hands up in front of me, "Ellie it's not that big of a deal, we can talk here, and then I'll leav—"

But the click of a gun and the cool metal pressed to my forehead shuts me up.

Out of all the things you thought may happen, I'm not sure why you didn't think about that one, dumbass.

But why the fuck would I?

"What the hell?" I raise my hands up higher, lunging backward in my seat.

"Get out," she tells me, gesturing with the handgun.

"Ellie, we can talk here; like I said, it's not that big of a thing. I just need to tell you—"

"Get the fuck out of the car," she repeats, looking up and pinching the bridge of her nose as if losing patience.

I think it over for a second, but something in her eyes makes me reconsider taking my time. Keeping one hand up as I unbuckle my seatbelt, I reach for the door handle.

"I'm not here to hurt you," I tell her, wondering what her friends in the car think of this.

She doesn't say anything. Instead, she looks me over from head to toe, studying me. "Look," I start.

But I don't get the chance to finish. Instead, my mouth and nose are covered with a cloth from behind. I try hard not to breathe, but it's impossible.

My vision starts to blur, my body wobbling as I strain to stay on my feet.

I don't last long.

The last thing I remember is a male voice telling her to help him get me in the car, the feeling of dirt and gravel catching my clothes as I'm dragged across the road.

My head hurts. Well, everything hurts, actually.

I try to open my eyes, but they feel so heavy.

The smell of sulfur and iron assaults my nose, and I try as hard as I can not to choke.

I try to rub my eyes with my hands but find that I can't move them. Wiggling, I attempt to move them again but realize they're cuffed behind me, the cool metal biting into my skin.

"Fuck!" I yell, the cuffs rattling against the pipe, the reality of the situation setting in.

Prying my eyes open, they take a moment to adjust. They're heavy, as if something is trying to hold them closed, and I can already tell that my right eye is swollen a little. I'm not sure why, and I don't really want to know.

When my vision clears and I can finally see clearly, I look around, realizing I'm really, truly fucked.

I'm in a basement, God knows where, cuffed against a pole.

And not just any basement, no.

The first thing I notice is the jail cell to my left, the door open with only a bucket and a thin, crimson-stained cot on the floor. The smell of vomit assaults my nose, and I choke down the acid rising up my throat.

The second thing I notice is the trickle of water running from one end of the basement to another, pooling at one corner of the cell. Following the stream, I find what looks like a well, the concrete deteriorating on the outside.

Concrete is porous, making it a terrible material to use for a well, making me think it isn't exactly used for containing drinking water.

There are a couple of thin windows on the wall above it, and one is opened just a crack, a hose slipped through it, no attachment on the end. Water drips from it, causing the liquid to overflow onto the floor.

On the wall opposite from me sits a large shelving system full of what looks like torture devices, and next to it, a rusty metal cabinet.

My heart slams against my ribs. This is some kind of serial killer's basement. What the fuck has Ellie gotten herself into?

"He's awake," comes a deep, gravelly voice from behind me, and I jump, my back cold against the pipe as my shirt rides up. It's only now that I notice my jacket is gone, and I can't feel my phone or wallet in either of the pockets of my jeans. I look down, noticing how my jeans are coated with dust and blood.

The man from the store walks into my line of vision, squatting in front of me.

"You don't look so good, man," he announces, smirking.

I glare at him, not dumb enough to be smart when he's clearly in control here.

"We just have a couple of questions for you. Nothing too serious," he assures, gesturing to whoever's still behind me.

I hear the creek of someone getting up and the light scuffle of feet before the two women settle before me. They stand behind him, the blonde looking as if she'd rather be anywhere but here, and Ellie, well, she just looks confused.

"You guys have to—" I start, but my voice is stifled as I choke, struggling with tightness at the back of my throat, clearly still coming down from whatever I was given. "You guys have to believe me," I croak, "I don't know what this is, but I believe Ellie is in danger," I tell them, my eyes likely crazed as I attempt to get my point across.

"The thing is," the man says, his voice trailing off as he looks at Ellie, "we had someone break in here the other night. We don't really know who he works for, but it definitely isn't the Agency. The only thing we know is that he was sent here to kill Amelia," he reports. *The Agency?*

I look at the blonde. "You're okay?" I ask her sincerely.

Her brows furrow as she looks at Ellie. "We probably should have introduced ourselves first. I'm Luisa," she says, scowling a little as if this conversation is physically painful.

Ellie purses her lips before squeezing her eyes shut, her arms unfolding as she places them at her hips. "Damon—it is

Damon, correct?" I nod. "How do you know my name?" A new wave of trepidation settles in my bones.

"What do you mean?"

"I mean, I don't go by that name anymore. No one has called me that since it happened." I open my mouth to ask what she means, but she beats me to it. "Before my death."

"I don't understand what's going on right now," I utter, shaking my head. My face feels hot, and I can't help but flex my fingers behind my back, wishing I could stretch out. Or, you know, *get out of here.*

"How do you know that I'm in trouble?" she asks, kneeling in front of me. The man stands, backing up as he lets her take center stage.

"Ellie, what's going on?"

She looks behind her at the other two, and without saying a thing, they understand. Turning around, they head for the door in the corner of the room and disappear.

Ellie doesn't face me until they're gone.

Her amber eyes penetrate mine with a curious mix of lethal intent and terror. All I want is to wrap her in a hug and protect her, no matter how tough she thinks she is.

Raising her hand, she rubs her forehead as if she has a headache. "What do you need to tell me?" she asks, her movements becoming more languid as the seconds go by.

"I think you need to explain what's going on before I can go into that," I tell her, closing my eyes and leaning back against the pole.

"Damon. This is serious," she tells me, her voice low, making me falter. "As Amare said, the night we spoke, and you called me by my old name, we had a break-in. Someone was hired to kill me. So, what is it that you know?"

My eyes pop open as I look at her, taking in the way her skin pales at the memory.

"Are you okay?" I ask her. "How did you get him out?"

A deep rivet settles between her eyebrows as she stares at

me, trying to read me. I keep my eyes locked on hers, waiting for her to reply.

"I killed him," she says finally, placing her hands on her knees with a sigh.

Wha—

"Look," she interjects, interrupting my thoughts. "I'm trying to be nice here, Damon. But my hospitality only goes so far. Tell me what you know and why people are after me, or we're going to have to get it out of you another way. I'd prefer not to do that." She stands, the motion stilted. Looking around, her eyes land on the far wall before sweeping back to me, her gaze intensifying.

I take a deep breath, wincing as my ribs cramp, not used to the position I'm in. "All I know is that your face came across my desk two weeks ago," I begin, my chest caving in as I slump over and focus on the floor. "When someone is seen in the area, if they're wanted, we get copies of posters so we keep an eye out. I'm not with the bureau anymore. Someone was distributing them. Your name wasn't on it, and you weren't in the system as a Wanted individual, but I knew it was you."

I glance up at her, hoping to find some semblance of the woman I used to know. Instead, I find her face twisted in a look of resignation, her jaw loose before she lets out a sharp exhale, turning on her heel towards the door in which the others disappeared.

"Do you know who was handing them out?" she questions, studying her white sneakers, a lock of chocolate-colored hair falling in her face.

"I don't know; it was some man. I've never seen him before," I answer honestly.

Her gaze meets mine again, and my breath catches in my chest. I shake myself mentally, trying to snap back into the moment.

Ellie scoffs. "Tell me, Damon, why we should believe a

31

single word that comes out of your mouth." My eyes harden, my chest constricting.

"You can look into it. I don't know what's going on here," I reply, my voice rising an octave in panic, "but Ellie, I swear to God I'm telling the truth. I have no idea who was handing them out. No clue." I shake my head vigorously, feeling light-headed as heat rises up my body in anger.

She takes a deep breath. "Where were you when this happened?"

"I was in Virginia. I live there, working as a small-town detective."

Her eyes narrow. "You said you worked at the Bureau before?"

I gulp. "I had to leave after everything that happened."

She looks me over but decides not to continue with that line of questioning. "I haven't been to Virginia. I'm not sure why anyone there would be looking for me."

I don't know either, which is why I've been so confused. She only has one family member left, and they couldn't give a flying fuck about her. There's no way they would have known she was still alive, much less cared.

"Ellie—" I start, but she waves me off, standing up and dusting herself off before looking over her shoulder.

"It's Amelia, Damon," she tells me, her voice void of emotion as she walks through the door, closing it with a slam.

FOUR

AMELIA

The whispers stop the second I appear in the doorway. Amare looks up, concern in his kind eyes, while Luisa studies her nails, working assiduously to pretend as if they weren't just whispering about me.

I walk to the fridge, opening it without a word, and snatch a yogurt before propping myself against the kitchen island. As I move, the belt loop of my favorite worn-out mom jeans gets caught on the bronze drawer knob, and I can't help the bubble of outrage flow through me as I slam the poor plastic cup onto the hard surface with a whack.

I can feel their eyes on me, letting me have my moment but concerned all the same. I take a second to sulk, allowing myself the opportunity to calm down before speaking. I study my hand carefully, only now realizing how pale I've become with nerves, my hand practically blending in with the countertop.

I take a couple of deep breaths, avoiding eye contact with the other two until I'm ready to speak.

That's when I smell it.

"Is that—are those brownies?" I ask, sniffing the air, the scent of warm chocolate enveloping me in a warm, fudgy hug, immediately boosting my mood.

Luisa nods, eyeing me warily. "I figured you needed them."

I take a moment to take them in, appreciating my two friends. Luisa picks at her long, blue nails once more, tucking her long blonde hair behind her ears before taking a breath and meeting my gaze. Her golden skin is marked with paint. She's been working on a large piece in her room for the last couple of days, and I'm sure the stress of this situation has inspired her a lot. Stress can do that to us. We just channel it into something else.

Amare leans on the counter, his large, corded arms crossed in front of him as he, too, feels the stress of everything happening. Neither of them like being unable to help me. They've been there before, helpless and unsure during dark, terrible moments. They care far too much for me.

"Are you okay?" he finally asks, clearing his throat.

I think for a second, careful with my words.

The clicking of toenails across the hardwood floor of the family room catches my attention, and Cooper's face immediately relaxes me even more. Sauntering over, the big doofus places his head on my belly, looking up at me with his big brown puppy eyes.

"I know, baby," I tell him, scratching his soft head.

Taking a deep breath, I look back up at Amare. "I think so," I tell him. "I guess I've never been this nervous about anything before. It's been, what, six years? I don't have any real memory of being called Ellie."

Luisa nods, popping a chocolate chip into her mouth. "I can imagine that's weird," she agrees.

"Someone I don't know just, well, knowing me as Ellie is just—" I trail off, unable to find the right words.

Amare fiddles with the oven mitt in front of him, thinking. "Did you get any information out of him?" he asks.

I shake my head, a couple strands of hair slipping past my ears and into my face. "He told me that someone is after me. He doesn't know who or where, but he said he has suspicions. I just needed to get some air, but I'll try to get more information out of him later," I inform them, turning around to open the oven and check the brownies.

"They should be done, I think," Luisa mumbles, getting up from her seat. I grab the oven mitts, pulling them out, the hot air hitting my face oddly comforting. "Do you know if he's someone you were close with, well," she trails off.

I shrug, placing the pan down. "I'm not sure?" I tell her. I honestly don't really want to know, though, if I'm being completely honest.

I look at Amare, who's been oddly quiet. "Do you have any thoughts?" I ask, starting to feel anxious again.

"I just think we need to get to the bottom of this whichever way we can." He tilts his head, snapping at Cooper as he peeks his head over the counter, sniffing the air next to the brownies. Coop lowers his head to the ground with a somber look up, realizing he was caught.

I eye the brownies, realizing that even the sight of them makes me feel the slightest bit better.

No matter how we were trained and for how long, we're human above all. I know my faults. I may not show others weakness, but I trust these two with my life.

We shouldn't, but we all trust each other above all.

But brownies also fix everything.

"I'll go back down there," I tell them, peeling the thin, crackled top off a corner of the brownies, too aware of the burn the hot sugar leaves on my skin. "I'll try to figure it out. Thank you, guys, for the brownies." I pat the counter, abandoning my yogurt on the counter as I head back downstairs.

As I reach for the door, I pause, listening intently as a voice echoes through the space.

"I don't know who I pissed off to end up in a fucking dungeon, but I need to have a word with them," Damon mutters, followed by a *pang* as he hits his head against the metal pole. "Damon! Go find the girl who's been dead for six years! Yeah, there's no *reason* she hasn't turned up in that time, right? There's no *danger* in finding her, that's for sure."

I almost snicker as I listen, practically hearing the eye roll through the door.

His soliloquy almost makes me feel better about him.

Not that I'd let him know that.

Whipping the door open, I amble through as if I don't have a care in the whole world, and I wasn't upstairs moments ago on the edge of a panic attack.

"Oh, hey El—I mean Amelia." He flashes a toothy grin at me. "Sorry, it's going to take a little bit to get used to that."

I give him a small smile before settling in front of him, crossing my legs as I sit on the cold floor.

"I want you to know that I don't think you had anything to do with the break-in," I start off, hoping to gain some trust. "But you told me in that bar that you had to discuss things with me, and I want to know it all."

He considers this for a moment before looking me in the eye. I take the moment to really take him in for the first time.

He's handsome, that's for sure. Too handsome to be as wholesome as he seems to be. With black hair, a dark, short, trimmed beard, and green eyes, I could tell that this man probably got every single thing he ever wanted in life.

"If I'm honest," he starts, clearing his throat and looking to the left, his shoulders slumping, "I don't know much. I saw you, realized you were probably in danger, and I came to find you." He looks up, finally meeting my eyes.

"How did you find me?"

He considers what he's about to say. "I used to work for

the FBI. I have friends high up still that do occasional, how should I say," his head tilts to the side, "favors for me."

"So, I assume you also have no idea how he found me," I state, not even asking.

"Nope," he says, popping the *p*. "I only know that he was able to find you on a camera somewhere and knew you had been seen at that bar. I was going there for a couple of days before you finally turned up. It was a gamble."

Interesting.

I nod, thinking it through.

"Why did you come here, Damon? Why really?"

His head hits the pole with a loud *pang*, and he shuts his eyes. "At some point, I'll tell you everything if you're ready for it," he tells me solemnly. "But I messed up. That day, I messed up badly. I figured if I got another chance to protect you, I needed to take it." He shrugs, his head still back as he closes his eyes.

I bite my lip, examining my hands. "I don't need protecting," My shoulders roll back as I sit up straighter.

He opens one eye, peeking at me. "How was I supposed to know that?"

Fair enough.

"You know, I think I deserve some answers, too," he says quietly, his green eyes burning a hole through my heart.

I'm not someone who usually cares about what anyone other than the two upstairs think. From the day I woke up in that cold, lifeless room and was told I was saved to the day I met Amare and Luisa, I've been incredibly careful to ensure I don't get too close to anyone. To feel anything other than the numbness we're told we must feel.

We could be gone at any moment. Whether it be sacrificed, used as pawns for the Agency's needs, or by the Agency itself if they decide to burn the whole thing to the ground.

"What do you want to know?" I ask him, my finger making circles in the dust covering the cold concrete.

"Do you remember anything from before," he pauses, not understanding what happened that day. I don't either, not really, "before that day?"

Pursing my lips, I decide to be honest with him. "I don't remember one single thing," I tell him, looking into his eyes. They flash with desolation, and I wonder, not for the first time, who I was to him. I don't want to know. Whoever I was, that girl is dead. Lost in the wind.

He nods, swallowing roughly. "So," he looks around carefully, "what is this?"

I wince. "I really can't tell you that right now," I state. His ashen face falls, and I immediately feel terrible, knowing that nothing good is going to come next for him.

"Black operations?" he asks.

"Something like that," I reply, getting to my feet. "I have to go upstairs and tend to some business, but I'll be back later with food for you," I assure him.

"You're not going to let me go?" he asks, shocked.

I shake my head. "We can't right now. We have to go through protocol. I'll have more information for you later, I promise."

I hear him sigh as I walk out of the room, and I can't help but feel for him.

Whoever he is, whatever he was to me, I can tell I meant something to him. For a split second, I allow myself to feel good about it.

FIVE

DAMON

It feels as though I've been chained up like a dog for a week, despite it being around twelve hours.

My wrists hurt, the cool metal digging into my flesh more and more every time I struggle.

It's been six whole years since I've seen Ellie—or, well, Amelia—alive. She was twenty at the time, finishing her first two years at community college and getting a full ride to Harvard to finish her schooling.

I was three years older than her, having graduated from John Jay only a year before. I moved onto the FBI Academy, graduating with flying colors after 20 weeks. I was living my childhood dream, young and naïve.

The very first case I was put on was Ellie's father. He had been caught taking bribes multiple times beforehand, but for reasons outside of our control, we couldn't do anything about it. The United States used to have a system of checks and balances in place, the FBI and other organizations having much more power than they do now. That wasn't that long ago, really.

It didn't take long to find out that the system I came to know growing up, respecting and looking forward to being a part of, was as unjust as any. Politics was about money, rapacity, and privilege. If you had enough money, you could get away with murder. Quite literally.

My stomach rumbles, and suddenly I become all too aware of how hungry I am having not eaten anything all day. My mouth is dry, my body is sore; at this point, I would be fine with simply being able to fully lay on the cold, dusty ground.

The door opens suddenly, and the other woman walks in. I try to suppress my disappointment that it's not Amelia.

She shoots me an easy smile as she walks over quietly.

And just stands there. She looks around before her hazel eyes land on mine again, her manicured hands slipping into the pockets of her black sweatpants. Her long blonde hair is tied up in a ponytail, swaying with every turn of her head.

I stare up at her, waiting for her to say something as she looks me over. "We don't know what's going to happen with you yet," she tells me suddenly, looking down at the ground. "We have to reach out to someone and see what to do, as you've been in our house and all that. Somehow you know way too much about the project, despite claiming to know nothing at all."

I swallow. That doesn't sound great for me. Despite the cold ground, sweat starts to form on my back, chilling my skin against the cold metal pole.

"I don't know who you are or why Amelia, the resident hard ass, seems to have a soft spot for you, but we're going to do whatever we can to get you out of here." She places her hand on her hip.

"Okay?" I'm not really sure what else to say. What *can* you say when someone alludes to not being able to let you go? Will I rot down here? Will I be put out of my misery?

"Between you and I, who were you to her?" Her head tilts to the side as she stands there, looking me over.

I shake my head. "I think that's for the two of us to discuss, not you and I."

Her eyes snap to mine, narrowing as she bites her cheek. "Listen. I've been here with her for the last five and a half years. We went through most of our training together. I love that girl like a sister, despite what we've been told to feel. We're a family, and the only," she pauses, bringing her hand up in front of her, "I mean *only* thing I truly care about, is my family," her voice dips. "I'm the only one in this house that remembers their life before I died." Her face melts, melancholy settling upon her features.

My brows furrow, and recognition flashes in her eyes. She messed up.

"What do you mean, before you died?" My eyes narrow. "What the fuck is going on here?"

"You may find out soon," she decides to say, flinching, and I can't help but add the silent *if you're going to die, anyways.* "Just, please. Who were you to her? I need to know what we're dealing with here. She can't find out."

I shake my head. "I'm not saying," I hold firm. But I can tell she knows she meant a great deal to me.

Nodding, she weighs her words carefully. "Just please, whatever you do, don't tell her anything about the past before she's ready to know." Her gaze feels like a gut punch.

Turning away, she takes a second as if deciding whether to say something else before continuing back to that goddamn door.

And I'm left, once again, alone with my thoughts.

Seven years ago

"Hey, is this seat taken?" I ask the blonde sitting at the circular table in the library. She looks up, her brown eyes meeting mine.

Shaking her head, she looks down shyly, blush spreading across her cheeks as she looks up at me from under her bangs.

"How's your day going?" I ask her, taking my books from my bag. It's been a little while since I graduated, and I wasn't thrilled I was told to go back.

Get close to the Senator's daughter, I was told. That's my one objective at the moment. If I'm able to do this, I will learn what to do next. But for now, I have to befriend her.

She sits up, looking down at the paper in front of her. "It's okay I guess." Her lip twitches, and I look at her a little closer. Her eyes are puffy as if she were recently crying. She wears jeans and a hoodie so large, she could disappear inside of it.

Maybe that's the point.

"Well, my day has been absolutely insane," I chuckle, grabbing my calculator in an attempt to look like I know what I'm doing. It's been ages since I've taken a math class. I'm not sure I even remember how to do PEMDAS, and I'm fairly sure it's pretty self-explanatory.

She watches me, her eyes curious as I solve a problem. I don't look up at her, but the intensity of her gaze is too intense to ignore.

"Um," she interrupts, and I glance up, meeting her eyes. She looks troubled, and for a moment I worry that she's in trouble. She takes a deep breath and closes her eyes before continuing. "Do you want help with that problem?" she asks quietly, curling into herself as I search her face.

"I think I'm doing a pretty good job," I grin at her, actually really impressed that I remember how to do it.

Her face goes slack as her eyes dart to her paper.

"Wait, I am doing it right, right?" I ask, suddenly unsure.

She shakes her head.

"How off am I?"

A small smile plays at the corner of her lips. "I mean, you're not even close."

"Not even a little bit?"

Another shake of her pretty little head.

"Well, fuck me then," I laugh, running my fingers through my scruffy hair. There were only a couple of things I was told about this mission weeks ago, and one of them was that I needed to look less "like a fucking cop," per my boss. Growing my hair out was apparently the solution.

Her eyes grow round as she looks down at my paper. "Well, I would really appreciate the help if you're offering," I tell her, leaning back into the table as I try to catch her eyes. She looks so frightened, and I'm not sure why. "My name is Damon," I say as I offer her my outstretched hand.

She looks at it for a beat too long, and I almost put it down, embarrassed. At the last moment, she takes it, shaking it. "I'm Ellie," she tells me as she tucks her hair behind her ear with her other hand, keeping her eyes down.

The first time I met Ellie in that library, she was a scared, injured girl who didn't understand what was going on in her life. Her parents were always fighting, and her friends would constantly bully her for her father's monthly mistakes.

Ellie had become a shell of herself at the time. She didn't trust anyone. But she trusted me.

I broke that trust, and I've been punishing myself ever since.

I think about how I got here.

My parents were great people. My dad had been in the FBI for 20 years before he was shot and killed on duty, taken from us far too soon. They were both older when they had me, despite marrying young.

My mother was never the same after my dad died, and I wasn't either. But it made me want to join. Graduating from the Academy was the one and only thing I wanted throughout my entire life. If I did that, everything would be okay. If I did that, I would know my dad was proud of me.

My mother was pissed. No, that's not a strong enough word for it. She was furious. It was about two months before she spoke to me again, despite me attempting to call her every day. She was scared of losing me, too.

But I threw the entire thing away. I only lasted a little over a year at the Bureau. I wasn't cut out for it. Not only did I fail Ellie and my first big job, I failed my father too.

It was all a waste of time. Every moment of it. If I hadn't gone to the Academy, if I hadn't met Ellie...

She could have suffered worse.

SIX

AMELIA

"What are we having for dinner tonight?" I ask Lu with a huff as I trudge back into the kitchen.

She eyes me suspiciously. "You doing okay?" she asks as she slaps a chicken breast onto the cutting board in front of her.

I watch as she turns to the knife block in the corner, choosing the largest option before returning, getting to work trimming the fat. "I'm fine," I say with a sigh.

It's been a couple of hours since I was last checking in on Damon, and I know that Lu had been down there a bit ago. I left the house to take Coop for a walk before returning and soaking in the bath, attempting to scrub away the events of today.

It's a silly thing, the past. For those who remember, it's a blessing. Remembering how you laughed as a kid without a care in the world, without worries or commitments, before the world gets complicated.

All I've ever known is complicated. All I've ever known is death.

Whether it be the moment I woke up in that room and was told I died, or knowing that every single time I get sent out to gather intel, every conversation I have with someone can result in my death... death is all-consuming.

I don't remember what innocence feels like. What it's like to laugh with siblings or friends. Hell, maybe I had a sibling. How many happy, carefree memories have I lost?

But then again, how many terrible ones? How hard would I grieve if I learned the truth?

I was put here in this big house with one purpose: to put my life on the line on missions the agency doesn't want their agents to risk theirs for.

The Agency chose us to protect themselves. The second we're unnecessary or they're at risk of being found out, we'll be terminated. They thought that making us forget would give us more of a reason to risk our lives. We have nothing to live for, right? Nothing at all. Like we were made in a lab for this purpose and this purpose only.

Yet it only makes some of us more human.

And here I am, presented with an opportunity to learn about my past. How many times have I prayed for this moment? How many times have I cried myself to sleep, trying to remember what happened to me? I can feel it. It's right there in the back of my mind, right there, just out of arms reach. I can feel it.

I can feel that that man downstairs was some part of it. I'm not sure who he is, what part he played, or what he wants now other than to help me, but what I do know is that at some point, for some reason, I cared about him.

And that little bit of knowledge, that little bit of rope... it feels like enough to hang myself from.

I desperately want to know everything, and yet nothing at all.

I drum my fingers against the kitchen counter, looking anywhere but Luisa. Ever since I got here, she's been able to read me like a book. Both could. When you spend every day with people, sharing secrets as we have, you become extraordinary at it.

She looks away from me finally, returning her attention to the chicken in front of her. "I need you to know that I support you with whatever you do, but I hope you make smart decisions when it comes to him." Her face is tight as she slices a piece of chicken in half.

I nod, understanding. She doesn't want me to hurt the way she does every day.

"And we're having lemon chicken and rice," she adds, not looking up. I nod, happy with that, and head back to my room, instantly relaxing as the floral scent reaches my nose.

Sprawling out on my sage blanket, I feel my mattress droop as Cooper jumps up, walking in circles as he paws the fabric, making himself comfy. I close my eyes, feeling him settle next to me, his large, warm body radiating heat. His head rests on my outstretched arm. I open my eyes, turning to look at him. His eyes are large and worried, and I wish I could tell him I'm okay. That everything will be okay, and that this feeling will pass as it always does.

There were times it didn't. But those times are in the past, long forgotten. I'm stronger now.

Instead, I turn over, my other arm draping over him.

We stay like that for a long time, and I drift to sleep.

———

A knock on my door wakes me up.

"Lia," Amare's voice calls, "dinner time!"

The smell of lemon and rosemary has infiltrated the air, and I feel my stomach rumble as I sit up in bed. Stretching, I pat Coop's head as he too sits up, letting out a lazy yawn.

"You ready for dinner?" I ask him, standing up and heading for the door. He jumps off the bed with a quiet bark, following me.

Amare is in the kitchen making plates as Lu sits at the dinner table, a glass of white wine in front of her. I head to the counter and pour myself a glass before taking a plate, setting it on the table, and going back to fill Coop's bowl.

He trots over, immediately getting to work.

Amare finally sits at the end of the table as I take my place across from Lu. We start digging in, allowing the peaceful silence to rest between us.

"Does anyone have anything planned for this week?" Lu asks, and I know she means for work. Each week we get a brief on anything we need to be aware of.

Political meetings, secret society meetings, any political issues moving into the area; it doesn't really matter what it is, we're supposed to find a way in and make sure that everything is going smoothly, the balance of power still in place.

I recently had a discussion with the handler after I had one too many weeks of seducing old men into rooms, only to get them drunk, force information from them, and leave. I'd rather do almost anything else.

"There's a secret society meeting this week," I tell her, taking a bite of chicken. "I think it's one of those big meetings with all the politicians, so it's going to be easier to get in and go unnoticed than the smaller ones."

The country had its fair share of secret societies, though they weren't what anyone thought they were. While social media buzzed with certain made-up groups, the real ones were usually less sinister. There was little to no bloodshed, and when there was, it was only their own. Normally, it was only secrets shared and alliances made.

"Yeah, I have a meeting with some banker," Lu says, pouting as she brings her glass to her lips.

Amare scowls, knowing she hates those. "I have to attend

some meetings," he tells us, "but I'm not entirely sure what kind."

Fair enough.

We continue to chat about what's coming up this week. Most of the time, we just hang around the house, doing whatever we want. I go for runs and read, while Luisa paints and bakes. Amare works on his car in the garage or goes on hikes.

We don't have that much in regard to work each week, but I think it's a rather small payment for being used the way we are.

When we're done, we gather our dishes and head into the kitchen, washing and drying them together as we talk about our latest jobs. Amare just had a black bag job, breaking into a local politician's home in order to gather intel the Agency wanted. He's been taking bribes, which the Agency doesn't look too kindly on.

Luisa has been working on a cipher for our handler, but also often acts as a cobbler whenever new agents need documents. Luisa has a nice setup in our office where she creates the false visas, passports, and more that the real agents will need to complete their missions.

As for me, I've been investigating dead drops around the city as more politicians, CEOs, and celebrities have met here.

Project Fallen Angel is a clandestine operation. It has stayed secret for decades, but meetings between government officials have been moving further and further west as time goes on, as more and more becomes uncovered. We're everywhere, in every state, and somehow, someway, it has stayed a secret.

When we're done, I look around, spotting the leftovers that need to be put away.

"I'm going to bring him food," I announce, knowing they'll know who I'm speaking of. I fix him a plate before heading to the basement.

Opening the door, I find him slumped over, his chin

resting on his broad chest. Damon is a large man, and the sight of his frame attached to the small pole is almost comical.

His jeans are ripped and dusty from being dragged along the gravel, and his t-shirt is rumpled and frayed. His dark hair is mussed and disheveled, and for one fleeting moment, I wish I could run my fingers through it.

I clear my throat, and his hard eyes snap to mine, immediately narrowing as he eyes the plate I'm holding.

"I brought you dinner," I tell him roughly, setting it next to him. My attitude feels bitter on my tongue, but I can't have him think I'm weak.

"I don't want this," he spits, his face twisting with rage.

I roll my eyes, kneeling next to him. "Damon, I—" I don't know what to say to him. How do you deal with a situation like this? We've never had to before.

I'm about to respond when the tapping of toenails echoes down the stairs, and I look back as Cooper enters the room, his tail between his legs. I knew I forgot to close the door.

Heading straight for Damon, Cooper drops next to him, placing his head lazily on his thigh before looking up at me with the most precious, adorable puppy eyes I've ever seen. Damon eyes him warily before looking back at me.

"He's a dog, not a bomb," I deadpan, fighting hard to prevent my eyes from rolling.

"I'm sorry for being suspicious but I've had an awful time with familiar things not being what they seem," he seethes.

I sit on the floor as Damon looks back at Cooper, his head tilted to the side as he speaks to him. "Hey bud," he starts, his eyes meeting mine with a scowl. "I sure wish I could pet you."

I let out a sigh. "Listen. I'm not sure who you are or what you want with me, but there's been a threat, and you can't blame us for starting with you."

"Actually, I can," he says, knocking his head back into the

pole. "No one is forcing you to kidnap people and tie them up in your fucking basement."

"Someone put a hit out on me. We're not sure who, but we're trying to figure it out. You called me by a name I don't go by anymore. The same name the man who broke into the house had on his phone. I haven't been called Ellie in over 6 years. We're only trying to get to the bottom of this," I tell him, an eerie calmness settling into my bones as I watch him take me in.

"That's what I've been trying to tell you," he tells me with an eye roll, his voice dripping with acid. "I could tell you were in trouble. There were people looking for you. I don't know who. That's the entire reason I came to find you. For the past six years, I've thought you were dead. I don't go looking for any random woman."

Okay, well, there are a couple of things we can address, and some we can't, it seems.

"Well if you cooperate with us, we'll let you go."

His brow furrows as he processes the information. "You see, I would believe you, but I haven't been told a single fucking thing about what's going on," he starts, nearly spitting. Cooper rolls his head to the side, looking at me now with a silent plea.

I know animals have the amazing ability to sniff out good people. Cooper wouldn't have approached him at all if he wasn't good. But I also know that if I let Damon go, it could result in all sorts of bad.

I open my mouth to say something and immediately shut it.

"I can't tell you anything right now. I told you that."

He scoffs. "If you're going to end up killing me, can't you just at least tell me what happened? What's happening now?" he pleads, pushing forward against his restraints, his muscles flexing.

His right arm is covered in tattoos, and if we weren't in

this situation, if I was a normal person who didn't belong to the Agency, I would move closer to inspect them. Instead, I avert my gaze, not wanting him to see I'm interested.

I shake my head sadly, and he flings himself back in anger, jostling Coop's head. He looks down sheepishly, apologizing to him. Cooper simply yawns, placing his head back in his lap.

"Well, I know you're not getting what you want," I tell him as I step closer, "but you have dinner. I'll release one of your hands so you can eat, okay?"

He looks at me, his green eyes cutting through me, and swear my heart skips a beat. There's something so familiar about them. But then again, maybe we've passed each other on the street.

Getting up and walking behind him, I take a key out and unlock one of his cuffs. He immediately brings his hand around front, shaking it out as he curses. I leave the other one attached to the pole.

"God *damn* that hurts," he whispers, smacking the back of his head against the pole again.

I nudge the food closer to him with my foot, and Cooper's head lifts in curiosity as he sniffs the air.

"What is it?" Damon asks as he looks up at me.

I scoff. "I hardly think it matters."

He nods, taking the fork and stabbing a piece of chicken before examining it.

"I swear to God it's not poisoned or anything," I promise him, about five seconds from losing my shit and forcing it down his throat.

Damon shoots me a skeptical look. "If it was, at least I'd be put out of my misery," he shoots back before taking a bite.

I take a deep breath, remembering that this man may know something he's not telling us. We need him. I can't hurt him. At least not right now.

"I promise I'll do anything I can to get you out of here," I say softly, making the words as sincere as possible. Am I telling the truth? No. I'm not sure if he'll ever get out of here. But that's not something he needs to know.

"You see," he says, dropping the fork on the ground with a clang and pushing the plate away. "I don't fucking believe you, Sweetheart."

I don't blame him for the anger. I really don't. But something about the way he says it, something about the way he spits the words while looking at me like *that*, causes anger to boil in my veins.

I'm not sure if it's my training talking, since if we're being honest, I would have beaten anyone else bloody by now, maybe even shot them in the leg a time or two before taking them out, burying them in the woods.

"You need to be extremely careful about how you talk to me," I growl, trying my very best not to reach my hand out and wrap it around his neck, feeling his pulse as it quickens in fear.

It takes everything in me not to threaten his life further. To treat him like anyone else who puts us at risk.

"This isn't a fucking game." I spit. "This isn't fucking fun for me, got it? This is life or death for us. I'm so fucking sorry you came looking for a girl who doesn't exist anymore, *Damon*, but maybe you should have let the dead stay dead."

Shock clouds his eyes. "The dead stay dead? Really? Do you think I should have just stayed home after seeing someone I saw die alive, knowing their life may be on the line *again*? You think I should have just left that be?" he grits, his jaw clenched.

"Yes," I say simply. "I get that I had a life before this one. I'm sorry you were wrapped up in it somehow. But I was never supposed to be found. I'm not that girl anymore, I don't remember anything about her," I take a deep breath. "And there's no way you can protect me better than I can protect myself."

His eyes bulge out of his head in shock. "Amelia please just tell me what's going on here."

I look down at my hands. "I can't, Damon. Stop asking." He opens his mouth to speak, but I cut him off. "I can't tell you right now. Maybe tomorrow. We're waiting to hear back from someone. Just stop. I'm sorry, but this isn't something that we can just fill you in on. If you want any chance of getting out of here alive, you need to honor that." I'm not telling him the truth. I know I'm not. But I pray he believes me.

He gapes at me for a moment before slowly nodding, looking at the ground. Picking his plate back up, he takes another bite before putting it back down, pushing it an inch, done with it for now. Coop looks at him expectantly, and Damon pats his head.

My heart bursts at the act, melting just a tiny bit.

I turn back to the door, about to call Cooper to follow, when I hear a glass shattering followed by the familiar sound of gunshots.

SEVEN

DAMON

The crash from upstairs just about gave me a heart attack. The first gunshot sent shivers down my spine.

Amelia stops, listening for a moment before pivoting quickly, heading for the side wall.

"What was that?" My voice wavers. I don't know what to do or how to help, especially not tied to this fucking pole.

"We're being raided. Stay here with Cooper." Like I had a choice.

She presses a panel on the side wall, opening a cabinet. The second it's open enough for me to peer inside, my heart stops.

Guns. So many guns. Some I recognize, some I don't.

Pistols, submachine guns, and everything in between line the inside of the cabinet, and Amelia only takes a moment to pick one of the bigger ones.

Looking over to me, she snaps her fingers and Cooper immediately gets up and trots to her, seemingly unphased. Pushing another button, a smaller door opens within the wall, and Cooper enters. She closes it, and it's as if there was never anything there.

Now, if only I could go, too.

"You know how to shoot a gun?" she asks, her posture tense.

I roll my eyes. "I know how to shoot most things," I tell her. The FBI Academy trains us to use pistols, shotguns, and carbines, but I haven't shot anything other than a small pistol in years. She doesn't have to know that.

She eyes me for a second more, seeing right through me before picking up a smaller handgun, tossing it my way.

"Are you going to untie me?" I ask her, bewildered. She only shakes her head, heading for the door and disappearing.

Holy shit what's happening.

If there was ever a time to try to escape, it's now.

Slowly, I start to realize that my only option is to shoot through the metal links of my cuffs, separating them. It's a bad decision. So many things could go wrong, but it's the only choice I have.

I get up, stretching my back before I pull the chain taut around the pole, placing the barrel of the gun against it. I brace myself, looking behind me and squeezing my eyes shut before pulling the trigger.

The barrel slips, the bullet ricocheting off the metal cabinet across the room and flying back at me, the sound echoing throughout the large space. I grimace, jumping back to avoid the wayward bullet.

I breathe out. "Let's try that again," I mutter to myself, placing the barrel on the metal chain once more. This time, I brace for impact, but I don't look away.

And it hurts like a bitch.

It takes me a minute to gather myself together and convince myself that no, my hand did not get blown off my wrist, it just *feels* like it did. When I'm able to think clearly again, I look around, trying to figure out what I can do to help them, the cuff still around my wrist. At least I'm free from the pole.

Taking a step forward, I sway a little but manage to steady myself after a moment, deciding I'm ready to go. Picking up the gun from the ground, I turn back towards the door, quick on my feet, the handgun gripped in my hands.

As I approach the door, it knocks open with a bang, and I jump back out of the way, trying not to get hit.

A large man dressed in all black steps inside, his gun aimed and ready. This is my one shot. It can't be good that he's down here.

I jump at him, knocking the gun down, but the man kicks me, and I drop to the ground like a sack of potatoes, my muscles feeling like noodles.

"Are you fucking *kidding me?*" I hiss, pissed off once more that I've been left for dead.

"Who are you?" the man asks. I'm so tired of being asked that question today.

I put my hands up. "I was kept down here, I promise I'm not associated with them, they drugged me and brought me he—"

BAM

My ears immediately ring as a bullet whizzes by my ear, lodging itself in the back wall of the basement. I see stars as I'm thrown off, the man in front of me going down. It takes me a moment to get my bearings, and I become more aware of the blood.

Warm blood and other unimaginables spread across the floor, and I only become aware that I'm gaping at the scene in front of me once I taste iron. I don't dare look down at myself, for fear that what I find will send me to the ground, too.

I've seen some terrible, terrible things in my life. I've worked as a detective for six years and things there are pretty tame in comparison, but before that I was the top student at the FBI Academy. We're trained to deal with some really terrible shit. But this? After years of only dealing with small crime scenes?

Seeing a man shredded by a bullet is another breed of terror.

My eyes slowly drift up, and I meet a pair of brown ones, hard as steel as she points her gun at me. I put my hands up slowly, licking my lips, gagging as I find them slick with blood.

"I'm sorry, I just wanted to make sure you were all okay," I tell her, sure she's going to shoot.

Without a word, she puts down the gun, resting it at her side as she looks around her.

"Our security was taken out," she deadpans, heading for the small room she put Cooper in. Pressing the button in the wall, the doors open, and he walks out slowly, looking around at the mess in front of him.

He looks up at her with big, brown eyes before she snaps, turning on her heel and heading out of the room again. I stand there, not knowing what to do.

She stops at the stairs, turning to look behind her. "You coming?" she asks me.

I look around me once more before following her, attempting to shake the image of the man's chest being blown out as I do.

"What do you mean your security was taken out, Amelia? Why do you need security?"

She turns around, shoving me into the wall, her arm at my chest. I could easily push her away, but I'm a smart man most of the time, and something about that idea after she just blew a man to pieces makes my skin crawl.

"I'll tell you whatever you want to know if you just fucking cooperate, okay? We need to get out of here." Her eyes stay on mine for another beat before she pushes off me, continuing up the steps where Cooper waits at the top for her.

You're a smart guy... I repeat to myself silently, willing myself not to say something stupid as she turns the corner. I follow her, but when I realize it's her bedroom, I stand back against the door, taking it in.

The smell of vanilla hits me hard, almost knocking me down. It's so familiar in such an unfamiliar place, I don't know how to take it.

Cooper jumps on her bed, his butt in the air as he bows down, ready to play. Amelia waves him off. I watch her pull a large bag out of her closet, stuffing it with clothes before I let my eyes drift over everything else. Her room is green. Really green. It was always her favorite color, but back then, it was more of a dark green. The shade has matured with her.

She doesn't keep much in her room. There's a pile of books on her nightstand and canvases stacked against one of her walls. My eyes drift back to her, and I can tell she's watching me, even as she packs. She doesn't trust me.

I glance down the hall.

And I wish I hadn't.

There are blood splatters everywhere, with three bodies stacked up in the family room. A loud crash comes from the other end of the hall, and I whip around, eyes wide.

Amelia's friend comes barreling down the stairs with a large bag draped over his shoulder. His tall, large frame looking much too big in the small space. At the same time, the other woman, Luisa, steps out of her room, a gun in her hand and a bag on her shoulder. They stop as they spot me, eyeing me warily.

"Hey," I say simply, leaning against the doorframe.

"The last guy got downstairs," Amelia calls from behind me. I glance back and find her flinging the bag over her shoulder as she grabs her phone and gun. She snaps her fingers at Cooper, who follows dutifully at her heels.

She looks up at me as she passes, and I take a moment to breathe in her scent.

She was always a vanilla girl. Her favorite perfume was

67

anything that had vanilla in it. Some things don't change, no matter what.

"Are you going straight there?" she asks the other two. They start walking down the hall towards the family room, and I follow behind them, a little lost at what's happening.

Okay, a lot lost.

But I don't dare open my mouth, fully aware that the three of them have deadly weapons and seem to know how to use them much better than I do. I'll ask about that later.

"Yeah, we're going to take Amare's truck, and you take yours. Sound good?" Luisa says as they stop in front of the carnage in the middle of the room.

"Yeah, that sounds good. Can you call Veronica on the way and tell her about this?"

Amare nods, looking down at the bodies. "Yeah. I'll tell her about the security, too. I have a feeling we're not going to be coming back here until we figure out what the hell is going on." He looks around their home sadly.

A silence settles between them for a moment as they see if there's anything else they need to pack up. Deciding there's not, the three of them head towards the open kitchen to the right. I follow them, trying not to vomit at the pools of blood spattered all over the white marble countertops.

"Jesus Christ," I whisper, taking in the scene. Somehow the light of the kitchen makes everything look so much worse. And it was already bad.

Filing out the door, we come into a large, mostly empty garage.

"Why is this so big?" I ask, looking around in wonder. The scent of rubber and dust fills the air, and I'm hit with the chilly Seattle air as the garage doors open.

"The Agency wants to keep us happy, so they give us big houses with lots of room for toys to keep us occupied," Amare tells me, opening the back door of his large pickup truck and throwing his bag inside.

I look at Amelia, who meets my questioning gaze as she pops open the trunk of her Bronco, throwing in her own. "I'll tell you later," she tells me with a sigh.

Closing the trunk aggressively, she rounds the side and opens the back door, motioning for Cooper to jump inside. He does without question, and she closes the door slowly, careful not to get his tail caught in the process.

As she grabs the driver's side door handle, her eyes flash to mine, her face twisting in confusion. "Are you coming or not?" she asks, pulling the door open and climbing inside with an eye roll.

I'm frozen in my spot, confused and in shock at everything I've witnessed in only a day. I try to shake it off, but it takes another beat before I can get my feet moving. By the time I'm at the passenger side door and climbing in, the truck is already started and moving backward.

"Where are we going?" I ask, "At some point I'll get answers, right?"

She looks at me from the corner of her eye before looking behind her as she backs out of her spot. She whips around, speeding through the garage doors and down the long driveway.

The trees blur past us, the misty haze lit up in the moonlight, and I settle into the silence, realizing I'm not going to get any answers today.

EIGHT

AMELIA

The tar-black sky above us cracks as the rain drums against my truck, the puddles on the pavement glowing from the lights of the city. A haze settles over the road, beautiful and haunting at once.

Damon looks out the window to my right, his face stoic.

I never cuffed his hands when we left. I'm not sure why, as I had another pair, but something deep within me screams to trust him. I don't want to listen to it. I can't trust anyone.

For the last six years, I've learned that important lesson over and over. We're not supposed to be here, on this earth, doing what we're doing. We shouldn't be alive. Yet we are.

The only two people I trust are Amare and Luisa, but even then, we could turn against each other in a matter of seconds if we had to.

I'd like to think they wouldn't, but something deep inside of me tells me I've been let down in the past.

I sigh, slouching in my seat as I beat my fingers on the

wheel to the beat of the windshield wipers, trying not to get too agitated before we get to the apartment.

"You okay?" Damon asks, his voice uncaring.

I glance at him before returning in front of me. "I'm fine. Just jumpy," I reply as I look out the rearview mirror.

He shrugs, turning back to his window.

Cooper grunts in the back, and I extend my hand behind me, feeling for his fuzzy head. "I know boy, we're almost there," I tell him.

"When do I get to find out where we're going?" Damon asks, his hands fisting in his lap. Metal catches my eye, and I realize he still has one cuff around his wrist.

He's going to find out eventually.

"We're going to our apartment in the city. When we have really late nights here and don't want to drive home, or we don't want anyone to track us back to the house if we think anything is dubious, we just stay at the city penthouse," I inform him. "I have universal keys for our handcuffs there. I'll get that off of you."

He nods, the back of his head hitting the seat with a thump.

A comfortable silence settles between us, and I wonder how long it'll last. I mean, he was almost silent for the whole thirty-plus minutes here, but now that he has a sliver of infor-mation, I have a feeling he's going to keep pushing.

I watch the clock as we sit in traffic.

It takes one minute on the dot.

"I just really feel like you're keeping something *big* from me. I don't know why, and I know that I'm not exactly owed an explanation, but I was told back there that I may not be able to go home. I clearly stepped in something insane, and I just want to know what," Damon rambles on, and I almost tune him out. Almost. "If I'm going to die either way, shouldn't I at least know why?" he adds finally, his green eyes puncturing my heart.

I can't understand why I let him affect me so much. He's like a small puppy I want to help.

I think for a moment, figuring out how I want to go about this. As the car in front of me moves just an inch, throwing on its brakes and sending fire through my body, I understand what I need.

"I want to say this first," I tell him, turning to him fully. I meet his gaze, holding it. "I don't know who I was to you, and I don't want to know." He looks at me curiously, but otherwise keeps silent. "I'm not that girl anymore, and there's no possible way I will ever be. I don't want to know who I was before, what I did, and what happened to me, got it?" I ask.

He nods silently, his eyes narrowing. "If someone is trying to kill you, do you think it's someone from the past?"

The thought crossed my mind. But it could also be so many other people. I've pissed a lot of people off over the years, and I've killed just as many, if not more. There's a long list of people who want my head served to them on a platter, they just don't know who I really am or where to find me.

"I think it could be," I reply softly, nodding as we drive forward finally. "But there's a reason we were made to forget. I don't want to remember whatever happened. I don't want to remember the life I had before."

Damon settles back in his seat, and I spare a glance at him. His mouth is pursed, his brows furrowed as if trying to figure out what he's about to ask.

"I'm sorry that I complicated things," he whispers simply as he stares out the window. "I didn't know any of this was going on. I just saw you and I just," he pauses. "I just really had to come see you. Warn you. See that you're alive myself." He turns to me, and I can't help but give him a small smile.

"I know. And I mean it when I say that I'm sorry for kidnapping you," he chuckles, and a smirk makes its way onto my lips, "but that's just how things are here. It's tight, and someone knowing us is a huge deal. I really don't want you to get hurt, I promise," I tell him, and I mean it. I really don't want him to hurt, but we also need to be realistic about the security threat.

"Are you able to tell me what's actually going on?" he asks.

I sigh. "I—" I don't want to, but he's going to find out one way or another. I decide to give him just a little. "We were recruited by the Agency," I tell him. "We're NOC Assets for them. We're not on the books. We're basically criminals that they house, giving us money and life in exchange for, well, for our lives, I guess."

"What does that mean?" he asks.

"It means that every single one of us died. On paper, we're dead. And most of us *did* die. I know I did. That's actually one of the only things I know," I chuckle darkly, "well, besides my old name. That's all."

"Have you ever looked your name up?" he asks, and honestly? It's a great question.

I shake my head. "No, we don't do that," I tell him. "Actually, that's kind of a lie. One time I did look it up on social media, but do you know how many Ellie Huxley's there are?" He shakes his head. "A lot."

His eyes go wide.

"What is this agency?" he asks me.

I look at him through my peripheral, my lips tightening. This is the tricky part.

"Which agency do you know has gotten into some deep shit in the past?" I ask him.

His eyes squint as he thinks. "I mean, a lot of them, quite frankly."

Okay, he has a point.

I roll my eyes. "There's one in particular. *The* Agency."

He looks at me curiously. "The only one I can think of is

the CIA and they haven't been allowed to operate within the States in decades."

I shoot him a look.

"Are you kidding me?" he cries, his voice rising an octave.

"Why would I kid about that?" I ask him.

"I'm not sure but holy shit."

His back slams back against his seat, his hand at his forehead. "You okay?" I ask him.

He groans. "Yeah. I'm just processing that I'm definitely a dead man." I chuckle, and he shoots me a glare. "You even told me so, Amelia. If you're involved with them then—" he trails off, his eyes closing. "That's some really, really illegal shit."

"Yes," I reply simply, gripping the wheel a little tighter.

He falls silent, processing everything I told him. I haven't even told him everything, honestly.

Though he's taking it like a champ, if I may say so myself. He may be a dead man, but he's a reasonably calm dead man.

Several moments pass, and we're finally close to the apartment. I take a left, and then a right, pulling into the underground garage of the building. We park next to Amare and Luisa who seem to have gotten here only a few minutes before us.

I turn to Damon. "If you knew what's good for you, you wouldn't say a word about what we just spoke about." I keep our eyes locked, hoping he understands the urgency of my request.

He looks at his hands and nods.

The ride up to the penthouse is tense.

Amare stands against the wall, his arms crossed over his broad chest, his eyes never leaving Damon once.

But Damon doesn't seem to mind.

In fact, he's just standing in the corner, a polite smile on his face.

Luisa looks at me, her eyebrow raised at the same time Cooper whines, letting out a large yawn.

I shrug.

After what feels like an eon, the elevator dings, and for some reason, it feels almost like a death sentence.

We enter a mud room of the penthouse, and Amare unlocks the door, his duffle bag in tow.

All four of us are dead silent as we enter. Amare and Luisa drop their bags to the ground with a thump, and I do the same. They go off to check the place out without a word, making sure nothing is out of place. Hoping no one has been here.

As I go to do the same, Damon catches my arm. "What do you need me to do?" he asks.

I look down at his hand before my eyes drift up, finally meeting his. "First," I grit through my teeth. "I need you to let go of my arm." He drops his hand, his face searching mine. "Second, you can stay here with Cooper," I tell him, and Cooper looks at me, his head cocked. "We don't need you getting into any more trouble." I spit, anger and hatred coursing through my body all of a sudden.

With that, I grab my handgun and head down the hall, flipping on every switch I can find before searching each room.

Behind the doors, under the beds, in the closets; we look everywhere.

What happened back at our home could be nothing. It could have been someone going astray. It could have been one of those someone's I pissed off looking for my head on that silver platter, and maybe they're totally fine with just scaring me. The amount of bodies left behind should be enough to scare them, too.

But there's a larger part of me that knows that this isn't

just nothing; that it's not just some small thing that'll get brushed under the rug soon enough.

This is serious.

"You guys done?" Lu calls from the family room. I head back that way, finding the three of them standing there, looking at each other. Damon looks sheepish, his hands at his sides as he looks up at the ceiling.

"Everything okay?" I inquire as I tuck my gun into the back of my jeans.

Amare's eyes narrow. "I'm not sure what we should do with him," he tells me, leaning against the back of the black couch.

"What do you mean what are we going to do with him?" I ask.

Even though I want him here just as much as they do, I feel some sort of protectiveness of him. I want to make sure that he's all right.

"I mean are we going to keep him locked somewhere," he replies, running his large hand through his hair.

"Why would we do that?" I ask, perplexed. "The man was alone with me in the car for forty minutes. He hasn't hurt me and all he's been is confused. I'm still suspicious of how he found me too, but he's with us. He's not going to hurt any of us, or he would have already."

"This isn't just about you," Luisa states, almost annoyed.

I stare at her, not understanding where that idea came from. "I don't think it's just about me," I assure her. "But the guy is fucked either way. I'm not sure what locking him up is going to do other than make him absolutely miserable for however long he must stay here."

Damon opens his mouth. "Thank you—"

"Shut the hell up."

He nods, backing up a step.

I look back at the other two, my shoulders sagging. "Look, guys," I sigh. "I don't know why I trust him, but I do. Some-

77

thing in me is telling me that he knows how he can help, and that he will."

Amare and Lu look at each other, silently coming to an agreement.

"Fine," Amare says simply. "But you're responsible for him."

My mouth gapes. "He's not a fucking pet."

"Amelia it's fi—" the voice to my right comes again.

"How many times do I have to tell you to shut up?" I turn back to Amare. "I'll make sure everything is taken care of," I say coldly before picking up my bag and tossing it over my shoulder.

I get to the hallway before I snap, commanding Cooper to follow me.

Instead, I get a two-for-one deal as Damon joins him.

I roll my eyes, turning back and heading to my room.

"Where am I sleeping?" Damon asks as I make my way into the large space.

I sigh, setting everything down as Cooper jumps on the bed, immediately making himself comfortable.

"I would say the couch, but I think it would be better if you were in here tonight," I tell him. He looks at the bed. "On the floor, dumbass," I add, grabbing a blanket from the closet and tossing it to him.

"Are you kidding me?" he asks, eying Cooper. "I have to sleep on the floor as the dog looks down at me?"

I nod, sitting on the edge of the bed and going through my bag. "Just for tonight. They don't trust you," I tell him, my eyes flashing to his.

"And you do?"

I stop what I'm doing, searching his face for any hint of disloyalty. I don't know who he was to me before I died, but I have a feeling I had him wrapped around my little finger.

I keep our eyes locked, the silence between us tensing. I can feel the tension growing thicker as the seconds pass, and a jolt of electricity runs down my spine, making me shiver. His eyes are intense, piercing mine, and I have to look away.

"Should I?" I ask finally, dropping my clothes on the bed.

We stay like that for what feels like minutes, sizing each other up. His eyes drift down to my lips, and a small part of me almost wishes he'd close the gap between us.

I can hear the others in their rooms, moving and shuffling around, but all I can *feel* is his eyes on me, burning me under their gaze.

I shake the thought off, struggling with what my heart is remembering and what my brain is forcing me to forget. I don't care if we were something before this. Maybe we were, maybe we weren't. I'm not that girl anymore.

Suddenly, he takes a measured step toward me, his eyes ablaze with heat. There's something so familiar about him, and it kills me inside.

He takes another step, his muscles tense as he comes to a stop in front of me. I look up at him, our breaths mingling between us. I take a step back, only for him to close the distance again. Suddenly, the wall is at my back, and I'm cornered.

For some reason, I don't want to get out of this. I want to see what happens. It's weakness.

I breathe in, taking in his masculine scent. He's dirty, bloody, and exhausted, but there's something about the smell that makes my muscles soften.

"I think you know the answer to that," he murmurs, his voice low as he brushes my hair out of my face.

I close my eyes, fighting what my heart wants and what my brain is telling me. Ignoring the heat traveling down my body as his eyes watch me, unwavering. My heart pounds in my chest, and my chest heaves. He glances down, his eyes raking over my body before meeting mine once more.

But I snap out of it. shoving him in the stomach, knocking him off balance as he falls onto my bed, a shocked look on his face as I step up to him, leaning over his body. I can feel his muscles against mine as I remove the gun from my back pocket, placing the barrel at his head. My eyes flash to the small scar above his right eye, but I force myself to look away, not wanting to be bothered by curiosity.

He looks at me as if I'm God, and I have the power of Creation. Like I'm powerful. And he's terrified of it.

"I don't want you to think for even one second that you're in control here," I hiss, my jaw clenching. "You are a means to an end. You are nothing, do you understand? I don't trust you. You haven't given me a reason to." I push away, grabbing a pillow from the bed and tossing it to the floor before grabbing my clothes.

"There's a shower through there," I tell him, pointing to the bathroom. "Get washed up, you smell."

He doesn't give me the satisfaction of a response. Instead, he simply walks around the bed and through the door, shutting it with a smack.

We're in for a long couple of days.

A knock on my door wakes me up. I squint as I open my eyes, the morning light blinding me. My back is stiff from this new bed, and I'm greeted by two different snores. For a moment, I forget Damon is sleeping on the ground below.

"Amelia, Veronica is going to be here in fifteen," Lu tells me from the other side.

"I'll be out in a couple of minutes," I groan, wishing I could get another hour of sleep.

"Do you want me to walk Coop while you get dressed?" she asks.

I only take a second to think about it. "Actually yeah, if you don't mind." I climb out of bed, nearly stepping on

Damon as I do. I grab Cooper's leash from my bag, opening the door to let him out.

"Thank you," I tell Lu, who's somehow bright-eyed and bushy-tailed like normal, despite the early morning.

"No problem," she assures me, peering around me.

"He's on the floor on the other side of the bed," I inform her quietly. "I'm going to have him stay in here while Veronica is visiting."

"What are we talking about?" Amare asks as he exits his room in nothing but a pair of maroon slacks. I furrow my brows at the outfit choice but leave it alone. Amare loves going shirtless around the house, but usually it's with something normal, like shorts.

Maybe he's trying to be cute for Veronica.

He notices my gaze and looks down at himself, rolling his eyes. "I'll put a shirt on before she gets here." I nod, my lips tightening into a straight line.

"Stop giving me that look, what were you talking about?"

"I'm going to have Damon stay in the room while she's here," I tell him, leaning against the doorframe. "Does she know we have him?"

"I didn't tell her anything other than the house was attacked," he says.

I nod, biting my lip. "We need to keep him from her," I say finally.

Luisa nearly chokes. "What are you talking about? Of course, she needs to know about him."

"If she knows about him, then he's gone. So is any help we're going to get from him," I argue.

"Did he tell you something? Are you okay?" she asks me.

"Goddammit, Lu I'm fine. I just want to get to the bottom of this and figure out who is trying to kill me." I can't hide the exasperation in my voice, and I just hope they take me seriously.

They both study me before nodding, Luisa looking down

at her shoes, Amare looking past me into my room.

I tuck my disheveled hair behind my ear. "You guys know it's true. We need him."

Amare sucks at his lip before tapping the wall he was leaning against, pushing off it and heading for the kitchen. Luisa gives me one last look before gently pulling Cooper along with her towards the door.

I'll take that as a win.

Taking a deep breath, I close my eyes, letting myself fall back against the wall.

"El—I mean Amelia? You doing okay?" a groggy voice asks from behind me.

I turn, catching sight of Damon's head peeking above the bed, his eyes heavy with exhaustion, his black hair sticking straight up. "Yeah," I tell him, returning to the room. "They were just telling me that our contact with the Agency is stopping by soon. You need to stay in here with Cooper and pretend you don't exist, okay?"

His eyes narrow for a second as he sleepily digests the information given to him. "Cooper has to hide, too?" he asks as I start gathering my clothes.

"She knows I have him," I tell him as I head for the bathroom. "I'm just technically not supposed to have him. She told me the first time she saw him that if she does not see him, she'll pretend as though he doesn't exist."

Damon nods but looks like the only thing he wants to do is pass out again.

"Go back to sleep," I insist. "Just remember when you wake up to stay in here. And stay quiet. No flushing the toilet, taking a shower, nothing. You stay on his bed and just," I look around the room, trying to find something he could do with himself. "I don't know. Make yourself busy. I don't care how."

At that, one dark eyebrow shoots up, and a smirk graces his lips. I roll my eyes, shutting the bathroom door.

"And you just, you just shot the first guy?" Veronica asks, her long manicured nails tapping the coffee mug in front of her, nonplussed. Her eyes search mine, waiting for me to tell her I'm joking.

"Yes," I reply, crossing my arms over my chest as I lean back in my chair.

"Why would you do that?"

Veronica is a great person, don't get me wrong. A bit of an airhead, Veronica is one of those people who constantly surprises you.

The first thing she surprised me with this morning is how much creamer she puts in her coffee.

Amare was able to find a bag of stale coffee beans in the cabinet, along with a little basket of those single coffee creamers. I swear Veronica used about twelve in her small mug.

The second thing she surprised me with is how against murder she is, apparently, despite working for the Agency and approving the assassination of multiple high-powered individuals in the last couple of years. Apparently, she draws the line at random men that come into our home with the intent to kill.

I gape at her as I pour my own coffee, my brows furrowed. "I mean, I'm not sure, probably because he admitted to being there to kill me?" I was never great at hiding my sarcasm.

She rolls her eyes, leaning back in her seat. "I just think you should have thought through it a little more," she tells me, "you guys could have taken him down to the basement and found out why he was there."

"Except for the fact that the others were asleep, and he was bigger than me," I tell her, looking at her incredulously.

It's extremely important in our field of work to be reasonable. I can be good at fighting, lethal even, and understand that I'm not a large person. Most of my power comes from being able to move, and move fast. I know I'm not the strongest person, and I'm not going to win a fight by brute force. That's just not realistic.

I take the opportunities I get in order to win a fight, and if I think that my life is in danger because someone is bigger than me, I'm going to take whatever opportunity I have in order to end them.

She clicks her tongue, her fingernails tapping on the surface again. "I just think that you could have gone about it differently, that is all," she tells me. I watch them, my mood souring with each tap.

I roll my eyes once more, turning around to wash a couple of dishes in the sink so I don't end up saying something I'll regret later.

"I think the bigger problem here is the men who came afterward," Lu tells her. I shoot a grateful look over my shoulder at her, thankful for her moving the conversation onward. "Who were they and how did they find us?"

Curious to hear what bullshit Veronica will spew, I finish scrubbing the plate, rinse it, and set it down before turning around and leaning against the sink, my arms crossed over my chest, my lips tight.

"We're not sure how they got past all the security cameras," Veronica shakes her head, looking at her phone. "We're not sure who they are, either if I'm honest." I roll my eyes. We told them as soon as we left. They should have more answers by now.

We stay silent as we watch her. She looks up at the ceiling before flipping her long black hair over her shoulder. "Okay look," she begins, pushing her mug away from her, the sound of the clay scratching against the marble deafening in the quiet room. "I talked to the higher-ups. You're not going to like this, but there's nothing we can do here. You guys need to figure it out."

Amare's eyes flash with anger as he stands, his hands fisted at his sides. "Are you fucking kidding me?" he nearly yells.

Veronica puts her hands up in front of her, rearing back just a little. Amare is usually the most level-headed of us. "You guys know the deal. You guys know why you're here. This is a security risk for us. We can't have the agency looking into why people were there, because that's a connection we can't have. You guys are off the books for a reason." What she doesn't say is that we're throwaways. We are quite literally labeled as expendable.

I knew it was coming, and yet it still hurts to hear. I know what we're here to do, I know why they saved us, but to actually hear that they don't really give a single shit about whether we live or die is a whole other situation.

"Is there anything you can do at all?" I ask her.

"No."

"Is there anything you can tell us in order to help *us* figure it out?"

She takes a second to answer, looking down at her lap. There's a reason she's a handler and not an agent. She's too open with her emotions and thoughts. "Until you guys figure it out, you need to be careful. Do whatever you need to do, just know that the Agency can't help you at all. You get yourselves arrested? We can't get you out. One of you gets killed? We have nothing to do with it."

"That doesn't really answer my question," I growl.

Her posture becomes rigid. "You do whatever you have to do. That's your answer. I would suggest you don't go back until you figure it out. I'll make sure the house is repaired and the security is set up, but you need to find out why this is happening because we can't. You have permission to go wherever you need to go, but you are not to use Agency resources."

Amare leans against the wall. "Can we connect with other

Fallen Angels if we need to?" he asks.

A loud thump from the other room interrupts us. Amare and Luisa's eyes flash to me as Veronica eyes all three of us.

"I think I left my bag on the edge of my bed," I explain. "It must have fallen off or something."

Veronica nods, taking a sip of coffee, relaxing a little. "I meant official Agency resources. The others are the same as you are," she answers Amare.

"Are we allowed to use any resources previously granted to us?" Lu asks. "As in, can we use the plane if we need to travel somewhere?"

Veronica eyes her, likely wondering what we have planned that we would need that. I also wonder, considering we haven't made plans at all.

Lu sees her confusion and shrugs. "I just want to make sure we cover our bases. These things are never simple, and I don't want to have to call you every single time we need something, especially when you guys aren't helping us any other way."

Veronica nods, thinking for a moment. "I'll make sure you have all the resources previously provided to you so that you can figure this out. You guys are important to us, and we don't want to lose you. You've done a lot of really good work here in Seattle, but you need to also understand the reason you're here," she tells us again, driving the wedge into my heart. "I've already talked to them, and as I said, do whatever you need to do to end this and make sure that you guys can go back to the compound. If this becomes bigger, they will not hesitate to act and wipe out the problem." She shoots me a pointed look, but she didn't have to. I know what she means.

If we don't figure this out and it becomes a bigger problem, risking the Agency, we're dead. They will not hesitate to kill us.

NINE

Damon

I've been staring at the ceiling for the last two hours, stuck in this room until whoever is here leaves. Cooper stretches out next to me, letting out a loud yawn.

I never knew how much I would miss things like my phone, or a book.

A book...

I saw a couple of them in a bag by the bed.

Rolling over, I search both sides of the bed, coming up with nothing. Leaning over a little further, I peek my head under the bed.

There we go.

Grabbing the bag, I pull it out, finding several books, a couple of thin canvases, and some paints. Interesting. Ellie was always into books, but painting must be a new hobby.

Six years and seven months ago.

"Your house has a library?" I ask, shocked as Ellie shows me around her home. She shrinks into herself, thinking I'm making fun of her. "That's so cool." I look around before my eyes meet hers, and

I see the small smile on her face. I've only been able to get a few out of her in the last couple of months, but each one has meant more to me than anything.

"Do you spend a lot of time in here?" I ask.

She shrugs. "I do when I can. Dad doesn't like me being in here if he's home. He hangs out in here all the time with his friends, drinking."

I nod, filing that in the back of my mind for later.

"What is your favorite genre?"

Ellie and I have become good friends in the last couple of months. Ever since that day in the library, we've bonded over how terrible I am at math, and how great she is at, well, everything. We spend a lot of time together outside of class, and I'm starting to feel horrible about lying to her.

This girl needs a friend.

Ellie is well-loved and has friends outside of college, but none of them understand her. All sorority girls and cheerleaders, her friends come from rich families who treat their kids like Gods. Ellie didn't have that good fortune.

Though her family is wealthy and her dad is powerful, Ellie's home life is nothing she would ever brag about. She hasn't come out and said it, but I know she's been abused in the past. It's written all over her face whenever she speaks of her family.

I want to protect her.

"I think it's romance." She flinches, as if admitting that is painful.

I shrug. "Nothing wrong with that. I've read a couple of romances recently actually," I'm not lying, either. I've been known to enjoy one or two once in a while.

She looks up at me, her eyes wide as she bites her lip.

Looking through the books, I try to find one that may interest me. Amelia won't mind, right? I mean, they're books!

The entire pile is romance books except for one thriller, which I take happily. If she was going to be mad at me for reading her books, she was going to be a little less mad at me for avoiding whatever romance books she has, right? Yeah, I'm sure.

So, thriller it is.

Cracking it open, I start reading, Cooper stretched out at my side, his paws digging into the side of my body.

Twenty minutes go by, and I feel my eyes growing heavy when I hear a door shut, the murmur of voices quieting. If I had gone closer to the door, I could have probably heard what they were saying, but if I'm honest, I didn't want to.

It's only a couple of minutes later when I hear footsteps walking down the hall, and Cooper lifts his head lazily.

The door opens, and Amelia comes in quietly, her shoulders slumped over.

"Are you okay?" I ask, putting the book down.

She eyes it, and for a second I think she's going to yell at me before she looks up, meeting my eyes.

"Yes," is all she says before walking over to the bathroom. I hear the sink turn on.

Climbing out of bed, I walk over to the bathroom, watching her as she splashes water on her face, her elbows propping herself against the counter.

"Amelia," I start, but she cuts me off with a glare.

"You're fine. They don't know you were with us. We're not going to kill you; you're going to be fine," she tells me.

"That's not what I was going to say."

"Then what?" Her tone is harsh.

"I want to make sure you're okay."

She pauses, watching the water fall from the faucet and make its way down the drain. Her back straightens as she stretches before standing and drying her hands off on the fluffy blue towel hanging on the wall.

"I'll be fine. We just have to work through some things," she tells me as she pushes past, her vanilla scent stopping me in my tracks.

I take a deep breath in, and my eyes close. I've missed that smell so much; I don't think I'll ever get over smelling it again.

"I have to go take Cooper for a walk. You can stay here and read my books if you want," she tells me as she gathers Cooper's leash, sending the book laid out on the bed a sideways glance. "But you're free to roam the apartment. You can't leave us just yet; we need to figure out a couple of other things, but you don't have to stay in this room anymore. You can sleep out on the couch tonight, I already talked to the other two," she tells me, heading for the door.

I nod, looking at my makeshift bed and back at the door as she leaves.

"Is there anything here to eat?" I ask Amelia.

It's a couple of hours later, and my stomach has been growling for the last thirty minutes. The dog has eaten more than I have.

"Yeah, there's yogurt in the fridge," she tells me, not looking up from her phone.

I nod, heading over to it. That's about all they have.

"How long are we staying here?" I ask her.

"I have no clue, but if you're worried about the amount of food we have, don't be. Amare and Luisa are at the store right now getting things," she tells me, finally looking up with a huff.

Grabbing a yogurt, I grab a spoon and rip the top open, shoveling it into my mouth as fast as I can. It dawns on me that I haven't eaten since I had a bite of whatever Amelia had brought for me the day before.

Amelia gets up from the couch and heads for the fridge, pulling an apple out of the bottom compartment. Grabbing a knife, she starts cutting it into slices next to me.

I smile.

"You know, before, you used to—"

In only a short second, my back is to the counter, the knife at my throat.

I look down at her, her eyes filled with rage and hurt as she presses the blade into my skin.

"What have I told you?" she hisses, her body pressing into mine harder.

"You've told me lots of things, I'm just trying to connect with you," I tell her, swallowing.

"I don't want to connect with you," she growls, the blade pressing into me harder. "I don't want anything to do with you if I'm honest. But I told you I don't want to know about the past. Not a single thing. Do not tell me anything, do you understand? That's the one thing I've asked. The one ground rule. No speak of who I was before, do you fucking understand me?"

It's only now that I feel her handshake and notice the apprehension in her eyes. She's scared. She won't show it, she won't tell me, but she's scared of the past. I can see right past whatever mask she puts on.

"What happened to you?" I whisper, careful not to move my head as I lift my hand, tucking her hair behind her ear.

"Nothing that concerns you." She bares her teeth, letting up just a little.

"You can tell me," I press, moving forward just a little, testing her.

She pushes me back against the counter with a smack, the knife pressing in harder, biting into my skin. Anger flashes in her beautiful brown eyes.

A couple of things run through my mind as she holds the knife to my throat.

One, she's beautiful.

Two, I should be scared.

Three, I would gladly let her slit my throat every day if it made her feel better. If it took this fear in her eyes away. If she was able to live a normal life, and not feel as if she was chased by the past.

I want to make everything better for her, no matter how much I must suffer.

And maybe that's my problem. Maybe that'll lead to my ultimate demise. But I've lost this woman once, and it was the worst moment of my entire life. Finding her again was something I never thought was possible; not in a million years.

In this moment, I know that I'm not going back. I'm not ever going back to how I used to be. I'm not losing her again. I don't care what's going on here, I don't care what I must sacrifice to make her feel better, I'll do it. I'll do it a thousand times over just to make sure that she lives a comfortable, worry-free life.

I'm not giving her up ever again.

"I don't want to hurt you," I whisper.

"You can't hurt me," she whispers back, her eyes never leaving mine. She holds my attention, not backing down. But I can see it. I can see the hurt in them, the years and years of confusion and despair.

Her fist clenches at her side as she holds the blade still, brushing against my jeans as it does, and I can feel my blood run south. Her lips part as she looks at my lips, her muscles stiffening.

For a long moment, everything is silent, only the sound of my heart beating in my chest for everyone to hear. It felt that way, at least. As if it were caged, desperate to be set free. It's the kind of silence rife with anticipation settling upon us in heavy ecstasy. We both know nothing will come from it, but it's thrilling all the same.

I lower my gaze, feeling the bite of the metal once more as I take in the rise and fall of her chest.

"It's okay if you are," I whisper. "But I don't want you to be. I'm sorry for mentioning it."

She looks at me for a couple more moments, only blinking

once before she forces herself to look away, dropping her hand with the knife, slamming it on the counter in the process. The metal rattles against the marble before it settles, so loud in the tense room.

She stays pressed to me for another moment before giving me her back, retreating into her room.

But that moment was enough for me to understand that she's in there, deep down. She has to be. I would embrace this new version of her, but she remembers me deep down. The scale has been tipped, and only time will tell if she'll come around.

I know enough about people not to follow her, but that doesn't mean that I don't want to. I do, with every fiber of my being.

But I meant what I said. I don't want to scare her. I want her to feel comfortable around me. I want her to let her guard down.

If I need to treat her as though I never knew her before, never knew a single thing, I will. I'll get to know her all over again.

I just want to be a part of her life.

Even if it kills me.

I was able to sneak into the room while Amelia was in the shower, grabbing the book I was reading and the blanket she gave me before heading back to the family room to set up my new sleeping arrangement.

Although the couch wouldn't exactly be my choice of bed, it was better than the floor, and who am I to whine about an upgrade, no matter how small?

Flipping off the overhead lights and turning on the lamp next to the couch, I settle in, opening the book to the last page read. I'm a slow reader, so I never got very far. In fact, I haven't read a book in years. But maybe I should.

Six years and four months ago

"I think you should read this," Ellie tells me, handing me a beast of a novel.

I look at it in confusion, turning it over in my hands. "What is this?" I ask her, holding it up.

"It's a novel." Her grin lights up her entire face, her eyes bright as she watches me try to understand what she's talking about.

"Ellie this looks like a textbook," I tell her, flipping through the pages, which all happen to look like a puzzle. The amount of footnotes is astronomical, and there's even some pages with only a simple word on it.

"It's a thriller," she starts, turning around as we continue to walk through the aisles of the bookstore. "it had a cult following at one point. It's really good, I think you'll like it. You love puzzles." She looks back at me with a smirk, fire alight in her eyes.

"I do love a good puzzle," I tell her, looking it over once more. Of course I'll buy it. I'll do every single thing this woman tells me to do for as long as she'll allow me to.

I hear the shower turn off, and the bedroom door open, a pair of bare feet padding down the hall towards me.

Amelia's head pops around the corner, her eyes tired. "I'm going to bed. Amare and Lu stopped at a bar for a drink, apparently. They'll be here a little later, so don't freak out if they come in late," she informs me.

I nod, not wanting to say anything else and make her angry.

She looks at me for another moment before turning around, making her way back to her room.

I let out a sigh before going back to my reading.

I get lost in the story for about forty minutes until I realize that something feels very, very off.

I can't figure out what.

Looking around the room, everything seems in place, as

far as I know. Tossing the blanket off me, I stand, walking to the kitchen. Nothing out of place here, either.

Peering down the hall, I notice that all the doors are shut, just as they usually are.

I turn back around, walking back into the center of the family room.

It's only when I look down at the book sitting on the couch that I see it.

There's a red dot on my chest.

TEN

AMELIA

I've been tossing and turning for the last thirty minutes. Cooper isn't helping as he kicks me in his sleep.

The past scares me, that's no secret. What also scares me is how familiar Damon feels. How much I want him to touch me. How much I wish I could hear what he has to say without breaking down.

But I know myself. I know that if I get a taste of the past, I'm going to want to know everything. When it comes to the Fallen Angels and what is required of us, knowing everything is just going to lead to pain. It'll lead to suffering down the road, especially if I ever have to make choices I'll regret.

Images of me pulling the trigger plague my mind. They always have. The idea that I'd have to kill anyone I'm close to has been one of my biggest fears since the very beginning of this journey. But those are platonic relationships. I don't want Lu or Amare to touch me the way I think about Damon touching me.

He just feels so familiar, and that kills me.

I don't want to do that to him, and I don't want to do that to myself.

For now, I can't know. I can't have those close calls where I almost let him tell me about who I was before.

I don't want to grieve her.

I turn over once more when fast footsteps stop me mid-thought. My door whips open, and Damon stands in the entrance, his hair disheveled, a panicked look on his handsome face.

"Amelia, I think there's a sni—" his words are cut off by the sound of a bullet hitting glass, and I roll off the bed immediately, pulling Cooper along with me, cushioning his fall.

"Get down!" I yell, crawling to the door.

Damon drops, covering his head with his hands as he flings himself against the hallway wall. Cooper is in front of me, crawling as I've trained him. "Room, now," I command, and he continues to crawl down the hallway until he reaches our saferoom. His nose nuzzles the button I had installed, and I only let out the breath I'm holding when he's safely inside, the door shut behind him.

"Is that bulletproof glass?" Damon asks as another shot rings out.

"Obviously, but one will break through any second. It can only handle so much." I peek around the corner as bullets ricochet off the glass, unrelenting.

He looks at me as if what I said was absurd. "I don't fucking understand what's going *on*," he groans. I raise a brow at him, encouraging him to go on. "How the hell are you not technically connected to the CIA, yet you live in a giant house, and have a giant penthouse apartment with fucking *bulletproof windows?!*" he asks, pulling at his hair. The last 24 hours have not been kind to the guy.

The shots continue to sound through the apartment. "Do you understand how much money can buy?" I wait for him to answer, but he just keeps his eyes trained on me, seemingly forgetting the dire situation we're in. "Do you know how easy it is to cover things up with money? We work for an incredibly rich man. He doesn't exist, but we do. If you're rich enough, no one will care enough to look into you. Fake documents are a thing for a reason. And do you really think that a government agency, no matter who they employ or how secret it is, will let us sleep in rooms overlooking a city without bulletproof windows? Are you fucking insane?" I ask finally, getting to my hands and knees.

His head hits the wall as he lets out a groan, and I look around, figuring out our next move.

"I don't know how they found us," I mutter mostly to myself as I look back into the room, spotting my phone on the bed.

Getting back on my hands and knees, I make my way back in slowly, trying to ignore how close the glass sounds to breaking. Grabbing my phone, I quickly make my way back out before telling Damon to follow me.

A second later, just as I'm back in the hallway, a bullet breaks through the glass, hitting my comforter, a cloud of feathers exploding into the air.

He obeys without question, and I open the saferoom door, letting him inside. I look out to the family room just as the window explodes, and more gunfire sounds through the apartment. I crawl in quickly just as bullets make their way through the wall, hitting the surface above my head. I shut the door quickly, hoping my cell signal is good enough for me to reach the other two.

Damon and Cooper sit in the corner, both looking eerily similar as they look at me with fear in their eyes.

"Good boy," I tell Cooper, rubbing the side of his face and kissing his nose. Damon looks at me expectantly, as if I'd do the same for him. I shoot him a look before glancing back at my phone, opening my group chat with Amare and Lu.

"What are you doing?" Damon asks me.

"I'm telling the others to stay out, and not come home. If they're on their way, they need to turn around," I tell him. "When the shooting stops, we need to get out of here as soon as we can, because the place will be swarming minutes after."

"How do you know that?" he asks.

I look at him quizzically, reminding myself that not everyone is used to thinking on their feet and figuring out life-or-death problems.

"If you were trying to kill someone, and wanted to make sure they were dead, you'd make your way in as fast as possible, wouldn't you?" I ask, trying to be as nice as possible.

He nods, looking down at his hands.

I look back at my phone, shooting a text off to the others before taking a second to think. "I'm going to tell them to meet us at Fredrick's," I tell him firmly. "We can all meet there and figure out what we're going to do.

He nods, not looking me in the eye. His black hair is unruly, his eyes look sleepy. I feel bad for putting him in this position, but not enough to let him go.

Who knows if he's even safe on his own anymore. He may be better off with me.

Two more minutes of constant gunshots pass before they die down. I wait about twenty seconds before opening the door and making my way out, telling Damon and Cooper to stay where they are until I tell them to follow.

The place is destroyed.

Pieces of drywall lay everywhere, dust and powder covering every inch of the place, but the silence is what feels the most crippling. Not the loss of another home, not the insecurity, no. The silence, despite the lights and traffic below.

I take only a second to take everything in before signaling to Damon.

Crawling to my room, I grab whatever I can, which isn't much. Cooper's leash sits behind the door, covered in drywall dust. Other than that, everything is destroyed. I have nothing left. Not that I had much to begin with.

Ducking under the bed, I grab two guns I had taped to the bedframe and tuck one into my pants. When I return to Damon, I hand him one, and he once again looks at it as if he's never seen a gun before. After a couple of seconds, he too tucks it into the band of his pants before nodding at me, our eyes lingering just a second too long for comfort.

Knowing Damon didn't have anything at all with him, I motion for him to follow me, clipping the leash onto Cooper's collar.

We've never been in this much danger before. At least, not in our own homes. I've been close to death more times than I can count out on missions, but it has never followed me home like this before. I'm going to have to find somewhere to keep him if this keeps up. I don't want to risk his life. We may not be able to help it, but he never asked for this life. I love him too much to bring him into these dangerous situations unknowingly.

Reaching the door, I turn to Damon. "Put your shoes on. We need to be quick. Like I said, there's going to be people on this place in seconds," I tell him before turning back, ready to go.

Peeling open the broken door, we run out, heading up the stairs toward the roof and around the corner just in time before several men dressed in black body armor break down the door to the staircase.

When they're safely in the apartment, we make our way quickly to the stairs. The elevator is too risky.

I shove Damon and Cooper in front of me as we go, constantly looking up to ensure we're not being followed. We're almost far enough away before I hear the clang of the door and footsteps echo through the stairwell. Yelling follows, and before I know it, bullets rain down on us.

"Run!" I call to Damon as he almost stops, shielding

himself and Coop. He looks at me, his eyes wide. I can see the wheels turning in his head as he tries to figure out whether he should stay and help me, but I shoo him away.

As he finally turns to do as I say, I crouch down, my gun drawn as I look above me. As one of the men peeks over, I take my shot but miss as he ducks back.

Slowly, staying in my crouched position, I make my way back down the stairs, keeping my gun drawn. A woman opens the door to my left, thinking she's fleeing from the gunshots raining upon the building, and her eyes grow wide as she sees me. I motion for her to close the door, and she does. I wonder how many people will be outside. They're safer in their homes, but they don't know that.

Another bullet whizzes past me, and I shoot, hoping I'll hit him this time.

"Fuck!" a voice bellows from above as footsteps boom around me, closer and closer as the seconds go by.

Turning, I start to run down the stairs, thinking I can outrun them.

But I stop dead in my tracks as I find Damon and Cooper at the door waiting for me. I never told them what to do when they get out, and there could be people waiting for us outside, their guns at the ready, all too pleased to put bullets in our skulls. It's reasonable they waited, but fear strikes me like a lightning bolt as my body tenses. Looking back up the stairs, I nod at him, silently telling him I'll be back in a moment, and run back up, ready to take on whatever meets me.

Once I'm far enough up the stairs that I feel comfortable no one will get to Damon if they get by me, I hide behind the corner, ready to strike when they get to me. Closing my eyes, I count, listening to the footsteps.

One… two… three…

Right when they reach the landing, I stand, the gun steady in my hand as I shoot one in the neck right between their body armor and their mask before they can even lift their weapon, blood spurting against the white walls behind them. They go down with a thump, a pool of blood collecting on the linoleum floor.

The other turns, and I grab their gun, pulling him toward me as I spin behind him, my left arm wrapping around his helmet and holding the bottom, the bulletproof material cool to the touch, my right hand wrapped around the top. I pull my arms back in opposite directions without hesitating, feeling his neck snap as I go down with him.

As the smell of copper fills the air, I turn, making my way back down the stairs as fast as I can, my thighs burning.

As I reach Damon, his eyes fill with concern as he looks me up and down. Attempting to see what he's looking at, I glance down, noticing the blood spatter covering my green shirt and shorts.

"You ready?" I ask him as I position to head out the door.

He nods, at a loss for words.

"I'll go first, I'll take out anyone I can, but you may need to shoot someone, got it?" I'm not sure what he did at his cute little detective job, but it's clear he wasn't super into the idea of killing anyone. I really hope I don't have to torture anyone in front of him.

Taking a deep breath, I get ready for a fight, whipping the door open, my gun raised.

"Was the job do—" I don't wait for the man to see me, shooting him in the neck before he can finish. Another man rounds the corner, and my gun goes off before he gets the chance to process what's happening.

I call out to Damon and Cooper, and we run across the pavement as I look around to make sure there's no one else following us. I'm sure there were building residents escaping, and I pray they were able to get out before having to deal with the men sent in.

Throwing open the back door, I all but throw Cooper in

before climbing in myself. I throw the keys into the ignition, backing up as fast as possible.

"I have no idea if we'll be followed," I tell Damon, who's all but clutching his chest in the seat next to me. "I'm going to drive around for a bit to make sure we're in the clear."

He nods, his green eyes still wide, his black hair practically gray with dust.

I almost want to smile. Almost.

After a couple of minutes, the man next to me settles down, his body decompressing as he slumps over in his seat.

"You doing okay?" I ask him, glancing in my rearview mirror for the tenth time to check if anyone is following.

"I've had more near-death experiences in the last two days than I ever have, and I've had my moments," Damon tells me, his hands holding his head.

Stopped at a red light, I look at him. Really look at him as the city lights highlight his tired face.

His high cheekbones appear even more intense in the moonlight as they've become hallowed from fatigue and lack of food, and his lack of quality sleep really shows as the rings around his eyes are dark. With the way the shadows hit him, it almost appears as if he has two black eyes. His beard has started to grow back in as he hasn't been able to shave for a couple of days.

If I'm being completely honest with myself, despite looking terrible, I still find him incredibly attractive, the magnetic pull that's been building stronger than ever.

"We'll get you something to eat when we get to the bar." If we can't, I'll stop when we leave. I'm not sure how long we'll be there, but we have to come up with a plan. We're not safe anywhere right now, apparently.

How were we tracked? The apartment isn't in any of our names. In fact, it's not in anyone's, really. It was bought by the Agency, just like the house, but it's not connected to them, either. I wasn't lying when I said money hides anything if you have enough of it.

I can't help but wonder what would have happened if Damon wasn't there in the family room. If he had been asleep too and hadn't warned me when he did. Sure, we hopefully would have woken up when the first round of bullets hit the glass, but it's reasonable to think about what would have happened if we didn't. We're both exhausted. Damon could be like Luisa, who has slept through our fire alarm on several occasions as Amare forgot about the bacon in the oven.

We could all be dead right now.

And did whoever was shooting at us know that Lu and Amare were out of the apartment? It was apparent back at the house that they wanted me. I still don't know why.

He might. You just don't want to know.

I fight back the thought. He made it clear he doesn't know who did it. If I can deal with this without knowing everything about my past, that's what I want to do. I don't want to have to grieve while dealing with any of this.

ELEVEN

DAMON

I know she's exhausted, but I also know that pointing it out will probably end up with me nursing a bloody nose.

Her grip on the steering wheel is tight as she constantly checks behind us, ready to act at a moment's notice if she sees anything suspicious.

I glance back and find Cooper sitting on the leather seat, staring out the window without a care in the world, like we didn't all almost die less than thirty minutes ago.

"You still don't have any idea who these people are?" I ask, rubbing my sweaty palms over my thighs.

She takes a second to respond, her eyes shifting to the rearview mirror again. "No."

"Is there anything I can do to help?"

She shakes her head, a few strands of her hair falling out of her disheveled, messy bun.

We sit in silence for several more moments, and I watch the cars go by through my window.

"I know we knew each other," she confesses quietly, and

my head whips to her, watching her carefully as her body slumps in her seat, her oversized blood-spattered shirt bunching in her lap.

I stay quiet, knowing she'll talk when she wants to.

"I don't know who you were to me, and I don't want to know. There's a reason we're made to forget. People who have no idea what they left behind, who don't remember what it feels like to have someone care for them, they make better weapons," she continues, taking a deep breath. "But I feel it, and I'm not sure what to do about it."

I look back out the window, not wanting to add anything for fear of her shutting down.

"Please don't tell me anything about my life before that day until I'm ready, okay?" Her voice comes as a hushed whisper, and it's one of the first times I've seen her truly vulnerable. She's not trying to be brave, not trying to pretend like she can kill me in a second. She's admitting she's scared, admitting that there are things that bother her.

I want to protect her from all of it.

"Do you want to know anything about me?" I ask, thinking it may make her feel better.

Her gaze flickers to mine from the corner of her eye before returning to the road in front of her.

"I know you worked for the FBI at one point," she tells me, her grip loosening on the wheel just a touch, her knuckles returning to their usual color from the white they were before.

I nod. "I did. It turns out it wasn't for me," I tell her, studying my hand in my lap.

"Why?" she asks.

The air around us becomes electrified with the unsaid as I contemplate what to say.

Finally, I look at her and shake my head. "It's a story for another time," I tell her, respecting her wishes.

Understanding me, she nods, pursing her lips as she thinks about what else she can ask me.

"What are you doing now?" she asks me.

I can talk to her about that, I think, without letting anything else loose.

"I'm a detective," I tell her before pausing, my face twisting, "well, I was. I'm not quite sure I'll have my job when I get back." A small chuckle escapes me as I lay my head back on the seat. I'm not sure I'll be going back. I'm not completely convinced I'll be alive.

"Do you like that job?" she asks.

"Yes and no. Like anything it has its perks." I get paid well, that's for sure. There's not that many people graduating from the FBI Academy looking for jobs as a detective anywhere. Depending on where you're looking, they'll offer you the big bucks. "I like it a lot, but like any other job like it, you see some horrific things. You must be a special breed to deal with some things you probably see every day."

She nods. "I've seen enough to last a lifetime." Her voice is soft in the quiet car.

"So, the CIA is up to its old tricks, huh?" I ask her, seeing how far I can push for information.

A moment passes, and for a second I don't think she's going to answer. Finally, she sighs, "Yeah. I can't see you not finding out in the next couple of days, so I guess I'll fill you in on a little," she tells me, and I suddenly become giddy with the idea of actually understanding what's going on. Her eyes flash to mine as she takes a right turn. "A *little*. I can't tell you everything. Honestly, you're safer not knowing everything you want to know."

I nod, trying to hide the smile fighting its way onto my lips.

"At some point I can fill you in on the history, because it's," she pauses, blowing a breath out, her cheeks puffing at the action, "a fucking mess. But we belong to the Fallen Angel Project."

I look at her, confused. "How many of you are there?"

I ask.

She shrugs, turning onto a dirt road. "I'm not sure how many there are, but I do know that we're stationed all over the country. If the Agency got caught operating in the United States all hell would break loose. We're the solution. We're off the books, not tied to them. They basically let us run around doing whatever we want to do other than our weekly missions."

"I mean, other than all the dead bodies and people trying to kill you, that sounds like a pretty good deal." I bite my lip, looking over at her. I can't help but notice the rise and fall of her chest, and the way she bites her cheek as she checks behind us to make sure we're safe.

"It does," she pauses, her grip tightening all over again, "but we're basically slaves to the Agency. We give everything to them." Her voice is almost sad.

"They took you after—" I can't say it.

"They took me in after I died. And I did die. I died for a couple of minutes. I was fully gone, but they were able to revive me. As I said, they take people who don't have any family who will come looking for them, so I assume—" She stops herself as she pulls into the bar parking lot. "I assume, well, that I don't have any family left."

I don't say anything to correct her. She's better off thinking that.

Instead, I decide to change the subject, realizing that nothing good can come of proceeding with that conversation now. Maybe another time, but not right now.

"Did the others text you?" I ask as she pulls into a parking spot, turning the car off. She pulls out her phone, checking her messages.

"Yeah, they're here."

Opening her door, she swings her legs out, and I take in her appearance once more. "Do you want my hoodie?" I ask, ready to give it to her.

She looks down at herself, pulling her shirt out by the hem. Her nose scrunches before she looks back at me. I may be covered in drywall dust, but at least I'm not covered in blood. The last thing we need is the police called on us.

She nods, her shoulders slumping just a little. I try hard not to smile a little. For someone so tough, someone who killed multiple men less than an hour ago, she allows herself to feel, and I like that. Even small amounts of disappointment show there's some humanity left in there.

Ellie is in there somewhere. I may never get her back, but small bits of her make Amelia all the more beautiful.

Gripping the hem of my, well, whoever had left it at the apartment's hoodie, I pull it over my head, handing it over to her. She takes it, murmuring a *thank* you, but her eyes are locked in on my stomach as my shirt rides up.

I quirk a brow. "See something you like?" I ask, smirking.

Her eyes whip to mine, her eyes narrowing into slits. "You wish."

My hand comes up to my heart in mock hurt. "You're wounding me," I tell her as she puts the hoodie over her head.

"If you're not careful, I really will wound you," she mutters under her breath as she reaches for her gun, tucking it into the back of her pants as if to make a point.

She did.

I shut up.

Opening the back door, she allows Cooper to jump out, grabbing ahold of his leash.

"Are they going to let him in?" I question.

"They love me here. I've brought him before. I probably shouldn't, but he comes anyways." She doesn't even look at me as she turns on her heel and makes her way for the door.

My lips thin as I nod. Maybe I shouldn't have joked with her. But if I'm stuck with her, I just want to lighten the mood a little bit. Take a crack at breaking her hard exterior. I know I can. She's shown signs of it falling before without me even trying.

I meet her at the entrance, and she holds the door open for me, allowing me to go through first. I look around, finding her friends in the back at a small table and start heading over as Amelia gets held up in the front.

"My favorite customer!" a large man bellows as he comes around the bar, making a beeline to Amelia. I stop, turning to watch as she grins from ear to ear.

The jealously I feel is unnatural, and I shove the ugly beast down. There is no place for that here.

"Hey James, how's it going tonight?" she says, enveloping the man in a firm hug.

My eyes narrow on their own accord.

"Going alright. It's always a good night when you bring this handsome man in." He rubs his gray beard as he bends over, petting Cooper.

I decide I don't want to watch anymore and turn back to the others, refusing to look back. Luisa keeps her eyes on Amelia while Amare eyes me. The way he looks at me makes me think I'm going to get punched into the wall.

Amelia told me they trust me now, but I think she's full of shit.

"You're safe," He says it almost like a curse. A filthy thing he'll regret saying the second it leaves his mouth.

"All good here," I say with a smile, holding my hands up in front of me. He simply looks me up and down, not hiding his displeasure. I'm sure it *would* be a lot easier for them if I died.

We sit in awkward silence for what feels like thirty minutes before Amelia makes her way back to the table. Sitting, she snaps, and Cooper dutifully sits next to her, looking around the bar with a careful eye.

"What happened?" Luisa asks her the second she sits, her eyes full of concern as she sips from her glass of beer.

Amelia looks at me for a moment before her gaze drifts back to her friends. "Damon knew something was wrong first. If he hadn't warned me when he did, we may all be dead." She shrugs, and I can't help but feel a little pang of joy in my chest at her admitting I helped.

I know she's only saying it so that they'll get off my back a little, but I know they're capable of making my life a living hell. I know that with everything that happened to them, they probably don't trust easily. I'll take anything I can get.

"That's good," Amare says, eyeing me again.

"They shot up the entire place. There's barely anything left. We can't go back." She shakes her head, looking at the table with a solemn look on her pretty face.

"Then where do we go?" Luisa asks, practically pouting.

Amare clears his throat, turning back to Amelia. "Do you have any idea who would want you dead?" he asks.

"You asked me that before." Her voice is stern and her eyes harden, narrowing at him.

"That was before you were attacked for a third time." He slaps his hand on the table, and it reminds me of a father speaking to a child, and although I understand where he's coming from, I know enough about Amelia to know she's not going to take it well.

"I know as much as you do," she hisses, leaning into the other two as her eyes narrow more. "And I would appreciate it if you stopped treating me as if I asked for this."

Amare holds up his hands in front of him, and I almost feel bad. "I didn't mean to allude to that," he tells her, "I just also don't know what we can do when they're going after you. We have no idea if this is personal or someone you pissed off on one of your missions."

She thinks about it for a moment. "There was that one man," she starts, "but I don't think he has the balls to come after me. And he certainly doesn't know who I really am."

"What man?" I ask her.

Three pairs of eyes flicker to me before returning to each other. "Wasn't that the club job?" Luisa asks.

Amelia nods. "Yeah, it was. He was a creep. He definitely got what was coming, but no, I don't think he knows who I am."

I'm so lost.

"What did he do?"

They ignore me once more, not even blessing me with a sideways glance.

"Okay well, then maybe it's personal," Amare states.

Amelia nods, thinking.

"It seems personal." They all stop to look at me again. "What?" I ask. "You said someone came into your house that first night and tried to kill you. That was one man. He clearly didn't know what he was getting into coming into that house, right? He doesn't know who you are or who you work for. What you're capable of. At least, that's how you described it to me."

She nods, looking down at her hands.

Before I can start again, a waitress comes over, asking if we want to order anything.

"Can I get a basket of wings?" Amelia asks without looking at me. I turn to acknowledge the woman, ready to order before I feel Amelia's hand tap my knee, the message loud and clear. The food is for me.

"Of course! What sauce?" the woman asks, pushing her blonde hair behind her ear as she glances at me, shooting me a flirty smile.

"Hot mess," Amelia states, a little rougher this time, her eyes on me.

"Fantastic, ya'll need anything else?" she asks, staring right at me. I shake my head, trying to avoid eye contact as I feel Amelia's eyes on the back of my head. "Fantastic, I'll be right back with that." She turns away with a wink.

I turn back to the others, and when I look at Amelia, a

small thrill runs through me at the look on her face. A look that she quickly wipes away as her knee grazes mine. It's such a small touch, something that wouldn't normally mean anything at all. But the chill that runs through me makes me think it's more. There's a touch of possessiveness there.

"Okay, well, what I was saying was that I think that someone who knows anything about what you're capable of would have brought more manpower the first time around. I'm not sure what you did to that man in the club, but it doesn't sound pleasant. Even if he doesn't know that you work for," I pause, lowering my voice, "who you work for," I whisper. "I feel like he would have sent more people in. I think this is personal. I can't tell you why, because I'm not sure, but that's what I think."

"You seem to think an awful lot," Amare accuses, and it occurs to me that I probably gave away a little too much about what I know. I look at Amelia, feeling bad for possibly getting her in trouble. She looks ahead, her head high. She can handle herself.

I lean back, folding my arms over my chest. "Listen. I know you don't like me," I say, and his eyebrow shoots up, "but I came here because I saw someone I knew died very much alive. I came here because I wanted to warn her that she was in trouble. I wasn't sure why, or what was coming her way, but I knew that something was happening, and I wanted to help. So, before you accuse me of shit you don't understand, just know that I've cared about this woman for far longer than you've known her," I hiss, done with his shit.

They can distrust me all they want, but I'm not going to battle them every fucking time I open my mouth to help. They can release me, or they can continue to hold me hostage. That's their decision. But I'm not going to deal with their bullshit, either.

"Anyways!" Amelia interjects with a clap of her hands as Amare opens his mouth, his eyes narrowed, all but shooting lasers through my skull. "I think we need to go to Texas," Amelia says.

"Why in the world would I ever step foot in that hell state?" Luisa asks, a frown on her face.

"I don't want to go any more than you do," Amelia promises, "trust me. I hate it there. But Henry has helped us in the past, and he can help us now."

"Who's Henry?" I ask, my brows furrowed.

I'm ignored.

"I mean, we don't have anywhere else to go," Amare says, leaning back in his chair and mimicking my pose as he eyes me.

My eyes roll into the back of my head.

"Okay, then we'll go to Texas." Amelia nods, biting her lip and looking down at Cooper, who licks her hand.

"Great," Luisa says, her smile tight.

Before I can ask them what's going on again, the waitress is back, handing me the bowl of wings topped with a separate bowl for bones.

I take it from her with a smile, immediately digging in. I offer a couple to the others silently, but they all shake their heads. I shrug. More for me. I groan as the spice hits my tongue, doing a little dance in my seat.

I don't miss Amelia's small smirk as she notices.

"Henry is cool, but his friend needs to keep his hands to himself," Luisa says, sighing.

"They're all hackers. What can they do? Just threaten him and he'll shut up," Amare tells her. "Or better yet, tell me and I'll take care of it." He grins.

"First, they're not *all* hackers. Some of them do other things, too. Timothy is a prick but I've heard about some of the shit he's done," Luisa stares into the distance, shaking as a shiver seems to run through her, her face twisting in disgust.

"We won't stay for longer than we have to," Amelia tells them, looking at the ground.

"You just don't want Henry asking you out again." Luisa grins, and Amelia's head whips up, her eyes staring bullets at her friend.

"He knows we don't date," she tells her.

Luisa scoffs. "You don't, maybe."

Before Amelia can argue further, the waitress is back with the receipt, and Amelia whips out her card, handing it to her. Her hand shakes, and I wonder if it's with anger or fatigue.

"Okay, we need a game plan." She wipes her face with her hand. "We need some things from the house before we leave. Clothes and the like. Amare and I are going to go there and get it. Lu, can you take Damon to wherever he was staying so he can collect his things? I'll call Veronica and request that the plane is ready for us."

"She's going to hate you. You know she goes to bed early." Luisa smirks.

"Yeah well, it's not like we have that many options right now. Anyways," she studies her nails, "I'll text Henry and let him know that we're coming. I'm not sure how many of them are there now, we may have to share rooms, but we should be safe." Her hands fall in front of her as the waitress walks back, handing her the card back.

Looking at the receipt, she pauses, her eyes finding mine as they narrow.

I go to ask her what's wrong, but her hand shoots out, handing me the small piece of paper.

For the handsome man with the tattoos, is written in flirty script in a blank space towards the bottom, followed by the name *Jessica* and a number. I feel my face heat up.

"Too bad you don't have a phone," Amelia deadpans, the corner of her lips lifting in a small smile as her eyes bear into mine.

I wish she understood just how much I can see through her.

"I'm sorry if we've been harsh," Luisa tells me as I direct her back to the motel I was staying at.

"It's fine. I just hope you guys know that I would never hurt her."

She nods, taking a turn down a dark road.

The hum of Amare's truck is peaceful as we make our way back, and I find myself so grateful for the ability to wear my own clothes in just a few short minutes.

"You know, I'm the only one who remembers what their life was like before," she tells me suddenly.

"You told me before." I nod.

"Well, it's traumatic. I'm jealous of Amelia and Amare. Always have been."

I turn my head to look at her. "It's that bad?" I ask.

She nods. "Knowing what you lost, what could have been if you made different decisions, it hurts." She sighs, shrugging. "I wish I died that day. That memory haunts me. I won't lie," she comes to a stop in front of the motel, "I've thought about ending my life here. Those two people back there? They're the only two who have held me together. They give me a reason to live. None of us have family anymore, but we have family in each other. Understand?" she asks, looking at me.

I nod, thinking about it.

She winces. "And Amelia, well…" she trails off, her eyes looking ahead but unseeing. "she's had it the worst. Mentally, I mean. And she doesn't even remember." She turns toward me.

I consider it for a second, deciding whether it's worth bringing something up with her. "If I know something that may change things, but Amelia doesn't want to know, is it safe to tell you?" I ask, hesitating.

Her brows furrow as she purses her lips, thinking about whether she wants to know.

"Tell me." She turns the car off and looks at me.

"I was there when Amelia died. She lost almost her whole family, but her dad."

Luisa's head tilts. "What do you mean?"

"I mean," I let out a breath, "that her father was the one to kill her. Or, tried to. He succeeded with the others. I thought he succeeded with her, too."

Luisa looks concerned for a moment before her features soften. "She doesn't need to know," she tells me firmly. "If we find out he may have something to do with this, we take him out like he's anyone else." There's a silence. "She doesn't need to know," she repeats.

"You think it would hurt her?" I ask.

"You don't think it would?"

"I think it would, but she likes to play tough."

Luisa grabs for the door handle, pushing it open.

"That's the key word," she tells me, "play. She likes to play tough. You read these stories of these spies that can turn their feelings off. Maybe some of them can; the ones who have jobs overseas, who actually work for the agency. Us? We're a means to an end. They do what they can to train us, to make sure we don't turn on them, but we're only human. We can't turn our feelings off. We're well aware of who we are and why we're still here, and sometimes that makes us feel even more." We walk towards the door, and I reach for my pocket, my heart jumping when I realize I don't have my keys. Why would I? They were left with my car.

I turn to Luisa, my eyes wide, but she's already reaching for her own pocket, pulling out a few tools.

"Not everyone goes somewhere without a plan." She shoots me a tight smile before getting to work on the lock. Thirty seconds later, the door swings open, and I make my way inside, collecting my things.

TWELVE

AMELIA

"The plane is ready."

I look up from my phone, spotting Amare across the small private room, his bag slung over his broad shoulder as he pushes his sunglasses up in an attempt to see me.

The room is dim as Damon snores lightly beside me, his dark hair messy, his face peaceful. He looks handsome like this. Serene, happy, quiet.

I almost don't want to wake him up. *Almost.*

Nudging him with my elbow, he jerks, his green eyes wide as they find mine.

"We gotta go."

His eyes cloud with exhaustion as he gets up and stretches, his shirt lifting up as he does. I quickly avert my gaze, not trying to have him catch me checking him out again.

"You guys good to go?" Amare asks, turning towards the door. I nod, lifting my bag and heading out, Damon right at my heels.

The moist air hits my face as we step out onto the tarmac,

the fog so thick I can barely see the plane just a little ways away, Luisa and Cooper standing in front of it waiting for us.

I check behind me as Damon stares forward, his eyes wide. "You guys really have your own plane?"

I shrug. "It's not really ours. It's just what we can use to get around to the other compounds so we don't have to deal with security and all that other bullshit."

"I feel like there's still so many things I don't understand about all of this," he murmurs.

The trip was uneventful. Everyone took the moment to sleep because none of us have had the opportunity to in what feels like days.

It was blatantly obvious that Damon had never stepped foot on a private plane before, which was cute. Most people haven't.

For me, it didn't feel like something new the first time I stepped on board, leading me to believe that it was somehow part of my life before. I'm not sure what that means, and I haven't cared to look into it more.

We touch down in Texas around four hours later, rested and ready to go. I've only been here once before, and if I'm honest, I could go the rest of my life never coming here again. That being said, our friends are here, and it's the base of some of the best hackers and computer coders in the entire country. Sure, there are some in other states, but there are not as many, and none as good as the ones here.

Including Stella Thomas, one of the women I trained with before being stationed in Seattle. I consider her one of my few friends in this world, and although I'd rather be anywhere but here, I'm really excited to see her again.

The second the door of the plane opens, we're hit with a wave of heat, nearly taking my breath away.

I'm not someone who enjoys the heat, and I can tell Damon isn't either.

Cooper, on the other hand, looks like he's thriving.

"We have about a thirty-minute drive until we get to the compound," Amare tells us, and I nod, making sure Damon is following us.

We walk down the stairs of the plane and towards the large black van waiting for us. The driver sits in his seat, his hands on the wheel, sunglasses on. He doesn't speak as we climb in, and he doesn't ask where we're going. Instead, he simply waits for us all to take a seat and pulls off, heading to our destination.

We sit in comfortable silence. Amare, Luisa, and I are used to living with each other, not really speaking to anyone else. We do our job, come home, relax and recoup. None of us are super social for obvious reasons. No one wants to make friends we'll lose at some point.

Knowing that we'll be heading into a much larger compound for who knows how long? All of us are just saving our energy to get ready for what's to come.

Damon sits next to me as he takes turns rubbing his palms with his thumb, his knee bouncing.

It's been extremely clear that Amare and Luisa don't like or trust him. I think Luisa has been warming up to the idea of him, but I know that deep down, she's not thrilled about any of this. I don't exactly blame them, I wouldn't either. I'm not entirely sure why I do, but I've established and accepted that somehow, someway, our paths were intertwined at one point. We could have been something, but the way he looks at me feels more like friendship, despite what I may wish deep down.

My head drops back into the seat as my shoulders pull back and relax while goosebumps settle down my arms. Crossing them loosely in my lap, I close my eyes, attempting to get another few moments of rest.

But my skin prickles, my hair stands on end. I can feel eyes on me. Prying them open, I turn my head to find Damon staring at me, a lazy smile on his face. I scowl at him, averting my gaze.

I don't want to be his friend. He's here to help me figure out what's going on, and that's it.

I close my eyes shut once more. *Promise me you won't open them again before we get there,* I think to myself.

But that's always when the memories hit.

"Do you understand what I'm saying?" the man in front of me says, his knuckle lifting my chin, forcing my eyes on his.

The room is chilly and smells like plastic and Lysol. The room is almost completely white, with only a table in front of me.

A shiver goes down my spine as my bare back brushes against the cold metal of the chair I'm strapped to, and I choke down a sob.

I squeeze my eyes shut, shaking my head. "I don't understand what's happening to me," I confess, a tear slipping down my cheek. My head hurts, my legs feel like jelly, and no matter how hard I try, I can't remember my name or what year it is.

"It'll get better." He gets up and walks to the window, opening the shades slowly. I feel the heat of the sun touch my skin, and I sink into it. I want to bask in it. My entire body. I just want the warmth.

I feel like nothing.

I feel like a ghost. Like I've died, and I'm no longer in my own body. I no longer have control of anything.

"You've been chosen for an incredibly important task," the man says, and I can feel his eyes on me once again. "You may feel like you don't belong now, you may feel like you're missing part of yourself, but you'll find it soon enough."

I don't open my eyes. Instead, I continue to feel the sun on my skin, my body tremoring.

"Do you remember who you are?" he asks once again. I shake my head. "You're name is Amelia Lorenzo. That's all you need to know."

My face twists in confusion. I don't remember who I am, no. But that, well, that feels wrong.

"Amelia, you're about to learn about this project. You're special,

and so incredibly important to our mission. You'll be serving the greater good, okay?"

My chapped lips squeeze together as my shoulders cave in. A sob escapes me. I don't understand what's happening.

"Amelia, welcome to Project Fallen Angel, and welcome to Texas."

I remember that day vividly. Later, I'd learn what happened. Well, I'd understand the idea of what happened. We're not meant to remember. We're not meant to have memories from before.

But we're also not supposed to have anyone that would come find us, either. Damon is an outlier.

The entire reason we exist is because we don't have anyone that cares about us. We have no other reason to be alive but to serve the Agency. None at all. They expect us to be robots. Expect us to be good puppets who do what we're asked.

And most of the time, we are. I am. I turn my brain off like a good little girl and go to war for them, putting my life on the line every single day.

And other times, I think too much. Like now.

I just want it to stop. So badly.

Suddenly, a hand hitting the back of my seat snaps me out of my thoughts, and my eyes fly open.

"Holy crap," Luisa says, looking at the compound in front of us.

A lot has changed in the years since I was here.

We drive down a large dirt driveway, a cloud of dust kicking up behind us. A large field lines both sides of the path, stopping in front of one of the most beautiful homes I've ever seen.

"They must have rebuilt since I was here," I murmur, amazed at what's been done.

"It's that different?" Amare asks.

I nod my head, taking it in.

The house is huge, white, and beautiful against the deep, cloudless blue sky. The mid-day sun beams down upon it, making it seem almost ethereal. It's gorgeous.

Behind it, I can see a large barn, and around it, several horses and a large cow.

The driver pulls up in front of the house, puts the car in park, and sits there, waiting for us to get out. He hasn't said a word the entire time, and he won't. That's how they like it. He wasn't hired by the Agency to speak with us.

The less we say around him, the better. Especially when it comes to Damon.

"Let's go," I tell him, grabbing my things as I open the door.

He looks out the window one more time before grabbing his bag and following behind Cooper.

The front door opens with a bang, and my head whips toward the sound. A tall man exits, his arms spread wide. "Holy shit. I never thought I'd see your ugly face ever again."

I smile, my hands on my hips. "And who are you calling ugly?" I laugh, walking over to him as the others get their things.

"God, I've missed you!" He envelops me in a firm hug.

"I've missed you, too," I tuck my hair behind my ears.

He looks me up and down, a twinkle in his blue eyes before he takes off his cowboy hat, wiping his hand through his blond hair. "Stella told me you were coming."

"Yeah. We're trying to solve a mystery." I shrug as I hear the others approaching behind me.

"And who are all these people?" he asks, his eyes lingering a moment longer on Damon, whose eyes are locked on me.

I introduce Lu, Amare, and Cooper.

"And this is Matthew," I tell them, smiling. "We had a mission together. My first one here, actually, before I was moved and met you, Amare."

"And who is this man?" Matthew asks, and I follow his gaze to Damon, who's looking around the property like he doesn't belong. He doesn't.

"Her pet." Amare snickers, bumping his shoulder into Luisa. She shoots him a look, but I can't tell if she's annoyed or just tired.

Matthew looks at Cooper as he sniffs his feet, his tongue hanging out of his mouth as he gazes up at him with giant puppy eyes.

"Her second pet," Amare adds.

I grit my teeth together, annoyed. "He's someone important. Well, hopefully. We're hoping he'll help us crack this." I shrug, ignoring the other two as they look at each other, something unsaid passing between them.

Matthew eyes us, his brows furrowed, but decides to drop it. His face relaxes as he claps his hands together. "Well!" he starts, "I know you're here to see Stella. I'm assuming you're not staying long, but we have rooms for you. Others are aware you'll be staying here, but as always, just try to lay low."

We nod, and I look at Damon as his face twists in confusion. I shake my head at him, warning him against asking any questions. I'd try to answer them later.

"I'll show you guys to the visitor's wing first, and Stella will come to you, is that okay?" he asks. "As I said, just lay low. We're a pretty private group here on the ranch, and we don't want no trouble. I know you guys had some issues up there in Seattle. We don't want none of that here," he tells us, his drawl creeping out the more he's comfortable in front of us.

We follow him into the house and down a long hallway. When we reach the end, he pauses, looking back at us before grabbing the handle and twisting it. "This is where you'll be staying as long as you're here. There are a couple of rooms for travelers, along with a kitchen so you don't have to mix with us."

I nod, understanding.

We've had a couple of visitors at our place as well, and each time we're always told to interact with them as little as possible. The less everyone knows about each other, the better.

The room opens up into a giant, spacious area complete with a dark, moody kitchen and family room. A hallway is directly across from us containing five doors, enough for anyone who needs to stay here.

"Jesus," I say, looking around. "This place has changed a whole bunch."

"You're damn right about that," Matthew says, his hands on his hips as he looks around, too. "Tore the whole thing down to the studs. She's a beauty, ain't she?"

Amare says something under his breath to Luisa behind me, and she chuckles. I can only imagine it has something to do with Texas being a shithole.

He's not wrong.

"Anyways, I'll let ya get settled in. Let me know if ya'll need anything. I have to go out later and tend to the horses, but I'll be back after. Go out and explore a little, get some sun, just, as I said, don't go lookin' for nothin'."

Matthew takes one last pointed look at us before tipping his hat, turning, and heading out the door. He's not gentle closing it, and Damon jumps at the sound.

"You said you're a detective?" Amare eyes him.

Damon rolls his eyes. I do too.

I'd be lying if I said a very small part of me, so minuscule I could easily ignore it should I want to, wants to defend him. Other people picking on him feels wrong.

I push the feeling down.

"There's five bedrooms," I deadpan. "Choose which ones you want. I don't give a shit."

Luisa and Amare head to the rooms while Damon hangs back. I eye him, motioning for him to follow them, eyebrows raised, but he doesn't. Instead, he keeps his eyes on me.

"What do you want?" I ask him finally.

"Can we talk?"

I turn to him, suddenly well aware of how close he's standing and how the light filtering in from the large windows light up his beautiful eyes, reminding me of the forest outside of our home.

"We already talked about everything. I gave you your answers," I tell him, my voice low, "maybe later."

"You gave me partial answers. You said yourself you'd tell me everything at some point." His eyes search mine for a moment more before realizing I'm not going to budge. His lips thin, and he runs his hand along his short beard, his eyes arcing to the ceiling in an eye-roll. He nods, gathering his things as he heads for the bedrooms, finding the first the other two haven't claimed. With one last look behind him, he walks in, closing the door quietly.

I sigh, allowing my shoulders to relax for the first time since we've gotten here.

"You ready to find out where we'll be sleeping tonight bud?" I ask Cooper as he yawns by my feet. He looks up at me, his big brown puppy eyes reminding me of Damon's green ones.

"Don't look at me like that." I roll my eyes.

We head to one of the other unclaimed rooms, the one right across the way from Damon's, and I'm so incredibly grateful for a real bed. I don't even look around the room before I fall into it, letting the thick bedding wrap around my body. I feel as though I'm lying on a cloud.

And that's when I drift off.

I wake up later to a soft knock on my door. I groan, turning over. Cooper is missing, which means Luisa likely came to check on me and took him. I make a mental note to thank her for helping me.

"Come in," My voice comes out gritty from sleep.

"Hey," comes a soft voice. I smile, instantly feeling a jolt of energy run through me.

I fling my legs over the edge of the bed, running to the door, feeling excited to see someone for the first time in so, so long. "Stella!"

She smiles, her blonde hair bobbing as she greets me with a jump. "It's been forever."

"It really has," I tell her. "I wish this was a more relaxed visit."

She nods, the corner of her lips lifting in a small smirk. "It's okay, we don't get many visitors here anyways," she pauses, "but when we do they're usually people needing help from us anyways. I'm used to it."

I sober a little, upset it seems like she thinks I only care about her for what she can do for me.

I open my mouth to clarify, but she holds her hand up. "I don't mean anything by that, I promise. You're the one person who has at least kept in contact with me."

I smile, not feeling as though I need to add anything else.

"Are you ready to go?" she asks, turning.

"Are we going somewhere fancy?" I ask, looking behind me at my bag.

She chuckles, "We're just going down to the computer room. Nothing fancy. You can come as you are."

I grab the smaller baggie of necessary items out of my bag before following her out, catching Damon's eyes as I go. When Stella notices him, she looks back at me, and I pretend not to see the question in her gaze.

I try not to see the questions in his, either.

"This is such a beautiful place," I tell her as we walk

through the main house. Despite the dead animals on the walls, everything is so dark, moody, and elegant. The perfect ranch.

"It's not bad," she says simply. "It's quiet. Peaceful." Her eyes darken. "Except for Timothy."

"What has he done now?" I ask her.

"You don't even want to know." She waves me off, walking faster.

Stella leads me down another hall and through a doorway with stairs leading down into a basement. The hair on the back of my neck stands, and Stella looks back at me, sending me a comforting smile.

We're used to being on edge. Questioning anything. It doesn't matter if they're other Fallen Angels. Anything can be a threat. Leading someone into a basement? Any one of us would be on edge.

"We keep the computers down here where we can monitor the temperature a little better," she informs me, flipping on the lights. "It's cooler down here, so we don't have to keep the AC on all the time in certain rooms. It's just easier, you know?"

I nod. I won't lie, I'm not really a computer person. It's part of the reason I didn't stay here, and instead ended up in Seattle. But I know enough to understand that nothing should be kept in a super warm room. It was enough of an explanation to allow some of the tension to leave my body. Some of it.

When we reach the bottom, we make our way into a large, dark room with giant screens lining the walls, and desktops along several long desks. "Welcome to the Hub." Stella smiles, her arms outstretched as she spins, showing the place off.

"This is amazing," I'm genuinely taken by it all. It's unlike anything I've seen before.

She leads me to the small sitting area in the corner, and I

plop myself down onto the dark leather couch, loving the cool feel against my back.

"So tell me, what's going on. What do you need help with? I've only been told you need help hacking into something." She grabs a laptop from what I'm assuming is her portion of the large desk, bringing it to the chair across from me. She sits, her tan legs crossed under her.

"I," I start, not entirely sure where to even start. "A couple of days ago, there was a man who broke into our home. I'm lucky I noticed in time, or I'm not sure what would have happened." I've thought about that a lot. What would have happened if he had found me and Cooper in our room. "I was able to take him out, but when I looked through his pockets, I found a phone. My face and old name was on the wallpaper, but I couldn't actually get into it."

"Do you have his phone?" she asks, her brows arched.

I nod. "I do, here." I slip the flip phone out of the small bag, handing it over to her. She flips it open, her eyes going wide.

"Well, congrats to you," she teases me with a smirk. "You're worth quite a bit, apparently."

I roll my eyes, but I can't help but let a small smile through.

She clicks her tongue. "Is it bad if I'm a little jealous that someone wants you dead that much?"

"It's only 600 grand!" I toss my arms up with a smile. "I've seen it way higher for way less."

With a chuckle, she tries a couple of codes. "It's definitely locked. I couldn't get into it when I found it. I was wondering if there's anything on it that could be useful," I add.

She eyes it, flipping it over in her hands before carefully inserting a cable into one of the ports. Her eyes flicker to mine before going back to the phone.

"So who's the man with you?" she asks, grinning.

"Amare? I've mentioned him." I study my hands in front of me, picking a piece of lint off of my sweater.

"You know damn well I don't mean him." She rolls her eyes.

My face twists in a grimace. "He's, I'm not sure who he is," I tell her. "I trust you won't tell anyone he's with us. I'm taking care of him after this whole thing, but he's necessary." I don't want to talk about him too much, because I meant what I said about wanting to keep him safe. I may not be the biggest fan of his, I may even think he's the biggest dumbass on the planet for coming to find me, but I feel that he cares, and that's more than I've felt with anyone in a very long time.

No matter how many times I tell myself I don't care what happens to him, I do.

She nods, pursing her lips. "You know I'm not going to say anything, I promise. But how is he necessary?" Her head tilts as she watches me.

I pause, thinking about it myself. How do I phrase this? We could probably solve this ourselves without him. That's true. But to me he's necessary. He feels necessary. I don't know.

"He," I grimace, deciding to just do it. I trust her, and I think she can help us. Trust can be used as currency here. "I met him at a bar, and he called me Ellie." Her eyes snap to mine. "It was a blow, that's for sure. But he knew me, back before everything. I don't know how; I told him I'd kill him if he tried to tell me. I can't deal with it, you know?" She nods. "But he knows something. He came to find me because there was a wanted notice that went out with my face on it. The only thing I know is that he saw me die."

She eyes me warily. "You sure you can trust him?"

A shot of adrenaline shoots through me, my body tensing up. I can't understand why I don't like other people questioning him. I don't want to acknowledge it, at least. "I can trust him," I reply crisply, and there's something in her eyes that says she believes me. She understands that something bigger is at play here, even though I don't even understand it myself.

She clears her throat, fiddling with the phone in her hand. "You know I adore you. We've been through a lot together." I nod. "I don't remember what my life was like before this, either. I haven't thought for one second that I would be better off knowing." She takes a deep breath. "But sometimes, just for a second, I think back, trying to remember if I ever loved anyone."

"I don't love him," I say it far too quickly, but I'm telling the truth. I don't know who he was to me. If I loved him before, I don't feel that now. All I feel is a familiar tingle deep in my bones. The same tingles I'd feel if it were a friend.

It's like when you see someone you definitely recognize from somewhere, but for the life of you, you can't place where you know them from. It could have been from anything. We could have crossed paths just briefly. He could have been an EMT that was at the scene—I know I was shot. There would be people helping.

He could have been anyone.

I once again shove down the idea that he wasn't just anyone. I can't be interested in someone like that, and I can't dig for information.

"I see that look, and I know what you're thinking." Stella sighs, putting the phone down. "You and I both know that that feeling of familiarity? It's home, Amelia. They can erase memories all they want, but they'll never be able to completely erase how you feel around someone. And that can turn into love real quick."

"I don't think that's what it is. I think I've been in such a dark place for so long that one person outside of this small forced, found family we have going on showing me any type of care has softened me, and if I'm completely honest, I feel like shit about it." I lean back into the couch cushions, closing my eyes for a moment.

Stella nods. "We're only human, I think sometimes we all forget that. If you're told you're not something enough times, you really do start to believe it. Trust me, I know." She places her hand over her chest. "Sometimes the greatest threat to humanity within is other humans. They rip it from us, expecting everything in return."

We fall into a comfortable silence.

"I haven't said this to the others," Stella starts, looking up from her computer. Her face is suddenly bleary. "I'm here to do my job. I'm loyal to the Agency, sure. But I just, I can't help but think there are consequences for playing God. For choosing people to save for their own Higher Purpose. Making us play Judge, Jury, and Executioner. There shouldn't be power like that."

The air is heavy as I digest her words, realizing it's how I've been feeling for the last six years. I feel my shoulders relax as a small weight leaves them, feeling a little less alone.

"I agree with you," I tell her, my voice soft, "though I think that after everything we've seen, I don't believe a God exists. If one does, how can they let this happen? Everything that goes on in this world. I just," I stop, slumping against the back of the couch. "I just can't think like that, or I'll get angry. I'm not sure there's any consequences for doing something God allows."

She nods, and for a moment, a singular, painful moment, I see the all too familiar look of grief pass over her features.

"I believe something exists, but I'm not sure what, and that's okay. It's hard to believe that millions of people have died in the name of something that doesn't exist. I have to believe there's something out there worth that."

Maybe one day I'll find something to believe in that much, but I can't imagine it.

"Alrighty," she perks up again as her fingers glide over

her keyboard, "I think I can get into this, but I'm not sure how much information is going to be on it. I've seen this type of thing before, which, well, that information may help you, too." Her eyes flicker across her screen.

"Where have you seen it before?"

"The man who had this phone was a mercenary. But not just any mercenary. These guys work for high-powered individuals. Mostly politicians, naturally." I nod, processing the information. It's good to have that confirmed, but it's not quite anything I didn't know before.

Her fingers click a few more keys before she throws her hands up, a grin plastered on her face. "Got it!" she yells, loud enough to make me jump.

"You got something?" I ask.

"Yep. I knew it! The guy worked for Atlee Enterprises," she informs me.

"Like the company that makes computer chips?" I ask.

She squints, "Yes, and no. Atlee Enterprises does make computer chips, but that's just a cover," she says, and my brows furrow in confusion. I've heard a lot about them, but I've never had to deal with them before. They're located on the east coast, so we never had to worry about making sure they're in compliance. I know they have their hand in government business though, and I know that some of the Fallen Angels in the East have had to keep their eyes on them.

"There's still not a ton of information on them, and we're still collecting info, so this honestly helps me as much as it helps you," she tells me, and she almost looks, excited? "but they run a larger business managing for-hire killers. Hit men. We're not sure where they're stationed other than on the east coast, and we're not even sure who manages that part of the company. All we know is that there's been someone else screwing with our job, and it's been making things difficult for a lot of the Eastern Fallen Angels. I've had to help them with a couple of things."

"I haven't heard anything about that at all," I watch as she types on her computer, her eyes glued to the screen.

"There's a lot none of us ever hear about parts of the country," she states.

I nod, leaning back in my seat. "Well, okay. So what does that mean?"

She shrugs, running her hand through her blonde hair, shaking it out. "It means that this person who hired them has friends in high places or they *are* in high places." She bites her lip. "It also means that they're likely in DC. Most of the contact we've seen comes from there. That's where we're almost positive they work from."

I nod, taking in all the new information, thinking about what our game plan is.

"Is there anything else on the phone I should know of?"

"There's a text asking if the job is done, but it's from an unknown number, and I can't trace it now," she tells me.

"Do you have any idea how someone would hire these people?"

She shakes her head. "That's something we've been trying to figure out, but we have no idea. We only know that Atlee Enterprises is a front, that's about it. It's a mystery for us, too."

I nod, resting my elbows on my thighs and propping my head on my fists. "I feel like I've learned a ton and nothing at all."

"I feel like that's our entire job," she retorts, her smile infectious. I grin.

"That's true," I tell her.

"I can try to see if I find anything else tonight, but that looks about it. They definitely wouldn't carry something with more information than they had to."

"They don't know about us though, it seems," I state.

She considers it. "I don't think so, no. They're old, don't get me wrong. I think they've been functioning for longer than you and I have been with the Agency, but they're not older than this project, and yet they still don't seem to know about us. Or they don't care."

"It's just strange that we don't know more about them. That's our entire job, right?" I ask, all of a sudden a little uncomfortable.

"I mean, it is. It isn't yours, though. Someone's been on it, but sometimes things just run so deep there's really no way of quickly figuring it out. It takes time. The Seattle compound is still fairly new. There's other areas that have a whole lot more issues to deal with."

It makes sense.

"And I assume this means we probably can't find *them?*"

She shakes her head vigorously. "Nope. And I wouldn't even try. It's going to be like a hydra. At some point we'll find them and try to stop them, but for now, all you'll do is bring attention to us while another couple of heads grow back to replace the one you cut off."

I slump back. "I guess we just have to go to DC."

She nods. "It seems like it."

I sigh, slapping my hands next to me as I get up from my seat. "I really appreciate the help, Stella. Whatever you need, let me know. I have your back."

She smiles, her eyes lighting up. "I'll definitely take you up on that. I'll be here today and tomorrow. I assume you guys are staying overnight at least?"

I nod, wrapping my arms around myself. "Yeah, we need some rest. We're staying in the visitor wing though; we need to stay low."

She smirks, "You're trying to hide your guest, too?"

I roll my eyes and smile. "I mean, yes. The others aren't too happy I'm bringing him with us."

"Just let yourself go sometimes. Give yourself some grace." She gives me a hug before leading me from the room.

"That's all we need," I respond.

"We have steak!" Luisa calls as I walk back into the visitor's wing.

Damon stands at the kitchen island, watching her cook with a lazy look on his face. The second his eyes find mine, they light up, and I can't help but feel a small fire start deep in my belly.

"How much do you wanna bet it's fresh?" Amare asks, grabbing a glass from the cabinet.

"What do you mean?" Luisa asks, her eyes wide.

Amare looks around, a confused look in his eye. "We're on a farm, Lu."

Realization dawns on her. "Oh my God you think they killed the cow here?"

I shrug, taking a seat next to Damon. "It would make sense."

Luisa looks from the steak and back to me, looking horrified.

"You may as well continue to cook it," I tell her. "You already disrespected it by not cooking it on the grill." Her cheeks turn a deep red at my teasing.

I can see Damon glancing at me from the corner of his eye next to me, a small smile on his lips. He moves just a touch closer, his knee brushing up against mine.

Lu and Amare continue to bicker like an old married couple in front of us as I turn to meet him, not saying anything.

He still looks like he hasn't gotten an ounce of sleep in the past ten years, and think it's a tragedy that I'm somehow attracted to it. And the sadness in his eyes? God I love it. What is it about tired men who hold all the melancholy in the world in their eyes? I'm just like any other woman. I'm not sure why we're all drawn to them.

A small part of me is sad that I'm the cause, though.

But I only feel bad for a moment. He was the one who got himself into this mess. I meant what I said before. He should have just let the dead stay dead.

"Are you doing okay?" I ask.

He eyes me for a second. "Yeah. I took Cooper out earlier and he, well, he loved the cows. It was like he was seeing his long-lost cousins." He chuckles. "But I guess I'm just a little lost."

"I know, I'm going to try to answer questions later."

He nods, turning back to the other two.

THIRTEEN

DAMON

We're staying here for one more day. I'm not sure why, as no one will tell me a fucking thing, but we're staying here until we go, well, somewhere. I'm not sure of that, either.

My patience is wearing thin.

I lay on my bed, the cool sheets feeling amazing against my overheated body. This place is far too warm for me, that's for sure.

It's been a day of being avoided, a day of wondering what I can do, and what is going to happen to me.

I understand the tough front Amelia has been putting up. I do. But part of me really wants to break it down, no matter what the cost. I know she'll hate me, but this back and forth that's been going on as she battles herself? I can't take it.

One second she's assuring me she'll tell me everything, and the next she pretends like I don't exist. Like I'm just some problem she's dragged along. Which, well, isn't completely wrong.

I know she doesn't need protecting. But I'm stuck here

with her, and I want to understand. I want to get to know her. I want to just feel like me being here means anything at all.

Getting out of bed, I walk out of my room, hoping to see any of them around, but there's no one. It's quiet, only the light hum of a tractor somewhere outside, the smell of bacon lingering in the air. The place looks pristine, like someone was here to clean it while I was in my room.

Is the place worth exploring a little more?

I take only a second to decide. Yes, it is worth it.

Looking around one last time to make sure I didn't miss anyone, I sneak out the main door and into the main house. I'm careful, making sure I don't run into anyone randomly. I don't want to have to explain myself.

But I'm a little too careful. Suspiciously so. Looking behind me, I sneak around a corner when I bump into a large body.

I consider myself a large man. I'm about 6'5 and mostly muscle. This man was another breed.

Taller than me, the man felt like a brick wall. His hands curl into fists at his side as he eyes me, his eyes narrowing.

I shoot him a smile, deciding my best option is to pretend like I belong here.

"Hey man, I'm part of the group staying here and was just looking for everyone."

He doesn't smile back, and my grin falters, my hand dropping to my side. My head cocks to the side, waiting for a response, but the man's brown eyes simply look me up and down, sizing me up as his brows furrow.

Just as I'm about to open my mouth again, the man points down a long hall. "That way," he grunts.

I shoot him a smile and thank him before heading off. I can feel his eyes on my back, and I just hope he doesn't follow me. Or tell on me. Honestly, I'm just hoping I don't run into the guy ever again.

The main house is bright and airy, and the smell of fresh

air wafts through the room, a light breeze rustling my hair. I make my way into the dark hallway, looking around for what the man could have been directing me to.

At the end of a long hallway is a door. I look behind me, finding the man watching. He motions for me to walk through. I open it, greeted by a long stairway down into what looks like a basement.

The first thing I notice is the stench of bleach, and the sound of water running. The stone walls on either side of the stairs glisten, and my hair stands on end.

I don't think anyone is down here.

"Hello?" a voice asks, coughing.

"Hello?" I reply back, straining my ears to listen.

"Please," another cough, "please help me. Let me go. I don't know anything." There's a scuffling sound, followed by a buzz of something electric. The person screams, and something hits the floor.

When I hear a gargling noise, I'm out of there.

Whipping back around, I close the door, my chest heaving. Is there a man down there? Do they have a creepy torture cave like Amelia does? What the fuck was that sound?

I look around for the man who pointed me this way, but don't find him. Speed walking away, I run face-first into another body, but this time, it's just Luisa.

"What the hell are you doing out here?" She scowls.

"I was just trying to get out. I was outside before and it was fine, I just, I ran into some giant guy and he told me to go down there," I point toward the door, "and there's someone down there."

She just stares at me, her mouth open but no words come out. She shakes her head.

"Let me get this straight. You were told to stay in the guest wing, decided to leave, bump into a large man who tells you to go down a creepy hallway, and you... you *do* it?"

I throw my hands up. "Okay yes, I know how it sounds I'm sorry."

She rolls her eyes, giving me her back as she heads toward the guest wing. "I'm about to bring Cooper out if you'd like to join. I think you should stay with one of us from now on." She shoots me a glare over her shoulder.

I look around, running a hand through my hair. Yeah, okay, that's probably for the best.

I follow after her, waiting at the door as she finds Cooper, clips his leash on, and walks past me through the door, scowling at me the entire way.

I don't say anything until we get outside, allowing Cooper to lead our way as he makes a beeline for the cows.

"Why do you guys hate me so much?" I want to know, because if I can, I'd like to win them over.

She looks me over, contemplating the best answer. I can't decide whether that's good or bad for me.

"I don't think I hate you. Amare might, I'm not sure. He's just overprotective. He's like a big brother on steroids. I'm just, well, I'm nervous. I've told you that."

"But I also thought we made progress that night." I look down at my shoes as we walk, kicking rocks ahead of us.

She shakes her head. "It's more than that. Amelia is soft on you because somewhere deep down, she feels something familiar in you. When you go through what we have, that means a lot. For me, well, I remember life before this." She looks down, her face scrunching as she tries not to cry. "I guess I owe you an apology, because I don't want you to think I hate you. I don't."

We come to a stop in front of a large fence. There's a couple cows eating grass on the other side, and Cooper sits, peacefully watching them.

We fall into a comfortable silence with him, sitting next to each other on the ground and basking in the sun. The large tree on the other side of the path throws some shade our way, and the breeze helps keep the heat reasonable.

The birds sing in a nearby tree, and one of the cows moo, causing Cooper to bark once before going quiet once more.

"I lost my fiancé," Luisa says suddenly, laying down on the grass.

"I'm so sorry," I murmur, not sure what else I can possibly say to that.

She shakes her head. "I'm the only one who remembers everything. I know I've told you that, but you have to understand that I wouldn't wish this on my worst enemy." She pauses, swallowing. "He was a third-grade teacher. He loved his kids so much, and he couldn't wait to marry me to have our own. He had one kid in particular that he could just, he could just tell that they were abused. It made him so mad." Her eyes squeeze shut, and I stay silent, knowing it's not the time to open my mouth.

"He did everything he could to get that little girl away from that family. Everything. Exhausted all resources. It was bad. Eventually, after she showed up to school with a broken arm, people listened. She was taken away from those monsters. Everything was fine." She falls silent, holding her hand above her, examining it. It's the first time I notice the thin tattoo on her ring finger.

"The father was livid. He was going to court because of the abuse. Things you just can't even imagine." She shakes her head, her eyes filling with tears. "He found our address. Showed up one night and shot us both."

Jesus.

"Luisa I—"

"Ian was one of the best men I ever knew. I've had a hard time trusting them throughout my life. But him? He was gold. I don't think I'm capable of loving anyone else. It's been six years and my heart still hurts."

"I'm sorry."

"You said that," she snaps, and I rear back, understanding my place. She can tolerate me without liking me.

She takes a deep breath. "I'm sorry. I'm just tired of apologies, too. I don't need them. All the sorry's in the world won't bring him back, you know?"

I nod.

"I was born in Puerto Rico. My entire family has lived there for decades. We met there but I was given a job opportunity here, so we came. I wish every single day that we didn't."

I stay silent this time, studying my palms.

"Something went wrong when they injected me, and I never forgot anything. I won't lie, I can be a jealous bitch about that. From the outside, I bet that sounds so silly, huh?" She lets out a dark chuckle.

She rolls onto her stomach, flipping her hair behind her, blowing a strand out of her face as she picks a wildflower, spinning it in her fingers.

"My parents are dead, have been for a long time, and my fiancé was murdered. I didn't have anyone left. I have no one at all that will come looking for me, much less six years later." She looks up at me, her eyes softening as her lips thin. "I don't mean to be an asshole to you, I promise. I just, part of me wishes I had someone like you. But Amelia deserves it. She really does. And I'm glad it's someone like you."

I nod, trying to process everything I've been told.

"It's really hard not telling her about everything. It's even harder not telling her about her dad with all of this." I shake my head, rocking back to stretch out my back.

"Do you think he has anything to do with it?"

I shake my head. "No. He doesn't give a single fuck about her. He's a piece of shit. I don't think he cares enough to pay attention to whether she's alive."

She nods, looking back down at the ground.

"I just want to make sure she's safe. I had no idea that this was so much bigger." I look around, taking everything in. "I promise I just came here to find out if she's safe."

"I know," Luisa says, smiling at me. "And don't take Amare too seriously. He's being an asshole, but he means well. He loves her, too. She's been through a lot in the last couple of years. I think she's been on the edge of remembering quite a few times. That can also do a lot of damage to someone."

"What happened?"

She waves me off. "She can tell you if she wants, but it's not my place. I'll tell you my story, but not hers."

Reasonable.

We sit and listen to everything around us for another moment before Cooper makes his way over, sniffing at my feet. "Want to go back, bud?" I ask, patting his head. He barks, and we both get up, making the trek back inside.

"You know, I'm not going to say I'm rooting for you to get what you want," she says as we reach the door.

"I'm—"

She cuts me off, her hand outstretched in front of her.

"That *is* what you want, and that's okay. I'm not going to say I'm rooting for you, but if it happens, just know that I'm happy for you and I'm happy it's you."

All I can do is nod, opening the door for her. We continue into the house before she stops, a smile on her face. "She's through there," she tells me, pointing to a door on our right.

"Who?"

"Who do you think, dipshit?"

I walk into what can only be described as the most beautiful gym I've ever seen.

Dark and moody, the gym is lined with some of the most top-of-the-line equipment. Racks upon racks of weights, benches, and more. A rock wall sits on one end of the room, and in the middle sits a large boxing ring, a large industrial-style fan sitting above it, casting an eerie glow over the space. At the center stands Amelia, her hands on her hips, her hair in two French braids that rest against her chest. She's breathing heavily, her gloved hands resting on her hips as she looks at me.

She looks absolutely stunning.

"I thought you'd be smarter than to come find me," she smirks, brushing a stray strand of hair from her face with her wrist.

"I couldn't sit in my room all day," I shrug, walking over to her, not wanting to launch into how I found myself out and about with Luisa just yet. "Do you want some help?"

She eyes me carefully for several moments before nodding, letting me up into the ring. Walking over to the side, she picks up a pair of punching mitts and hands them to me. It's now up close that I notice how absolutely perfect her body is.

She's put on some weight since that day, likely from all the training she's done. She used to be so thin I worried about her disappearing within her clothes, and now she's lean and muscular. She has the body of a killer. Literally.

The thought is sobering.

She shakes her shoulders before stretching her neck. "Where is everyone?" I ask.

"I didn't think you'd care where they are." It's a statement, not a question. She doesn't seem to like asking questions.

"I don't. I saw Luisa before this but haven't seen anyone else." I don't mention the large man. Or whoever is trapped in the basement.

She stops and stares at me before launching a punch toward my face, and I bring my gloved hand up, blocking it.

"I clearly haven't gotten very far with you, have I?"

She doesn't answer, instead narrowing her eyes and launching another punch toward me.

She continues launching punch after punch at me, and I block each and every one. Sweat beads on her skin as her breathing becomes more ragged, her chest rising and falling faster, catching my attention.

Suddenly, I'm on my ass.

I sprawl out, looking up at the ceiling, attempting to gather my thoughts and process what just hit me.

A second later, Amelia's face appears over me, her hand coming out to grab my wrist before yanking me up. "You can't take your eyes off the target like that." she slaps my arm before putting her glove back on.

"I'm pretty sure my eyes *were* on the target." I roll my eyes.

She turns, a spark igniting in her eyes as our gazes lock for a moment before she looks me over. Starting at my feet, her eyes roam up my body, only stopping when they reach my face. She smirks, and if it isn't for the way her eyes darken, I may feel hurt.

"You like what you see?" I grin, dropping the mitts on the ground.

Her head tilts as a mischievous smirk plays at the corner of her lips. She turns, and I go to follow her but stop as she whips around, launching a punch right at my chest.

I block it with ease, grabbing her arm and pulling her into me. She's not a large woman, and I easily hold her to my body. For a long, torturous moment, I think I win.

I shouldn't have been so stupid.

Amelia isn't a large woman. Despite her muscles, she's short. There's almost no way she can take down a man just from sheer force. Yet, I know she has. I shouldn't be surprised as she whips around, her knee coming up to my stomach, knocking the air right out of me as she spins out, punching me in the arm as I go down. I bring her with me, and she lands on top of me with a huff, her lips just inches from mine as she scowls at me.

But I see the way she glances down. I see the way she looks at my lips when she thinks I'm catching my breath.

She could have done worse. Way worse. She's taking it easy on me.

Satisfaction courses through my veins as I catch my breath. I don't care that she beat me, all I can feel is the warmth burrowing into my bones, the smile creeping onto my face. We're making progress. I can feel it.

It may also be because I haven't done this type of workout in a long time, and getting the shit beaten out of you can really humble a person.

We get up, and she brushes herself off, turning around.

"You can do better than that, Sweetheart," I tell her.

She whips around, her eyes narrowing, fury sparking inside of them before she runs at me, whipping her body into the air and catching me around the waist. Using the sheer force of her legs, she pulls down, and I go tumbling over her as she lands on her stomach behind me.

Honestly, it's the scariest and hottest thing that's ever been done to me.

"Holy shit," I groan as I attempt to get up, failing miserably.

"Want more?" she asks, crawling over to me.

I breathe heavily as my jaw tightens. "I don't think I can handle more. Won't lie to you." I tap my head against the cool surface of the ring, waiting until my body doesn't feel like it's on fire to roll over.

She sits next to me, her legs outstretched in front of her as she leans back, waiting for me to get up. When I finally can, I crawl next to her, laying on my back.

She looks at me for a long moment, her beautiful brown eyes baring into mine as if trying to figure me out. She could have any information she wants. I'm an open book for her. All she has to do is ask.

"Where did you learn all of that stuff?" I ask her, still struggling to breathe enough oxygen. She looks away, bending her legs at the knees and laying her arms over them. Her hair blows as the fan blows cool air onto us from above.

"Agency training is," she pauses, "a lot. Well, it is for actual agents. It's hard for us to but in a different way."

I quirk a brow, pursing my lips. "What do you mean?"

She sighs, laying down on her back next to me. She continues to look up at the ceiling. "I mean that they don't care what happens to us. But we're the first line of defense. The pawns that won't get them in trouble if something needs to be done here on U.S. soil."

I nod, trying to understand everything.

"Are we in a place where you can tell me everything?" I ask, crossing my fingers.

Her head turns towards me as her eyes meet mine, and I instantly know the answer. "Not here. Not right now," she whispers, and my eyes drift to her lips, wishing I could taste them.

Like old times.

I've tried so hard not to think of her that way while I've been dragged along, but here, alone with her, it's all I want.

My eyes lazily drift back up to hers. I watch her pupils expand, her eyes darkening as they take me in.

And as I'd expect, she sits up, turning her back to me.

I follow, my hand reaching out to her shoulder. "Amelia," my voice is quiet, "just talk to me. Please."

She looks at my hand before looking over her shoulder at me. Her eyes flicker to mine once more before she stands, dusting herself off and stretching.

"Meet me in my room in twenty." Her voice is barely a whisper as she looks ahead, walking off without a glance back.

I count the minutes. All I've wanted this entire time is answers, and the thrill of finally maybe getting them has my head spinning.

The second twenty minutes is up, I exit my room, heading right across the hall to hers. I knock softly, avoiding Amare's questioning eyes as he looks up from the couch, confusion clouding his eyes.

"You good man?" he calls out, putting down the files he was looking at previously.

I turn, shooting him a thumbs up. "Oh yeah! Totally good. Just, uhh, checking on something," I tell him. His eyebrow shoots up in question before he decides to let me be, going back to his files.

The door opens a crack and I slip inside, shutting it quietly. "Amare saw me," I told her, scratching my head with a wince.

She rolls her eyes. "Amare doesn't own me, you're good."

She sits on the edge of her bed, pulling on a pair of white socks. She showered, her hair wet, dampening her soft, light blue t-shirt that fits her like a glove. My eyes travel down her body before she sits up, and I can't help but feel some of my blood run south.

It's hard to see someone you had something with not remember you. It's even harder when you can't tell them about it.

All the past memories, and all the past desires come rushing to the forefront as I desperately attempt to ignore her nipples peeking through her shirt. I shove them all down with a cough.

I sit on her bed, crossing my legs in front of me, my hands behind my head. "Have I been a good enough boy to get some answers?" I ask with a cheeky grin, hoping joking will lighten the mood.

She rolls her eyes, turning towards me as she folds one leg underneath her on the bed, the other handing off. The room smells like coconut shampoo and her vanilla perfume, and I shut my eyes, breathing it in.

"What do you want to know?" she asks.

I look around the room, my face twisting. The answer is obvious. "Literally everything. Start at the beginning. You said that this is an illegal project. I know you told me the name of it. I just, I don't know I've never heard of it."

She flinches, her shoulders slumping. "It wouldn't be Top Secret if they told every idiot who graduated from the Academy about it, Damon," she deadpans, and I open my mouth to protest, but she cuts me off. "You could have been one of the smartest people there, but you were easily caught by us. You're an idiot. There's a reason we took you in for questioning. No one is supposed to know outside of the people involved. We're not on the books."

Seeing the confusion written across my face, she sighs before adjusting, getting comfortable.

"The CIA was formally created in 1947, right?" I nod. "It was after the National Security Act was signed into law. Truman saw how important the Agency was, but he was afraid of it leading to political abuse, which," she shrugs, grimacing, "obviously it would be. Obviously, it *has* been."

"The CIA was prohibited from spying on the American people because of that," I say, digesting this new information.

"Yes and no. The CIA has never been one to play by the rules, you know this. Everyone knows this. If people found out about this project, most wouldn't bat an eye. It's just the Agency up to no good again, but it *is* illegal and people finding out about it has way more ramifications politically and globally than it does in the court of public opinion." She leans back, breathing deeply before continuing. "They never actually stopped operating in the country. Everyone knows this. They've been fucking with things for decades."

"The Bureau is supposed to be the government's investigative agency," I say. "Are you saying that they have all of these operations going right under our nose, and no one knows?"

She nods, biting her lip. "I mean, as I said, they never stopped. After 2001, intelligence failings made sure of that."

"Politics became more unstable," I say mostly to myself.

"Project Fallen Angel was created in 1950 in response to the 1947 charter. The Agency couldn't technically legally operate within the states because Truman thought they would mess with politics. The problem is, sometimes people need something to keep them in line. All of these powerful people doing horrible things, and there's no one to keep them in check."

"So the Project was created as a sort of balance of power? What about everything that happened in the 70s?"

"They were caught. Simply put. But this project wasn't found out. There weren't that many of us."

I nod, taking it in.

"As I said, we're off the books. No one knows about us. We get paid through dummy accounts, fake organizations, the like."

"How do they choose who to use for this project?"

She pauses, her lips tightening as she looks up, thinking about how to phrase whatever she's about to tell me.

"They can't just take anyone. Secrets don't keep for very long when you have people close to you wondering what you're doing every day. Because of that, they take people who they know have no one who will look for them.

"The only thing I know about my past is that I was dead for several minutes. I assume the rest of my family is dead." She doesn't look at me when she says it, not wanting the confirmation. "They take us in, give us new identities, and use us to do their dirty work. The things they don't want to waste their actual agent's lives on, you know?"

I look over at her, noticing how her face twists as if she's anxious about this conversation. Warmth spreads through my body, and all I want to do is grab her, cuddling her into me. I want her to know she's safe with me.

"Is there a reason it's called Project Fallen Angel?" I ask, thinking of any silly questions I may want answered to get my mind off the ones I can't ask.

"Fallen Angels are angels who were expelled from heaven. We were given a second life, something that many frown upon. Our mere existence is illegal, and what we do is absolutely a sin."

I grimace. "So they're basically calling you demons?"

She shrugs again, looking away. "It's just a name. Something that sounds a little less intense unless you know what it is, you know?"

"I didn't think spies are normally violent." Her eyes flash to mine, and I put my hands up, stopping her before she lashes out at me. "I just mean that I know that spies don't normally shed blood. They get in and get out. If they need to, sure, but not normally. That draws attention to them."

She tilts her head, her eyes narrowing. "That's part of being off the books, though. We're black ops. We do what has to be done no matter what."

I don't understand, but I'm not supposed to. I don't think anyone is, including the people wrapped up in this clusterfuck.

I nod slowly, studying the frayed edge of the blanket next to me. "I don't get why you can't just leave."

"What part of they saved my life and now own me don't you understand?" her voice raises, and my eyes shoot to hers. "Damon, this is an Agency that told us they would rather kill us if someone finds out about the Project to protect themselves. All of us. They would rather kill every single one of us to protect themselves."

"You don't have an out at all?"

Her nose crinkles as she looks down. "Once we reach a certain age, we can get a job with the Agency and live a normal life or we can take our papers and go wherever we want, as long as we never speak about any of it ever again. And still, if they wipe all assets out, that means those people, too."

"If you're not official and work off the books, how do you operate?"

"We have a handler that works with us. She gives us our missions for the week, we let her know of any issues. If we get in trouble, arrested, or killed, the Agency doesn't have to worry about it. We didn't work for them, they're not at fault for anything, it was simply like we never existed. No one will miss us, and no one has to answer to families."

Good God, there's so much to unpack.

"I hope that one day I can have the words to describe how incredibly sorry I am that you have gone through everything you have," My hand reaches for hers. She stills at the touch before relaxing once more, her eyes meeting mine. She looks down, breathing out as she readjusts herself on the bed. I watch her, feeling as her pinky caresses mine in a butterfly-like touch. I move my hand up her arm, and she pulls away, a pained look marring her beautiful face.

"There's nothing to be sorry for," she starts, "it is what it is. They do what they can for us. Lu remembers her past, and she's right when she says that erasing our memories is a kindness they offer us."

I scoff. "All they're doing is turning you into robots."

Rage clouds her features in an instant, and I know I've fucked up. "We're human," she whispers as if I can't see her in front of me.

"I know that, but taking away decades of memories, they took everything from you." My voice gets louder and louder as I go. "They took, they took away—"

"You?" she interrupts, her eyes ablaze. "Did they take you away, Damon?"

I'm silent. She doesn't want to know.

I look down, opening my mouth to speak, but nothing comes out. As time ticks by, I finally look at her. "They left you with nothing but what they want you to know and remember, taking away every piece that makes you yourself. For that, I'll never forgive them. But I can only hope that one day, once you're free, you'll find that again."

"Look, that girl is—"

"Not that girl," I shake my head. "It's fine if you're never Ellie Huxley ever again. That version of you is dead. I want you to find *you*. Find the things you love. The things that give you a reason to live." A tear falls from her eye as she looks down, her upturned nose red, her full lips red from biting them. I move towards her, placing my hand along her face, wiping the tear away with my thumb. She doesn't look at me. "I want you to know," my voice is soft, barely above a whisper, "that you can never be that girl ever again, but I pray that one day you'll see yourself as whole."

"Would you still wish that for me even if it means I run away? That you never see me again?" she chokes.

"I still mean every word. Especially if I never see you again."

Her breath tickles my wrist, and I want nothing more than to close the space between us and taste her lips. Nothing more than to whisk her away to safety where the harshness of the world can't touch her. I want nothing more than to make her mine. To show her what real love is like.

Her jaw locks, and she looks up at me, her beautiful eyes brimming with tears. "Thank you." Her voice is meek.

"You don't have to be strong all the time, Amelia. Not with me."

She nods.

Closing the door to my room, I turn, almost jumping out of my skin as Amare greets me, his arms crossed over his chest as he sits on my bed.

"What are you doing here?" I know he's not my biggest fan, but it seemed like we were getting along a little bit better earlier. I'm hoping that's still the case.

"I just wanted to talk to you quick." He purses his lips, looking around the room.

I gesture for him to go on.

"Look," he starts, his voice low, "Amelia is like a sister to me. I care about her. We're a family. One that has only had each other for the last six years. Now," he stands, sauntering over to me and landing his hand on my shoulder, "I think you're a good guy. I do, stop giving me that look. I think you're a good guy, despite how things started. Do I think you may know a little more than you let on? Yeah, but that's neither here nor there. It's clear you've known Amelia for a long time. I want her happy, and if, somehow, someday, that means you're in the picture, I support it."

I'm shocked, my back rigid.

"But that doesn't mean that that's what's good for you," he says finally, dropping his hand. "This life isn't for everyone, and I can tell it's not for you. If she cares about you, that puts her in danger. You have to understand that."

I nod, swallowing a lump in my throat.

He pats my arm before slipping silently out the door.

FOURTEEN

AMELIA

I don't know why I defend the Agency. I understand what they have done is horrible. That what they are doing is horrible. But I've also seen the horrors of this world. Of what human beings can do to each other. I understand the need for something to happen.

But when Damon was criticizing everything, it felt almost like he was wishing I had just died.

But I know I'm projecting. I know I wish I was dead more often than not.

I trudge into the bathroom, leaning against the counter as I splash cold water on my face.

I don't know everything about the history of the Agency. I don't need to. In fact, we've been told at times that the less we know, the better, which is fine by me. Half of what I know I've learned on the internet. For people who have historically been terrible at keeping secrets, they've kept this one pretty well. But the less shit I have to learn, the better.

The thing about erasing memories is that there's no way to

165

pick and choose what someone remembers and what they don't. This may be by design, I'm not sure. But each of us has struggled to learn things over again. Basic things. Thankfully, as long as we have the knowledge deep in our subconscious *somewhere*, we do just fine.

I've never had to explain it all to someone before, and it was weird.

I lay in my bed thinking about today. Seeing Damon in the gym was unexpected, and I can't deny that seeing him in his form-fitting shirt, his muscles on full display, did something to me.

When I praise the Agency for wiping our memories, I'm lying. Right through my teeth. And I think he can tell.

I wish I could remember him. It's like having a word stuck on the tip of your tongue. I can feel him right there, I just can't conjure the memory at all. No matter how badly I would like to.

Because God, I would love to.

I know I'm going to spiral if I don't shut my brain down, but thankfully, I don't have to as someone knocks on my door.

"Come in!" I call from my bed as I pet Cooper's soft head. He's been with Luisa all day, running around outside as Matthew showed her around. Apparently, he took a keen liking to the cows and almost got head-butted by a baby goat. It was a long day for him.

"I found something," Stella says as she steps in, her laptop in her hands as her sandy hair bellows behind her.

I sit up, interested. I've never seen Stella so excited about anything. She must have found something good.

"What is it?"

She sits on the edge of my bed, pulling up windows on her computer. They're all numbers and letters, codes I don't have any hope of understanding. "I found where the hit originated, and I was right. The call came from DC. But I can get you more than that," she tells me, her eyes meeting mine.

"Do you know the exact location?"

"I know a bit. It originated here," she points to a map, "It's a bunch of offices. I can't see who works there, and their computers have about a million different safety features, so I can't get in to see who the hell they are. But I know it came from there. Well, at least that text did. I think you may find your answer there."

I nod, thinking.

"There's a compound in DC. I'm friends with the head, Jerry. I can give her a call." She gets up from the bed, wiping her palms on her jeans before looking at me, an almost crazy look in her eye. "I really think you need to go. We usually can't get an exact location like that, but you know I care about you," Her shoulders slump, "I don't want to see anything happen to you."

I don't want to see something happen to me, either. If anyone is going to take me out of this world, it will be myself. I won't let anyone else have the privilege.

"Can you contact her and see if they have room for us to stay with them?" Cooper picks his head up. "And do you know if they'll be okay with him? I'm nervous about bringing him into more danger."

She looks at him for a moment before her gaze returns to mine. "I know they have a dog. I think they'll be good friends. Just keep him there and don't bring him on missions, obviously." She rolls her eyes. She knows I wouldn't dream of it.

"Thank you," I tell her quietly. "Let me know what she says and then I can arrange to leave tomorrow if that's okay? Either way, we need to figure something out. If we can't stay there, we'll stay somewhere else."

"You got it," Stella shoots me a grin before picking up her

closed laptop from the bed, turning on her heel, and walking out the door.

The silence lets my mind drift to Damon again, and for a moment, I want to follow her. To overload my brain with thoughts of other things. Anything, really, to keep my mind from thinking of the handsome man in the room across from me.

And his sweaty body under mine…

God, I need help.

Flopping back on the bed, I cover my eyes with my fists, groaning.

A moment later, there's a knock on the door, and I'm almost certain it's Stella again, telling me she talked to her contact in DC and we'd be able to stay there. I call for her to come in, only to be met with the face I least want to see.

"What do you want?" I roll my eyes, propping myself up on my elbows.

"I just heard things from the room, wanted to make sure you were okay." His eyes rake over my body. I feel alight under his watch, and I hope and pray the feeling will pass.

I want him, and that's not a feeling I'm used to.

"I'm fine," I breathe out, all of a sudden at a loss for words.

His eyes meet mine and he nods, backing up to close the door.

I wish I invited him in.

Who *am* I?

That's a human emotion, you're fine, I think. But it's not fine.

I've gone for so, so long not thinking about anyone like that. For me, it's survival. I can't have feelings for someone, and I know I'm not the kind of person who can sleep with someone and get away unscathed, not a feeling in sight.

At some point, I'll lose the people who matter to me most, and I'm not ready for that to be a possibility. I'm just not. Maybe one day, when I'm released, I'll settle down with a nice guy I meet at a bar playing pool. But that time isn't now. Right now, I need to be on my game, ready to take on whatever challenges are thrown my way. The way to fail that? Getting attached.

Cooper lets out a sneeze as he looks at the door, his eyes sad. "I know buddy, I know."

It doesn't take me that long to drift off.

When I awake, the room is still dark and Cooper is still passed out next to me. I look around, feeling around the bed for my phone to check the time. Three a.m.

I should go back to sleep.

I reach for my water bottle on the nightstand but find it empty. I had forgotten to fill it before I went to sleep.

Sighing, I slip out of bed, looking down at myself. I'm still wearing a cropped cami and shorts. Not something I'd walk around in during the day, but it's enough to make a short run to the kitchen. No one else should be up anyways.

Sneaking out quietly, I tiptoe down the hall. When I'm safely in the other room, I let out a breath, heading for the fridge.

"What are you doing up?" a deep voice asks from the counter. I jump, whipping around to face them.

But it's only Damon, his voice groggy with sleep.

My eyes scan his shirtless torso, my mind drinking it in like I haven't had water in ten years. I've thought about what he looks like under his shirts, sure, but I haven't seen all of it with my own two eyes.

His green eyes watch mine as I straighten, my breath catching. I can feel the heat move from my cheeks to my neck before drifting down my body, right to the one place I'd rather not feel anything right now.

Traitor, I think.

I shake my thoughts, but it does nothing.

His bare chest and six-pack abs are only the beginning. His shoulders are broad, and his arms are roped with muscles. I've been pressed against him before. I've felt them, but it's a whole other experience to actually see them.

The thick black lines of his tattoo wraps around his bicep, and I can feel my mouth start to water as I attempt to keep it from dropping open as my own muscles tense.

"I—I umm," I start, and I hate the smirk that snakes onto his face, slowly stretching into a full grin.

"You okay?" he asks, tipping his gaze down as it makes its way up my legs slowly. A shiver runs down my spine, and I lick my lips.

"Obviously. I'm just tired. I, umm, I just needed water." I turn around with my water bottle, breaking the trance.

I'm just about to grab the pitcher of water before I feel a body behind mine, and my skin prickles. Before I know it, it's pressed against mine, my body thrown against the counter.

"We need to talk." He breathes into my neck. My eyes close as I feel every inch of his skin against my back.

Snap out of it.

"There's nothing to talk about." My breathing becomes labored.

Grabbing my shoulder, he turns me around, quick to push himself back into me, pinning me so I have no way out.

But I do have a way out. I can get out of this in two seconds. If I wanted to, that is.

My brain and my heart have two very different ideas of what I want. Clearly, I have to have a little talk with my heart about this newfound sexual confidence.

"I want to be as careful as possible with you," he starts, his eyes burning into mine, his lips hovering an inch or two away.

"I don't need anyone to be fucking careful with me," I growl, annoyed.

He pushes into me harder, his arms going up to grip the cabinets above us as he leans into me, caging me further. I try as hard as I possibly can not to lick my lips at the sight.

"So you want me to tell you about the past?" he asks, chuckling as the horrified look crosses my face. "That's what I thought."

I squeeze my eyes tight, wishing for once that I knew everything. Maybe someday soon, but not right now. Not when we have so much to do. So much relying on me. I don't need it.

"I, I need to get back—" I start, but he presses into me harder, and I once again lose my train of thought, feeling every inch of him.

Oh.

"Damon please, we need to get back to bed. I can't take this right now, let's not wake the others up. I thought our talk earlier was good," I whisper, unable to look into his eyes.

"It was good," he says, his breath fanning my face, "but I don't think it's a stretch to say that there's something unsaid between us, Sweetheart."

My breath quickens as he eyes my lips, and I can't help but angle my face up at him. For a brief moment, I let whatever be, be.

But it doesn't get there.

Instead, he lets up, stepping back.

"I'm trying to be good, I am. But I never got closure from your death. Not once. I spent six years grieving you." His face twists with anger, his fists shaking at his sides as his eyes twinkle.

"I—"

"There's only so much someone can take. I've been fine with the way you've treated me the last couple of days. It was my decision to come and find you. I'm sorry I stumbled into something I didn't understand. I just want you to promise

171

that today will last. That you're not going to go back to treating me like you were before."

"Damon please—"

"If you just chose one, if you just chose *one*, I would be okay. Either hate me and treat me like a problem or treat me like a person. I see it. I see that you remember me deep down. I see the desire in your eyes, the need to fight. I'm more familiar with your body than you think." His eyes drift to my chest before roaming back up. It burns my skin.

I take a deep breath, my eyes welling with tears. "I don't know what to say," I admit after a moment. And I don't. For the first time, I'm speechless.

I want to feel. I want to let someone in. I want to understand what he's telling me. I want to get rid of the stain the agency put on me. Not for the first time, I want to scrub my skin of any trace of them.

Not for the first time, I want to know.

But I can't.

"I need you to get the fuck away from me," I snap, and I instantly regret it as rage fills his eyes. He narrows them, taking a step towards me.

"You don't mean that." His voice is low, danger dripping from every word.

"I do." I try to shove past him.

In an instant, a hand is at my throat as I'm forced back into the fridge, his other arm resting above my head on the cool metal.

"You don't want to do that," I warn him, narrowing my eyes as he tightens his grip, forcing me to look up at him.

"I think I do." He drops his head, his lips at my neck. I shiver. "I think," his lips caress the sensitive skin below my ear, "that you've been in control for so long, you desperately want someone to take it away."

My body arches on its own accord, and I can't stop myself

from grinding my hips into his as I look up at him from under my lashes.

"I don't think that's the case at all," I practically moan.

"Yeah?" he pulls away, his lips less than an inch from mine. I can feel the warmth from his breath, the softness of his skin as he brushes them against me.

"I can see it in your pretty little head, Sweetheart. You want to let go. Do it. Let me help you."

We're alone in this room, the others safely tucked into their beds, hopefully asleep. We're not alone in this house, but it feels as though we're alone in this universe. It's only us. We're the only two that matter in this moment.

His green, hungry eyes alight a fire in me that I didn't know existed. I've never felt it before. I want him to devour me.

I think about it for a second as we stare at each other, his face highlighted by the moonlight out the giant windows. I want to, God, do I want to. He feels so goddamn familiar. I want nothing more than for him to throw me on this counter and take me. To show me how much he desires me.

But the reasonable side of me screams for me to walk away.

"Damon I've never," I pause, unsure I want to admit this. "I've never been with anyone before. I know I haven't."

He looks surprised for a moment before biting his lip, moving away.

I don't know how I made it to twenty-one as a virgin, but I did. After that, it was the one thing I could control about my life. I chose who I let in, and no one was ever worth it. No one was ever worth the loss that would happen after.

"I'm sorry," he says as he walks away, but I grab his arm, turning him around.

"I'm the one who should be sorry," I tell him in a whisper, a tear escaping.

His eyes close tight, and he looks as if he's in pain. "This is what I'm talking about. You can't tell me to fuck off one moment and then treat me as if you actually care the next. I know they messed with your head, I understand, but I'm a person. I can only take so much." His eyes open as he tips my chin up, forcing me to look at him. I can't help but feel my own heart twist.

He breaks from my hold, giving me his back as he returns to his room.

I let all the pent-up tears escape.

FIFTEEN

Damon

Six years and eight months ago

A short honk sounds through the silent night, making us stop. Our eyes meet each other's, wide with worry that someone will come find us. After a moment, we know we're safe.

We shouldn't be nervous. We're in the middle of nowhere. But her father has been keeping an extra careful eye on her for the last couple of months, and I worry I've been made.

Her lips return to mine as she holds my face between her hands. They move back, her fingernails scraping my scalp, and a guttural growl escapes me as I deepen the kiss, devouring her tongue as she lets out a moan from deep in her chest.

She sits on my lap, and I run my hands over her spine, arching her back so she doesn't hit the steering wheel of my classic Camaro. Her hips grind into mine, and I swear it's been so long since I've been inside of a woman, I feel as though I'll combust at any moment.

She breaks the kiss, pulling away just an inch, looking into my eyes. Her ash blonde hair glistens in the moonlight, her brown eyes staring into my soul.

I always loved brown eyes. The rich softness of them makes me feel warm, safe, and loved. They feel like home.

"I want to feel every part of you," she whispers into my lips, and I breathe in, not knowing how much more I can take.

"I know Sweetheart," I rest my forehead against hers. Her hands run down over my shoulders, snaking around my neck. I wish I could keep her here, just like this, forever. She's safer here than anywhere else.

"I don't want to marry him." Melancholy drips from her voice, and I wish I could make all the pain go away.

"I don't want you to, either." I kiss her scrunched nose.

"I just wish I could give everything to you."

I brush her hair from her face.

"First, I want you to understand that what he's told you is bullshit. Virginity doesn't impact your worth, Ellie. You're worth more than gold whether you are or aren't. If you listen to one thing I say, please listen to that."

She nods, looking down sheepishly.

"Second, any man that requires you to have a hymen is a fucking creep." Her gaze snaps to mine, a small smile on her lips. "No man should even be able to feel it. If someone cares so much that you're in pain your first time for them, checking for that small amount of blood, they're a creep and honestly, should probably be put on some kind of list." I chuckle. "Third," I hold up three fingers, grabbing her small chin in my other hand, making sure she can't look away, "I want you to know I'm going to try to get you out of this, okay?"

She doesn't nod this time. She doesn't say anything. She doesn't have to. Instead, she leans into me, her cheek caressing mine as she settles into the crook of my neck.

"I just want to run away with you," she whispers.

I knew she was a virgin before her death. Her father was strict and made sure it stayed that way. She was to marry a politician, a sick bastard her father adored, and he would only take her hand if he could be the first.

It made me sick.

It made me even sicker that she's internalized it, believing it's the one thing she's had control over. But I understand, too.

I watch as she packs, careful not to make eye contact with me.

I felt a shift last night, and that's all I can hope for, right? All I want is for her to be safe. I don't care if I ever get to make her mine. I want her safe and happy, no matter what. But the life she's been leading now, whether it's her fault or not, is destroying her humanity.

I don't want to save her from it. When it comes to her, my morals fall to the wayside. I would gladly kill for her. I just want to save her from what they've done. Her memories, her soul. They took her humanity away, wiping away any trace of her, only to use her.

That's not the way people should live.

"Is all your shit packed?" Amare asks me, looking between us. Amelia glances up, her eyes meeting mine for a brief moment before drifting back to Cooper as she adjusts his harness.

"Yeah, it's all here," I gesture to the small bag before me. It's not like I had a lot.

He looks me over one more time, and I can tell he knows something is up. "Good," his tone is curt as he turns away to find Luisa.

The blonde woman I saw the other day makes her way through the large doors, her steps light and bouncy as she makes her way to Amelia. Handing her a file, they exchange a couple of words before hugging.

And Amelia smiles. An instant shock of jealousy flows through me. I want to be the one to make her smile. Just once. A true smile, like she's happy.

I used to make her happy.

I shake it off, turning back to my things as I look around, my hands on my hips. Feeling something brush up against my legs, I look down to see Cooper's dark brown eyes staring up at me.

"Hey bud, you doing okay?" I ask, patting his head. He lets out a sneeze, and I smile. At least I have one friend here, right?

Luisa walks into the room, announcing the car is here. Picking up my bags, I watch as Cooper trots back to Amelia, his tail wagging, his tongue hanging from his mouth as he smiles.

Clipping his leash to the harness, Amelia looks at me, allowing a small sheepish smile to creep onto her face. It freezes me in my spot. Does she actually feel bad for last night? Are things actually going to change? I'm not sure. I'm definitely not going to hold my breath, but it would be nice if I could actually speak to her without feeling as though I'll be tied up in her basement again the second she gets the chance.

I understand where she's coming from. I completely understand that the Agency has done a number on her. If I was being used as they are, I'd shut down completely, too. She's become more like a robot than anything, and the most frustrating part is I'm positive she could save herself. She doesn't need me. She's strong enough to pull herself out of it.

I also completely understand not wanting to learn about the past. I respect it. But it's so incredibly hard when I see how she reacts to me now, and how she used to.

I think about the late nights in my car and I, well, I can't think about it. Not without getting flustered.

We walk out of the house, waving goodbye to Matthew, who stands in the foyer, cowboy hat on his head, a coy smile on his lips as he and Luisa make eye contact. For a bunch of spies, they don't have great poker faces when they're not actually on the job, that's for sure.

She catches my eye, and I smirk. "What's going on there?" I whisper.

"Fuck off, West," she says with a smile, pushing me.

We make our way into the same car we were in just the other day, packed in like sardines as the same driver looks at us from the rearview mirror. I wave at him, shooting him a smile.

"Thank you so much for the ride, sir, I really—" I don't get to finish as Amelia shoves me back, shooting me an annoyed look. I don't miss the slight shake of her head. We're not supposed to talk to them, I suppose.

I'm not sure if that's for their safety or ours.

Finally, we're on the road, the beautiful Texas compound behind us.

I almost want to go back and explore the place more.

The ride is silent as usual, and when we get to the airport, we're escorted to the plane without going through security. I'm not entirely sure how we get that pass. I look around as the employees check us out.

Amelia is in front of me, Cooper next to her as Luisa and Amare take the lead, their eyes shielded from the hot Texas sun by sunglasses I wish I had, their bags slung over their shoulders lazily.

Hitting the tarmac, I can feel the heat through my shoes, and I'm suddenly so happy we're going somewhere cooler. I wasn't made for the hot sun.

"You ready to get out of this place?" Amelia asks, hanging back so she's next to me.

"You're talking to me now?" I ask, glancing at her.

She looks down at her shoes, letting out a sigh. "Can we call a truce?"

I consider it for a second. "As long as it's actually a truce, and not just me letting it go. You need to stop whatever this has been," I grit out quietly, trying not to let the others hear.

But Amelia sees the way Amare's head tilts to the side, picking up on a conversation happening. She shoots me a look before continuing ahead of me again.

I roll my eyes as we approach the small private plane, making our way up the steps.

The others throw their bags down, and I take a seat towards the back. At least it's a window seat. I settle into the cool leather of the seat, getting comfortable.

Looking around, I take everything in. I'm not exactly used to flying private, and although I wish the situation was a little better, it's still a cool experience. Behind me is a bedroom, for God's sake. I'm sure that there are long flights and the need for some rest. The bathroom is next to it, and there's a small kitchenette with snacks and water.

The others are up further toward the front of the plane, talking in hushed tones. I don't even try to listen to them, knowing whatever they say will likely annoy me.

I close my eyes, attempting to get some rest early.

"You okay?" Amelia interrupts my peace, sitting down in the seat in front of me, resting one leg over her other.

"I'm fine." It doesn't come out as friendly as I intended.

"You seemed a little worked up earlier." I open one eye, peeking out at her again.

"I'm as fine as anyone would be in this situation." I close them again, not wanting to continue this conversation.

"Damon, talk to me."

I sit up, meeting her eyes. "I told you what I want. You either treat me like a prisoner or you treat me like an actual person. I'm not doing this hot and cold bullshit," I hiss, biting back more angry words.

Her head tilts to the side, her beautiful brown eyes meeting mine as the sun lights them up. Even from here, I can see the flecks of gold in them, and I want more than anything to stare into them for the rest of my life.

I've missed them so, so much.

"I want us to get along." She sighs, studying her hands.

I throw my hands up. "Doesn't seem like it." I want to hold firm, but I can feel my resolve breaking.

Her eyes flash to mine before looking back down, and I can't tell if it's because she feels bad, or she simply doesn't care.

"I want to know," she mumbles, not looking up.

"What do you want to know?" I ask, my brows furrowing in confusion.

"I want to know who I was to you before." She meets my gaze for a moment. "But that's it," she adds, "that's all I want to know. Nothing else."

I nod, thinking about whether I actually want to tell her now. I know she'll be angry.

"Where do you want me to start?"

"From the beginning." She settles into her seat, tossing her legs over the armrest, her sweatpants bunching up at the ankles. She props herself up on her elbows against the opposite armrest, eyeing me.

"Okay." I clear my throat. "You were a mission, but you didn't know until the last few days of your life," I tell her, crossing my arms over my chest. She bites her lip across from me, and I wonder if I should continue. When she doesn't say anything, I decide I should. "I was assigned to watch your family. I won't get into why. It was undercover. My first mission after graduating from the Academy. Most don't get cases like that right off the bat, but I was young and showed I really cared. I would fit in there, unlike some of the guys that were a little older. Some people went through the Academy in their late twenties, after they had some work in the field under their belts.

"Well, I had to befriend you to get access to your family and watch over you. It was the only way. You'll understand if I ever eventually tell you why this was needed." I take a deep breath, making sure I don't let anything slip that will make her angrier than she already will be. I would be upset, too. Someone pretending to be my friend. Except it wasn't pretend. Not for me. Not after a while.

"You were beautiful," I smile, leaning my head back against the seat. I can feel her eyes on me. "You had this short blonde bob at the time, but you were trying to grow it out. You were brilliant. Straight A's, you constantly talked about going to Harvard. I loved that. But you were so shy that first day. You continued to be for a long time until I eventually cracked you." I leave out that she got a full ride there before she died. She doesn't need to know.

"You had this hoodie on, and I remember seeing your freckles for the first time and thinking they were so cute before slapping myself. I had a mission, and my mission wasn't to fall for you.

"But I think I did. I think I did quickly, even if I don't want to admit it." I look at the ceiling of the plane as the engine kicks on. "It wasn't long. You had," I pause, trying to figure out how to word this. "you had some issues going on, and I quickly became your shoulder to cry on. That's why I was there. To listen to you. I would have given you the world at that point."

I sigh deeply.

"I always thought I would be a great agent. I was at the top of my graduating class from the Academy, I took my job seriously, and I was absolutely positive I was going to do great things at the Bureau. I had been wanting it for so long." My eyes feel prickly at the memory. They weren't things I really thought about often, as they hurt. My dreams went down the drain that day I lost her.

"Things got heated, and I got too attached. We never did anything other than kiss," I tell her, meeting her eyes, "But there were some really late nights in my car, where all I did was hold you.

"Then one day, I was at home when I got a call that some-thing awful was going to happen. It had nothing to do with me, I promise. I should have been around that day. Closer. I got there as soon as I possibly could, but it was too late."

I keep her gaze, not wanting to continue further and upset her. She doesn't need to know the circumstances, who she lost, or what I saw when I got there. She asked who she was to me, and I told her exactly that.

Her eyes are bright, glistening with tears as she looks down at her hands and back up at me, her tongue peeking out to wet her lips.

"I know you said you don't, but I have to make sure. Do you still work for them?" she asks, and I shake my head, not wanting to tell her that she's the reason for that, too.

She nods, getting up and heading to the back room.

"Amelia?" I turn as I watch her.

"I need a minute,"

But I know that the second I leave her alone, the second she comes back, she's going to greet me with those cold eyes again, closing me off from ever seeing who she really is. I can't have that. I can't live with that anymore. And as much as I hate when she does it, I really do understand.

So I follow her. I don't give a shit who sees me enter after her. I don't care what they think. All I know is she's upset, and I want to comfort her. She knows the truth; she knows how I felt about her back then. I want to make sure she understands that I'm here because I still care about her. I never got over her. Not when it ended the way it did.

I felt guilty for the last six years over what happened. I let it eat me alive. I'm not going to let her go after that. Never.

I follow her into the bedroom, watching as she sits on the edge of the bed, her head in her hands as her shoulders shake. I sit next to her, wrapping my arm around her.

"Shhh," I comfort her, bringing her into my chest. "I'm sorry, I just wanted to tell the truth," I whisper into her hair, holding her head to my body.

"I just, I don't know what to do." Her voice is barely audible, shaking as sobs rip through her.

"What do you mean?"

"I don't want to be here." The sob she lets out breaks me.

My heart shatters into a million pieces.

All I want is to pick them up and put them together again. To help her. To heal her. To give her back all the time she has ever missed.

"I've tried before. I've tried to end it. I'm not strong enough for this." She sniffles, looking up at me, her eyes red and puffy.

My brows furrow in confusion.

"There have been times it's gotten too much. I've seen too much, I've experienced too much. There's been times our missions have led to learning some really awful things about the world." She sighs, more tears escaping. "I just wanted to end it. I was supposed to be dead. I just wanted to be dead." Her body slumps over again as another sob tremors through her.

"You're one of the strongest people I've ever had the pleasure of knowing Sweetheart," I tell her, running my fingers through her hair like she used to love me doing. She used to say it comforted her. I hope nothing's changed. "You were before this happened, and you are now. Do you know how many times you've looked at me over the last couple of days and I've seen my own life flash before my eyes?" I let out a chuckle, tears blurring my vision.

"You're one of the most special people on this planet, and I'm so goddamn sorry you've ever wished to end it. This world is far better with you in it."

Her tears fall, soaking my shirt, and the tightness in my chest refuses to loosen. I feel myself crumbling with her.

"I just want this pain to end," she whispers.

"I know. I know love." Her hair is soft beneath my cheek as I hold her shaking body. She turns, her hand grabbing my shoulder as she turns into me more.

"They took everything from me." Her voice is soft.

"They did,"

Under the guise of giving her everything, they took the most quintessential parts of her.

And there's only one person at fault for it.

SIXTEEN

AMELIA

I've never felt at home before. Felt truly safe. Felt it in my bones that I was secure.

But this feels pretty close.

And it's petrifying.

"I don't want to hurt you," I whisper, the beat of my heart sounding so loud over the hum of the plane engine as we fly and the low murmur of voices in the other room.

"How would you hurt me?" he asks, raking his fingers through my hair. I close my eyes, taking comfort in the action.

I sigh, wiping my tear-stained face on his shirt. "We've been told not to make connections. Not to care for anyone. We can be gone at any point. Or they could be in danger. I don't, I don't know what to do."

He nods, pressing his cheek back onto my head. "I got you. I don't know what this means, I don't know what's going to happen in the next couple of days, but I got you, okay?" His low voice is soothing.

I look up at him. "How did you get your scar?" I ask. It's

189

not the most noticeable. A small scar over his right eye. It's not angry, not prominent. Just... there.

He searches my eyes, cupping my face with his large hands. "I can't tell you that right now," he tells me. "Please trust me on that."

I nod.

I can't tell him that I'm terrified for him. He hasn't seen what I have. Heard what I have. He doesn't understand that death will come for him. A punishing death. For both of us.

What terrifies me more is the life I feel deep in my bones for the first time. For the very first time, I have an actual will to live.

From the very second I woke up on that table, I wanted to die. I wished for it. For an entire year, Luisa and Amare watched me to make sure I didn't hurt myself. That I didn't take my own life. That was four years ago.

I never got better. I simply learned to live with the pain knowing it was never going to happen.

But I can now say with absolute certainty that feeling alive is the scariest thing of all. Especially knowing the person who brings me life will be my downfall.

"Please don't push me away," he whispers against my skin, his lips on my forehead.

"I won't," I lie.

"We can be friends, okay?" He pulls my head back, looking into my eyes. They linger, waiting for my response.

I nod, burying my face in his chest again. Lying is part of my job, but it doesn't usually taste this horrible on my tongue.

He holds me tight. As I drift off, I hear him whisper, "I'm going to find a way to keep you safe. You're going to be okay. I'm going to make this right. I lived for six years thinking you were dead... the next time your heart stops beating, mine will too."

And I drift off to sleep in his arms, my heart squeezing in my chest.

Four years ago

"There's absolutely no way you're getting out of here alive," I tell the man in front of me. His head is hung low as blood, sweat, and saliva drip from his face to his tattered jeans.

"I told you before, I don't know anything," he grits out, his eyes meeting mine, full of anger and resentment. Spitting at my feet, the man lurches back, leveling me with a stare intended to make me sweat. He still doesn't understand what he's gotten himself into.

I lean against the wall, my dagger clutched at my side. With a knowing smirk, I reach into the back pocket of my jeans, withdrawing my lighter. "I think we can work together to find out the truth," I start as I flick it on, watching the flame jerk. His eyes go wide as I focus back on him, shrugging.

"You have one minute to give me the information I want.

"You crazy fucking bitch, I don't know anything, I fucking told you," he spits, his lips pulling back in a snarl.

"So you're telling me that twenty girls have gone missing right after meeting with you, and yet, you don't know anything about it?" I ask him, stepping forward as I place the blade over the flame.

"I was set up, I don't know. Why the fuck am I here?" he asks, pulling against his restraints, attempting to get out of them.

Irritation flickers deep within me, and I wish I could kill him now. His time is coming, but sometimes it's just so hard to keep them alive.

"Most humans only think of how to survive in times like this," I click my tongue, squatting down until I'm at eye level with him. "And yet here you are, doing everything you possibly can to die. Why is that?"

He doesn't answer, instead focusing his attention on the dagger in my hand, and the flame dancing beneath it.

Putting the lighter down, I move closer to him, and it takes everything in me to ignore his repugnant, sickly smell wafting from him. A mix of blood, sweat, and sheer terror.

"I'm sure you'll remember the details in a minute," I tell him, bringing the blade across his cheek.

He screams, rearing back in the chair. He shakes, and I can hear his teeth grinding together as he tries to stifle his pain.

"I need you to tell me what I want to know, or things are about to get so much worse for you."

Instead of answering, he looks at me, a smirk on his bloodied, split lips. Slowly, he smiles, his teeth red with blood.

I stand, grabbing hold of his cheeks with one hand and squeezing, forcing his mouth open. Pulling his jaw down, I place the blade at the entrance of his mouth. He clamps down, and I wish one of the others were here to help me.

There's only so much a woman can do herself.

"I wouldn't do that if I were you," I warn him. "This blade will slice you open in two seconds. Open up."

The man reluctantly opens his mouth, his eyes squeezed shut. I place the burning blade on his tongue, and he thrashes in pain, kicking his bound feet in front of him.

I leave it there for a minute before taking it out, wiping it on my pants before turning my attention back to him.

Saliva drips from his mouth, his eyes bloodshot as he glares at me, lighting a fire deep in my belly.

"You have one more chance. Tell me what I want to know, or I'm carving into your forehead and leaving you dead on your family's doorstep, letting them know exactly what kind of girls you go after when your wife isn't looking."

His nostrils flare, and my excitement peaks. "I don't know what the hell thith ith," he lisps, his tongue swelling, "but if you kill me, they'll come after you."

My head tilts, my eyes never once leaving his as I watch the fear creep into them. For some reason, he's been so incredibly confident that somehow, someway, he'll find his way out of this.

Men like him should know that this will be their end. Any man who dares mutilate women, throwing them away as if they're nothing should know that someone is coming for them.

I wish we could have sooner. The government and the Agency don't tend to care until a mass amount of people go missing at once. If it's enough to stir up some news, we're the first ones on the case, instructed to shut whatever is happening down before it becomes a larger issue.

It doesn't matter how powerful the man is, their death serves a higher purpose. It keeps the peace. It keeps everyone in line.

The only time anyone will ever know about us is before they die. Otherwise, we're ghosts. People who don't actually exist on paper. We're shells of our old selves, long forgotten.

We're credible threats to every rule this fucking country has, and yet we were created by the CIA.

I stand, slamming my bloody, busted fist into his jaw one more time for good measure, feeling the crack as his head falls back, the legs of the wooden chair breaking.

"You know, I've never been one to get along with men," I tell him. And I haven't been. Ever since I can remember, almost every man I've come across has been a sleazeball. Amare is one of the good ones.

That being said, I don't normally speak to people outside of our missions, and the men we come across are almost always in way too deep with the wrong people, thinking they can take advantage of me or use me.

The man bares his teeth, and I bring my foot down on his elbow, taking pleasure in the crack of his bones. His screams ring out, and for a second—just one moment—I'm filled with dread and horror.

I shove the feeling down, focusing back on the task at hand.

"I'm feeling generous today," I tell him, kneeling next to him, my dagger still in my hand. "You have one more shot, but just one."

I take the blade and brush his hair from his forehead, tapping it to his flesh. "I always fulfill my promises."

He coughs up blood, his body lurching as he tries to catch his breath. Closing his eyes, he steadies his breathing as he winces in pain, flexing his shoulders. When he opens them, his lips pull back with a growl. "Carl knowth thomething. He'th the head of—"

"I know who Carl is," I snap, looking at the ceiling in annoyance. Carl was how I found this guy. An older man with a taste for hookers, Carl didn't seem like a threat. But if there's one thing I've learned, it's that some people are capable of weaving the most intricate webs. It was simply our job to torch them.

"What is he doing with the girls?" I ask him, slapping the blade against my thigh in impatience.

"I told you. I don't know anything other than that. I juth know he hath thomething to do with it."

My eyes narrow as I consider this. "And how many women have you assaulted?" I ask. He wouldn't be here if he was completely innocent. We don't need high-powered individuals using their privilege to hurt people. This man is far from innocent.

He takes a deep breath before he brings his attention back to me, glancing at the blade in my hand once more. "There wath only a couple," he chokes out, looking down, his eyes welling with tears.

I smile, bringing the blade under his chin, tilting it up so he's forced to meet my eyes. "I'm so sorry someone as pathetic as you was allowed to walk on this earth while so many innocents were taken from the streets," I tell him, turning my wrist so the blade is against his throat, cutting into his flesh.

Rage rips through me, bursting out of me, and for a moment, I can't see. I'm blinded by it, consumed. Blood runs down his neck and onto the floor as he gargles, gasping for the last breath he'll ever take on this earth as his beady eyes stare blankly back at me.

I bring my hand up to shut them just as the door to the basement opens with a bang. Two pairs of footsteps descend the stairs, and I can tell they're dragging something.

I stand, wiping the blood from my hands onto my clothes, not caring how I look. It doesn't take long for Luisa and Amare to appear, a man slumped between them, his hands and feet bound.

"Another one?" I ask. He's in rough shape, his clothes blood-stained and crinkled, his button-up ripped open, his tie tight around his neck, his pasty skin turning the most vile shade of purple. "Jesus Christ, did you drag him with his tie? Is he even alive?" I ask them, eyeing the man as they toss him hap hazardously in the cage, slamming the door shut and locking it.

Luisa's eyes snap to mine before drifting down to the man beside me. "Is yours?" she asks, knowing damn well he's not.

Fair.

It's been three weeks, and none of us have gotten any closer to finding out why so many women are going missing. It's become a big enough problem that the Agency is worrying about it becoming national news.

The news will always care the more white women disappear. The disappearances have been happening for months to others, and there hasn't been a peep until this change.

It should have been a priority from the start.

"He told me Carl has something to do with it," I tell them. "That's all I was able to get out of him.

"Well, this is one of Carl's assistants. We're getting closer," Amare tells me, narrowing his eyes as he watches the man twitch.

My chest heaves. It's been so long since we've even gotten a sliver of new information.

We know who's been involved. They may not be the men in charge, but we know who has been working with them. We were told to take out whoever necessary in order to make this go away.

If it's someone who will be in the press, we need to make it look like an accident. That was the one and only stipulation.

Amare and Lu share a look before taking a step toward me. "How are you holding up?" Luisa asks in the same tone you'd use on an orphan.

My eyes thin, knowing what's coming. "I'm fine," I grit through my teeth, not wanting to talk about this right now.

"You're not fine," Amare snaps. "I found you trying to kill yourself just days ago and here you are torturing a man to death."

"Do you want information or not?" I question, throwing my hands up in exasperation.

"Amelia. You know what I mean. We just want to make sure you're okay with everything going on."

I'm not okay. I know that, but there's no way in hell I'll ever admit that.

Amare walked in on me with a mouth full of pills just days ago, forcing me to throw up the ones I already swallowed. I wish he wasn't home. I think about it all day. What could have been if he just let me do it?

I just want to be free of this suffering.

"I just need some rest, that's all," I tell him, looking down. They both think it happened because this mission has been too much. In a way, they're right. It has been too much. But it's also allowed me to focus on what the Agency wants me to be. The reason I exist in the first place.

If they want a monster, I'll be a monster.

I wake up with a start. It's common for me to have nightmares, but they're not often flashbacks. Moments of my life I wish I could forget. Not because I regret what happened, but because they led to much larger issues. I've seen some of the darkest of humanity during my time in the Fallen Angels. Moments I don't care to ever tell a soul.

It was two days after that day that I went to the shelter and got Cooper. He was almost fully grown at the time, and when the woman warned me that he was sometimes skittish around men since he was abused, I almost lost it. I knew at that moment that he was mine.

Despite what Cooper went through as a puppy, I needed him more than he needed me. I still wished for death more than any human should. I still suffered. I still do. But for once, I felt like I had someone relying on me. Someone who needed me and who loved me. It was selfish. But who are human beings if not selfish?

I love Luisa and Amare. I do. But when you're told not to trust people for as long as we've been told, when we've dealt with the most vile, wicked of humanity, it's hard to not think that at some point the people you grow close to will happily stab you in the back.

As it is, we have to. Three years ago, if the Agency told me to kill either of them, I would have. And they would have done the same. We've spoken about it.

Things are different now.

Back then, I took pride in being the Agency's pet. I loved being the judge, jury, and executioner, not caring who I hurt. It was gratifying. It filled me with pride. Now I question things more. I saw too much, did too many terrible things. If there's one thing I never want to be, it's a puppet.

I look around, breaking out of my trance enough to notice the arms around me. The body next to me breathes deeply, a small snore escaping him.

Damon was able to get us turned around on the bed, and I've been curled up into his side, his arm wrapped possessively around me, falling as I turn over.

He twitches at the movement, and I can't help but smile. For a second, I allow myself to be in the moment. To not think about the future.

But reality comes crashing down on me as always moments later, and I roll out of bed, careful to not disturb him too much.

Creeping to the door, I look behind me. He looks so peaceful, the last thing I want to do is wake him.

But I give him my back, exiting the room. I close the door gently, and when I turn around, I'm met with Amare and Luisa's eyes.

"You look happy," Luisa says with a smug smile, looking me up and down.

"I'm willing to bet any amount of money my face is red and puffy from crying," I tell her with a small smile, rubbing my under eyes. My skin feels tender to the touch, and I feel the exhaustion settle into my core. The type of exhaustion that only comes after a good sob.

She pauses, her smile growing wider.

"They were not those kind of tears, Lu," I tell her with an eye roll.

Amare closes his book. "Why were you crying?"

My face twists as apprehension curls in my stomach. "I'm just stressed, that's all," I tell them weakly.

"And you went to him about it?" Luisa asks, glancing at the door to the room.

The plane hits a small bout of turbulence, making me lose my footing. I sit down in an empty seat across from Cooper, who's passed out taking up two seats of his own.

"He was there." I shrug, not letting them see that he's gotten to me.

We're friends, but I'm not quite ready to talk about what we discussed with the others. Not right now, at least. We'll figure all of this out, and then I'll tell them.

In the meantime, I can try to get them to treat him kinder.

"He's a good guy, I think. I really don't think we have anything to worry about with him."

They both eye me, their eyes narrowed in suspicion.

Instead of answering, they go back to their activities. Amare reads his book, Luisa plays a game on her phone, and I look around, thinking about the conversation we had in the room, trying not to cry again.

A couple of hours later, we're landing in DC.

SEVENTEEN

DAMON

I was woken up when we landed in DC. I hadn't gotten a lot of sleep last night after my conversation with Amelia, and it was clear my body needed the rest. I'm not sure how much we'll be getting in the coming days.

I was a little sad when Amelia wasn't in my arms when I woke up, but she was still there, lightly shaking me. It was clear she had been up for a while. She was kinder to me, more open. It seemed like she actually may care.

Exiting the plane, the chilly DC air hits our faces, a welcome feeling after the abrasive Texas temperature.

A woman stands propped against the sexiest red classic car I've ever seen, seemingly completely restored. A large van sits behind her, a young man in the driver's seat. I eye it, wondering what we're about to get ourselves into.

"You know that's one of the most expensive cars to restore, right?" I whisper to Amelia as Cooper pulls on his leash, almost making me stumble.

"I told you, the Agency gives us money to shut us up. It

could be a hobby for them. Amare has worked on cars for a bit to pass the time." She shrugs, pursing her lips. "Or it could be stolen. Some of us like to take advantage of our skills and just take things. The Agency rarely intervenes. As long as we're doing what we're told they don't care."

"Wouldn't they get arrested? If they're off the books they're on their own, right?"

"Money gives people incredible power. We don't need the Agency themselves to step in most of the time." She looks at me, her eyes bright in the sunlight. "Do you know how many privileged people do horrible things and get no time for it? Same for us. Besides, spies are really good thieves. I haven't heard of a single one of us even needing to wave money around to get out of trouble." She focuses in front of her again, walking up to the woman waiting.

"You Amelia?" The woman asks, her voice gravely as her lit cigarette hangs from her lips. She takes it out, letting out a puff of smoke as she throws back her jet-black hair, a stark contrast from her red roots.

"Yeah, you're Jerry?"

They shake hands, the woman, Jerry, looking at her skeptically. "You gonna be here long?" She crosses her arm over her chest as she sticks the cigarette back into her mouth, taking a long drag.

"I'm not sure. Hopefully not," Amelia tells her, stretching her neck.

"Well, I got a van for you. Ronan is gonna bring you to the warehouse." She gestures behind her, ashes flying to the ground.

"What year is this?" I ask her suddenly, stepping around Amelia as I eye the Challenger behind her.

Her attention whips to me, and I immediately feel ice down my back. Her blue eyes send shivers through me, and I instantly wish I hadn't opened my mouth. Amelia seems to feel the same way, as she shoots daggers my way.

"You know about cars?" she asks roughly, a smile creeping over her red lips.

"I know a little."

"1970."

So I was right, it is one of the most expensive cars to restore.

"I haven't seen one this beautiful," I gape, wishing I could run a finger over the exterior without the risk of being shot in the face.

"Oh boy," she says with a throaty laugh. She pokes me with a bony finger, and I step back as hot ashes land on my shirt. "You're gonna fucking love your stay with us."

Amelia shoots me a look before ushering me toward the van behind the others.

"You know about cars?" she hisses.

I shrug. "I know a bit." What I don't tell her is that half is from one particular movie franchise, and the other half is from a video game.

Sometimes you have to omit truths to look a little more badass.

I'd say around a bunch of spies who kill people for a living is one of those times.

We settle into the van and the man up front looks us over. "Welcome to DC guys," he says, winking at us through the rearview mirror.

I nod, shooting him a smile as I settle next to Cooper, my arm over his body.

"It's not that long of a ride, I promise. About twenty minutes."

I want to thank him, but I stay quiet, following the lead of the others, not interested in getting whacked again.

Fifteen minutes later, we pull up to a giant warehouse, each and every one of us clutching our chests after seeing our lives flash before our lives.

Jerry drives like a fucking maniac, which means this guy does, too. He tried hard to keep up with her, but she was gone before we knew it.

Getting out, the man rips the doors open, letting us out. Standing there, he helps the women out before giving both Amare and I fist bumps.

"Ronan," he introduces himself.

"Damon, nice to meet you." I smile. He's one of the first people who has actually acknowledged me in the last couple of days.

Turning back to the warehouse, I take it in with the others.

"Are we in the right place?" Luisa asks, flipping her hair over her shoulder, her head tilted, hands on her hips. Her eyes squint as she tries to figure out what she's looking at.

"Yep," Ronan says, heading for the door. "We leave the van out here."

The place looks abandoned. The aging, faded brick is crumbling on the outside, and the whole place is surrounded by junk. It's a *large* building, and there's no possible way only a couple of people need this much space.

The entire property is completely enclosed in a tall barb-wire fence. Small devices sit on the top of fences, and I can only imagine they're motion detectors because they sure aren't lights.

"This place is a fortress," I whisper.

"Sure is. Just wait till you see inside," Ronan says, hearing me.

As we approach the large warehouse doors, Ronan turns. "You guys ready?" His words seem to put Amelia on edge as her back stiffens, her face hardening.

"Relax, I just overheard your boy toy asking about her

car." He turns around before we can correct him, whipping the doors open.

And we step into one of the largest, brightest rooms I've ever laid my eyes on.

It seems as though most of the warehouse is hollow, as I can see all the way up to the top ceiling. Parts of the old floors still stick from the walls, and I wonder how sure they are they won't fall.

There are cars all around us. Most of them only cars I know from my video game, ones I would never see anywhere other than a fictional world. Some I've never seen before in my life. The one thing I do know, however, is that they're all very expensive, and some very collectible.

"Holy fuck," I whisper.

Ronan smacks me on the back. "You like them?" he asks, a bright grin on his face.

"How the hell did you get all of these?" I ask as I eye one that looks eerily like a Lykan HyperSport.

"We have our ways," he replies, following my gaze. "Just pretend like you don't see that one." He chuckles.

"That's, that... that's a 3-million-dollar car," I spit out, unable to stop myself as I walk over to it.

Ronan considers this. "A little more, actually."

My head whips in his direction. "There's only seven of these, aren't there?"

"We have our ways," he says, crossing his arms over his chest.

I take one last look at the beautiful car in front of me before continuing to look at everything else. "This is insane,"

While there are dozens of cars lining the walls of the warehouse, there is living space in the middle. A staircase sits on the left wall, leading up to what would be the second floor. Along the second-floor wall are what looks like rooms, which wrap around to the back wall as well. The metal walkway continues across the compound, over top of one long wall that sits in the middle, the kitchen. Another staircase leads up to a third floor, where the rooms do the same.

Over on the far wall, I see a small door that leads to what I'm assuming is the bathrooms, judging by the crude sign outside of it.

In front of the kitchen is a large living area, which includes a large couch, table, flatscreen TV, and a couple of chairs surrounding a large, rustic coffee table, and a plush rug underneath. A small, expensive metal table sits right off to the side, a beautiful glass chess set on top of it.

Amelia looks around too, gaping. It really is something, that's for sure.

I breathe in, taking in the scent of new car. I wonder if some of these have ever been driven.

"You like?" Jerry asks, climbing out of her Challenger. Despite driving as fast as we did, we were too far behind her to see her driving into the building.

I nod.

"Well, I guess I'll introduce you all," she says as if it's paining her to do so. "Aye! We got company!" she yells, grabbing a new cigarette from the box before tossing the rest into a nearby car.

Two doors on the second floor open, and one woman and two men emerge, eyeing us warily as they descend the stairs, coming to a stop in front of us.

"This is Kim," Jerry introduces the woman. She takes Luisa's hand, shaking it with a smile. She looks nice enough.

When she's done, she goes back to the man, wrapping her tan arm around him.

"And that's Zach and Brandon." She gestures to the other two as though they don't matter.

Zach, a pasty white man with dark circles under his eyes —a man who could somehow steal any woman here—reaches out to me, shaking my hand. "Nice to meet you, man."

I nod, "Likewise."

"And you met Ronan. He's my right-hand man." She flicks her bony hand toward him. "Elena is monitoring your little," she pauses, "situation. She's at an event right now gathering some intel after Stella asked very nicely." She flicks her cigarette ash on the floor. "Brandon, show them their rooms and," she waves her hand, gesturing around the place, "everything please." He salutes her before turning, expecting us to follow.

A loud bark sounds at the other end of the warehouse, catching Cooper's attention. His ears perk up, the hair on his back rising just slightly. Jerry turns, snapping her finger.

A large, mean-looking Doberman approaches, his head down as he bares his teeth at us.

"He's literally a marshmallow." She rolls her eyes. "We rescued him from some bad circumstances, otherwise he wouldn't have clipped ears." Her mouth twists in disgust. "He'd look a whole lot less intimidating, that's for damn sure. Anyways," she waves towards us, "he's a good boy, and he'll get along with your," she eyes Cooper, "mutt."

Amelia's brows furrow as she processes what she just called her dog.

I urge her forward before she gets in a fight.

"What the fuck?" she whispers. "How the fuck do you look at him and think he's a mutt?"

I look at Cooper, who's too busy eyeing the Doberman to care.

"I don't know but I can assure you, you do not need a fight with that woman."

Her eyes meet mine, alight with fire. "I could take her,"

I shake my head. "I'm sure you can Sweetheart, but let's not find out."

"What's his name?" Luisa asks.

"Maverick." Of course.

Brandon turns as we make it to the top of the steps. "We have three bedrooms open right now, as we're expecting a guest tomorrow. You won't see them, they're just staying here and lying low. But there's two down here and one upstairs. You can choose which ones." His eyes drift between Amelia and me. "It doesn't matter which ones, they're all sound-proof," he smirks.

Amelia rolls her eyes, turning to the other two. "Damon has been staying with me the past couple of days other than Texas. He can stay with me now."

Luisa tries hard to repress her knowing smirk. Amelia is a little easier to read than she thinks.

Meanwhile, if looks could kill, I'd be six feet under after Amare's glare.

"We'll take the top floor," Amelia declares, turning to go up the steps.

"Second room up there," Brandon chirps before showing the others their rooms.

Cooper follows after us, glancing back every couple of steps.

I try not to think about what being in DC could mean.

EIGHTEEN

AMELIA

The place wasn't what I expected. That being said, I'm not sure how it could have been anything expected at all.

I pull the heavy wood door open, nervous about what's inside.

But the room is gorgeous.

A large, fluffy-looking bed sits on top of a rustic wooden crate bedframe, which, though may be creaky, definitely matches the theme. Was it probably thrown together with whatever they had laying around here? Yes, but it's kind of charming.

A plush rug is centered in the room, and it even has a bathroom and TV. Most likely so no one goes over the edge of the rail while trying to get downstairs half asleep.

"This is nice," I say, dropping my bags.

Damon follows, nodding. "Yeah, it is." He sits on the edge of the bed, rubbing his hands together. "Do you know what's going to happen next?" he asks, his eyes meeting mine.

I shake my head. "No, we'll see what happens tonight."

He nods, flopping down on the bed as Cooper jumps up, nuzzling him.

"Amelia," he starts, looking everywhere but me as I turn to him, "at what point do you want me to tell you, you know, about everything?" he asks.

I think about it for a second. Ideally, never. "I don't want to know unless I absolutely have to. But if I ask, tell me." I lean against the wall. His head turns to me, and I feel heat rising throughout my body as his eyes travel down, lingering at my hips before drifting back up. "I just want to be able to do whatever we have to do without emotion, you know?"

"I just want to be sure."

I nod, tucking my hair behind my ears.

"Okay." He sits up, watching me as I unpack a couple of things. Finding my favorite shirt, I pull off the one I'm wearing. After Texas and the airplane, I feel like I need fresh clothes before meeting new people.

Damon clears his throat behind me, and I look over my shoulder, quirking a brow. "You okay?"

"Do you want me to turn around?" he asks sheepishly, wiping his hands on his jeans.

"I have a bra on," I reply, pulling the new shirt on. "Are you telling me you're shy now?" I chuckle.

I hear the bed creak as he gets up, his footsteps light behind me before his large hands grip my waist. I bristle at his touch, my eyes closing. A large part of me wants to tell him to let go of me, but the other, much bigger part of me wants him to pull me closer. Wants him to take my shirt off. To feel his mouth against my skin again.

"I don't think it's a secret that I want you." His breath tickles the back of my neck.

I move back into him. "I think we need to stop whatever this is," I tell him, moving away from him suddenly. He only grips my hips tighter, keeping me in my place.

"I think you need to let go."

My breathing becomes more ragged as my back arches, pushing into him more. I feel his length press against me, and a fire ignites deep in my belly.

"We agreed to be friends," I mumble, having trouble keeping my composure.

He hums into my skin, his mouth at my ear, nipping at it. "We did. But I know that's not what you really want."

I turn around, and as he loses his grip on me, I shove him back. "And how the fuck would you know what I really want, huh? You've known me for days."

"I've known you for years," he hisses, and in an instant, I'm thrown back against the wall as he presses himself into me. It's a familiar feeling now after the previous night. His skin radiates heat through his shirt, but it's not the uncomfortable kind. I feel safe. "I think you've been fighting for so long, my love, that you can't see anything other than the fight. Let go. Let me ruin you for anyone else. You're mine, Amelia."

"I'm not anyone's," I say, but my voice falters as he sucks at my skin, and I can't help but let my head fall to the side, allowing him easier access. "Damon," I start, but all thoughts are lost as he runs his tongue up my flesh, biting at my jawline.

No thoughts, just the unmistakable rush of lust. Lust I've never felt before. At least, not that I remember. And yet it feels so familiar.

"We're stuck in this room together for I don't know how long. We can't be doing this." My voice comes out in a whisper. It's all I can manage.

I know that he's right. I need to let go. I need to allow new experiences in. I've gotten a small taste of being alive, and now I want more. I want more from him. It's terrifying.

"I want you," I tell him, my mouth hovering just under his, "but I can't handle this right now. I need," I take a deep, shuddering breath as I squeeze my eyes shut, my fists balled at my sides. "I need a second," I tell him as I push past, sitting on the bed with my head in my hands.

I feel the bed dip as he sits next to me, his arm wrapping around my shoulders. "I'm sorry," he whispers.

And something about the sincerity about it, something about how it sounds like he's telling the truth, that he *cares*, makes me lose my head.

And it only takes me looking into his darkened green eyes for me to twist around, throw my leg over his lap, and straddle him, crushing my lips to his.

It's not a nice kiss. It's not kind or pleasant.

His hands come up to cradle my face as I sink into his hold, the fire deep within me spreading as he deepens the kiss, his tongue consuming me. The throbbing between my thighs is foreign, something I don't understand how to control.

I'm so, so used to controlling every situation. From what I eat to how I kill a man, control is the only thing that makes me feel like I can live in this world. But I never thought that losing it could feel so delicious.

Damon's hand runs down my body, slithering around my waist before my back hits the soft mattress. He props himself up over me, running his hand over my forehead, pushing my hair away from my face. I go to wrap my legs around him.

"No," he commands, shaking his head. "You're not ready for that, and I'm not letting you get ahead of yourself."

"But you said—"

"I know what I said, and your reaction proves you're not ready for that," he murmurs gently, rubbing his thumb over my lips. "I promise you this is so hard for me, but it's for the best, Sweetheart." He presses a soft kiss to my lips before pulling away again. "You taste just as I remember," he whispers, and it feels like a bullet to my chest.

"You were right." I close my eyes.

"I mean, usually, but what about this time?"

"I'm too controlling. Too calculating. I, I don't know how to change that. I don't know how to let loose. Whatever just happened, I don't know," I say, shaking my head as I refuse to look at him.

He grabs my chin. "Look at me," he commands.

And I do. I don't want to. But I do. He doesn't have to ask twice. My eyes open without my permission, staring up into his beautiful eyes, and I can feel the throb between my legs become stronger.

"Tell me what you want," he asks, his gaze searching mine.

"I want you to show me." My voice is barely audible.

He cocks his head, a knowing smirk spreading across his full lips. "Show you what, Sweetheart?"

I roll my eyes. "I want you to show me what you meant by giving up control."

He stares at me for another moment before sitting up, allowing me to prop myself on my elbows.

"Are you sure?"

I nod.

And just as he opens his mouth to reply, I hear a knock on our door. I run my fingers through my hair, making sure it doesn't look insane before getting off the bed, throwing the door open. Luisa stands on the other side, her arms crossed over her chest as she looks between me and Damon sitting on the bed.

"You okay?" she asks, looking me up and down.

I nod. "Yeah, was just about to head downstairs. What's up?"

"Jerry says that Elena is back. She wants you to come downstairs to talk." I nod, shutting the door and turning back to Damon.

"You can come down when you're ready. I have to meet someone," I tell him before making my way downstairs.

Jerry and another woman stand in the middle of the building, talking in hushed tones as I approach. When she sees me, she takes one last puff from her cigarette, flicking it onto an ashtray. "Elena, this is Amelia. The one with the issue." I'm once again confused as to whether she actually likes me or she thinks I'm an inconvenience.

"Nice to meet you," Elena smiles, grabbing my hand. She tosses a loc behind her as she sits on the couch. "I was just at an event with some Senators. I was able to get a little bit of information. Nothing huge, but it's somewhere to start." She crosses her legs.

The guys all make their way out of their rooms, causing a commotion as they file downstairs, laughing and carrying on. We look over at them, smiling as Amare has joined them. Damon steps out of our room, looking over the rail. I wave him down, hopeful he'll join the other guys and get along with them.

"The call came from a Senator. We know this. I'm not sure which one, but the building the call came from? A bunch of them meet there. Some kind of secret society thing. It's a little creepy, but they don't seem to be doing anything too illegal."

"Do you have a list of Senators in the society?" Jerry asks, her arm hung over the side of the couch, her legs spread as wide as they can go as she reclines on the couch.

"No." She shakes her head. "They're really secretive. But I do know that they're all going to be at a fundraiser tomorrow. It's a masquerade."

"That sounds fun. Do we have an in?" I ask her curiously.

"Of course, I wouldn't be doing my job if I didn't come prepared for you." She grins. "You guys are already on the books. I'll be going with you because, well, I have to. Then I have you, Amare, and Luisa all on the guest list.

I cringe, secretly upset that Damon wasn't also invited.

But she wouldn't have known to, and I don't want him in danger anyways.

So instead of saying anything, I nod. "That sounds so great, thank you so much, Elena."

She smiles again, getting up. "You don't have to thank me, it's my job. I just hope we're able to figure this out for you. I heard what happened to your home, that's awful."

I grit my teeth, looking at my shoes. "I know. I miss home. I can't wait to go back," I tell her honestly.

"Oh, we'll make sure you can go back in no time," Jerry lets out a throaty chuckle, and I can't help but feel as though it's not because she cares about my well-being.

"Thank you." My lips tighten into a tense smile.

"You're welcome!" she singsongs before getting up and heading to the small bar on the other side of the couch. She takes out a glass and a bottle of what looks like whisky, filling it to the brim before putting it to her lips.

"Want one?"

"Maybe later," I reply tensely, looking for Damon.

Walking around the couch, I find Damon behind the other guys in the kitchen as they cut vegetables for dinner. Damon has been put on potato duty and looks intensely at the starch in front of him as he runs the peeler over its skin. "You doing okay with the guys?" I ask as I approach.

"He's safe with us, cross my heart," Ronan promises me with a smile.

I chuckle. "Thank you, that means a lot."

"Yeah, I am." Damon smiles. "I still don't think Amare likes me," I glance his way, only to be met by a scowl as he eyes us. "but the other guys seem super cool, and I would hope Amare will warm up to me, right?"

Well, hopefully, you won't be around for that long, I think, but I can't help the little stab in my chest at the thought of not having him at some point.

It's not like I didn't understand that at some point he's

217

going to have to go home. It's just that I don't want to think about it.

I've known how this is going to end. I can't let myself forget it.

NINETEEN

DAMON

There's no doubt that this is the very first time in the last couple of days that I feel as though I belong. As though people like me, and that I'm not some problem to be dealt with.

"You should have been there," Zach tells me, a smile on his face, "it was so incredible. We were in and out in under five minutes I swear." He holds a cue in one hand, the neck of a beer bottle in his other.

We stand in the space behind the kitchen, which is home to a giant, beautiful pool table, a couple of shorter couches, and another bar. The light is dim as the night has gone on, and although I'm having fun with the guys, a part of me just wants to go upstairs and go to sleep.

"Impressive," I bring my bottle to my lips, taking a long sip. "How did you guys pull that off, by the way?"

Ronan chuckles. "We're able to push the envelope a little bit here," he starts, looking around at all the cars around them. "We don't get in trouble for much. But we may get slapped on the wrist sometimes, that's for sure." They laugh.

"Which one did you get in the most trouble for?"

Ronan looks around. "Definitely the HyperSport. One hundred percent. We almost had to give it back, actually."

I look over at the beautiful car, appreciating how beautiful it is. It's the kind of car that most people will never see in an entire lifetime. "It's insane that you were able to get that."

He clicks his tongue. "I know man," bending down, he lines up his shot, missing his target. "So how did you end up with Seattle?"

I pause, thinking about how to respond. I'm not sure there's any correct way to, because frankly, I'm not sure if it's safe to tell them much of anything. I'm not sure what will get me in trouble, and I don't want to upset the others.

Amare crosses his arms over his chest across the pool table, his eyes narrowing.

I shrug, deciding to tell the truth. They already know I'm not one of them, what is my story going to change? I could just leave out a few key details. "Well, I thought I knew Amelia before everything, and saw that she had caught someone's attention. I'm a detective now for a small town. Sometimes I get news. I'm not sure if Amelia had passed through at some point, or if she grew up around there, but either way, a notice crossed my desk, and I thought she had died. I went to go find her, not knowing that they had been attacked." I set the bottle down on the pool table and taking my shot, sinking the cue ball. I groan, leaning back as Brandon takes it out of the pocket, placing it in front of one of their balls.

"Seems like you bit off a little more than you can chew," Zach says, sinking one of the solids.

I nod. "Yeah, it's been a wild couple of days."

"I'm sure you wish you were home," Amare says, his eyes thinning even more.

"No not really," I say, getting annoyed.

"I can tell this has been a whole fucking thing," Ronan chuckles, looking between us as he lifts a muscular arm to run his fingers through his hair. God, I wish I had muscles like that.

I pick my bottle back up, angrily bringing it to my lips. "He's protective of her. I get it," I say, spreading my arms.

"I just think you shouldn't be here."

"But I am," I reply shortly, acid dripping from my tone. "And I understand that you have all been through a lot, and I'm not ever going to say I've had it harder, but I don't exactly want to be here. If you want to settle this, let's settle it."

I watch him as his eyes soften, a small smile forming on his lips. "I just want to make sure she's okay, my guy. We're all good."

I stand there, perplexed. "What do you mean we're all good? You've been an asshole to me for days."

"Testing the water," he shrugs.

I roll my eyes.

I'll see if anything changes. I'm not holding my breath.

"Hey! Boys!" Jerry calls from the other side of the wall. We put down our pool cues and head back around, finding all of the girls there, dressed to the nines.

I find Amelia in an instant, noticing how uncomfortable she looks in her short, glittery mini dress and heels. It makes me uncomfortable that she's uncomfortable, so much so that it takes me a moment to even realize how unbelievably sexy she looks.

My eyes rake up her toned legs, almost sad the dress just barely covers the part of her I have yet to feel. The dress cinches at her waist, somehow making it look even smaller against her wide hips. The dress is low-cut, and my mouth goes dry at the sight of her chest.

Brandon bumps into me, shooting me a knowing smile. "You haven't heard a word she's said, have you?" he laughs. I shake my head. "We're going out tonight."

"I hate this."

"I know you do. We'll be home in no time."

Amelia hits the back of her head against the seat of the car we're driving. No one could agree on what time we'll be staying out until, so we all drove separately. They let us pick a car to drive but were quick to tell me no the second my eyes flashed to the HyperSport.

"We will one-hundred percent get arrested the second that thing is on the street." Zach laughs. "That thing is purely for show at the moment."

Instead, I picked a Maserati GranTurismo. Nowhere near as cool, but still a fancier car than I could ever dream of driving.

"I'm sure it'll be fun," I assure her, glancing over. She sits in the passenger seat, one leg crossed over the other, her head tilted to the side as she stares out the window. Her hair cascades down her chest as she chews on her thumb, deep in thought.

"I feel like an idiot," she mumbles.

"Why?"

Her head whips to me, her eyes giant. "Do you see what I'm fucking wearing?"

"You don't dress up or go out at home?" I ask, surprised. Most people would go out all the time if they had all the money in the world at their disposal.

Her face twists in disgust. "Absolutely the fuck not," she scoffs.

Okay then.

We pull up to the club behind Jerry's car, and I watch as she gets out, handing the keys to the valet. I do the same, rounding the car and opening the door for Amelia. She gets out, unsure on her feet, pulling the dress down with a grimace.

"Didn't you say you had a job at a club?" I question.

"Yes, and I hated every fucking second of it. Which is probably why the man went home to his wife without fucking balls."

That's… a lot to unpack. I make a mental note to ask her more about *that* later.

"Okay well, you got this." I link my arm with hers, leading her to the door where the others wait.

The line of people waiting to get in wraps around the building, but we're let through with a wave from the bouncer as Jerry kisses him on the cheek. I want to like her, I do, but the woman is terrifying. I wonder if anyone here actually likes her or if she just scares them all to death.

The second we step through the doors, the floor shakes under my feet from the bass of the club music. It's nothing I've ever heard before, but I'm not exactly a clubber.

"We're going to go get ourselves some drinks!" Jerry yells above the music, taking a cigarette from her purse and lighting it. She wears a bright blue suit that matches her eyes, a stark difference from the other women in the group's dresses.

Taking a puff of her cigarette, she breathes out, a ring of her dark lipstick around the paper. Grabbing Amelia's arm, she pulls her away. Amelia reaches for me, her eyes crying for help, but I shrug, unsure what I can do.

"You need a drink and stat," she tells her with a rough laugh. "Gotta get that stick outta your ass."

I grimace, knowing I'll be hearing about this later, but I trust Jerry to put a bullet in someone's skull if they so much as look at her wrong. She feels like the kind of person who would do that.

"You guys want to get a table?" Zach asks, but he doesn't wait for a response, instead heading down the stairs to one of the booths.

The blue and purple lights around me are overwhelming,

and I blink, trying to make sure I'm not going insane under them. Women in tight skirts and dresses dance everywhere, the men hanging back to ogle them as they talk. My eyes scan the room until they find Amelia's purple sparkly dress in the distance, a cup of alcohol in her hand as she looks around, unsure of herself.

She bites down on her full lower lip, her shoulders hunched just slightly. It's amazing how much different she is when she's not on the job having to pretend.

And yet she still looks lethal. And so incredibly beautiful.

It didn't take long for the club to bring out strippers. They all walk out at once, heading to the booths to find whatever sad men need attention, and my gaze flickers to Amelia. Her eyes are locked on mine as she takes a sip of her drink, dancing between Kim and Jerry, Luisa and Elena to her left.

Jerry has forced at least three drinks into her hand, and I know she doesn't normally drink a lot. I'm starting to get a little worried that they're going to get her plastered, and I'm going to have to carry her up those steps back at the warehouse.

Not that she weighs much, but those stairs terrify me, and there are a lot of them. Throw in a drunk woman? No, thank you.

"Would you like a dance, handsome?" a woman asks as she places a hand on my shoulder, leaning down to give me a better view of her cleavage.

I shake my head, leaning back. "No thank you."

"Are you sure?"

I roll my eyes, my hands in my lap. "Yes, I'm sure."

She looks me over, clicking her tongue as she flips her hair over her shoulder and heads to the next man. I find Amelia again, her eyes locked on mine, shooting daggers through them.

Great.

"Everyone want another round?" Ronan asks, and I shake my head. I don't need anything else, I've been nursing this beer for the past hour.

I'm going to have precious cargo in the car. I can't risk it.

While Ronan, Brandon, and Zach rush off to get beers, Amare slides next to me. It feels warmer, or maybe it's just my anxiety over needing to impress him. I pull the sleeves of my Henley up a touch.

"Hey," he calls over the beat, raising his bottle.

"Hey," I reply awkwardly, suspicious.

"I just want you to know I'm sorry. I don't want to like you man, I really don't. But I know you've done nothing wrong. We just haven't had outsiders in our circle before."

I nod, taking a sip. "I get it. I just don't appreciate being treated like shit."

He doesn't say anything for a long time, instead watching the girls dance. "You know, I know Luisa told you her story. I don't have any story to tell you, man." He chuckles. "I don't remember *shit*. But I do know that that girl over there," he points to Amelia, "deserves more than she has ever gotten. I know what happened to her." I whip my head around, watching him. "Looked it up when you came into the picture. That's wild." He shakes his head.

"It was," I agree.

"Well, I hope she gets some sort of revenge. If there's one person who deserves it, it's her.

The men return, handing Amare another beer. I've lost Amelia during our conversation, so it takes me longer to find her this time. When I do, my blood runs cold as I find a man's hands around her waist.

She wobbles against him, clearly drunk, and anger shoots through my body, taking over my mind.

And then her eyes find mine, and I see the small smirk on her face as she grabs the man's hands, clutching them to her tighter.

Well, I won't have this.

Getting up from the booth, I leave my beer on the table. I don't take my eyes off hers as I make my way over, intent on claiming what's mine.

"I'll take over from here," I tell the man as I reach him, and she looks up at me, her eyes dark as she watches everything unfold.

"I'd watch it if I were you," the man hisses, clutching her tighter. She winces, and I can tell he's hurting her, no matter what she'll say.

"Take your hands off of her, turn around, and leave," I growl, and something in my eye must have set him off because he does. Backing away slowly, he scowls at me before giving me his back, finding a new woman to harass.

"He wasn't doing anything wrong," Amelia pouts.

"Doesn't matter," I say as I pull her close, dipping down to whisper in her ear. "If you want me to show you how to let go, I don't want you flirting with other men, okay?" I ask.

She can do whatever the fuck she wants, of course. But I'm also not an idiot. I know she doesn't want that man or any other man, for that matter. She just wants to make me jealous so she can get what she wants. And it works.

It'll work every single time.

"So you'll do that for me?" she asks, looking up at me with those giant eyes I love so much.

"I'm thinking about it," I reply, tugging on her hair a little.

"You want to take me into the other room right now and have your way with me?"

My breath is knocked out of me, my stomach in knots as I look at her, stunned. I wasn't expecting that out of her.

I shake my head. "No Sweetheart, I'm not having sex with you in this club."

She pouts. "I keep having dreams about your cock deep inside of me. I just, there's nothing in this world I want to feel more."

Okay, it's time to get her home.

I can feel my dick shift in my pants as it grows hard, and I don't need to be miserable at this club and also have a raging boner. I'm not sure how the young kids deal with this.

"Okay let's get you home."

"So you'll finally fuck me?" she asks, swaying in her heels.

"No, not tonight. Let's go," I tug on her wrist, leading her forward. When I look behind me to make sure she's still okay, I find her eyes on me, never wavering.

We get outside and she shivers in the cold. I call for our car before going back to her, wrapping my arms around her freezing body.

"I want to go home," she sighs, looking out into the night.

"I know Sweetheart, we are."

"No, I mean really home. Back to Seattle," she hums.

A wave of sadness sweeps over me. I really hope she can go back after this is done. I hope it's safe for her.

The car pulls up and I open the passenger door for her, letting her get in. When I'm sure her hands and feet are inside the vehicle, I shut the door, smiling at the man.

The second I climb into the driver's seat, we're off.

Amelia sits on the bed, hungrily looking me up and down. "You made me come home early." She pouts, her arms crossed over her chest.

"You didn't want to be there in the first place," I remind her, my eyebrow arching.

"That was before I realized how hot you are tonight." Her voice is low. I turn, watching her undress me with her eyes as she bites her lip.

"Let's get you cleaned up and in bed."

She shakes her head. "I really want you, Damon."

I reach out for her, kneeling in front of her as I grab her shoulders. "I know, and I want you too. But this isn't going to happen tonight. You're drunk."

"I'm fine,"

"No, you're not. You're drunk, and I'm not taking advantage of you when you're drunk. Especially not for your first time."

Her eyes dip down to her hands as she whispers, "You just make me feel safe. I want this."

"I know Sweetheart, and if you still want it tomorrow, we will, okay?" I fight the excitement that rips through me at the prospect. "But right now, I don't want to hurt you."

"How would you hurt me?"

"It's your first time. I don't know if it'll hurt you—"

"It won't," she interrupts, vigorously shaking her head.

My brows furrow. "Why do you say it like that?"

"I made sure it won't."

"What does that mean?"

She sighs, rolling her eyes as she stretches her arms out above her head before dropping them into her lap again, letting out a lazy yawn. "I made sure no one would be able to hurt me. I took care of it, I promise."

I grab her face between my hands, trying to understand what she's telling me as ice chills my bones. "Baby, why would you need to do that?"

"I just figured," she hiccups, "that if I were to be taken and someone tried to do something to me, I didn't want it to hurt more than it already would, you know?" She shrugs.

And I feel the ground fall out from under my feet as it dawns on me just how much she's gone through. Just how much she's had to endure these last couple of years. The fact that that was even a worry for her; that it was ever a thought in her mind that she could be taken and raped, the fact that she made sure it wouldn't hurt—it shatters my heart.

"Damon it's not that big of a deal. I'm sorry that I—" But I shut her up quickly with a fast, hard kiss.

"Don't you dare finish that sentence," I tell her firmly, tipping her head back so she's forced to look at me. "You don't ever apologize to anyone for that."

And I wonder why she feels as though she has to. Does a part of her remember what her father put her through? Is that still ingrained in her mind? Out of all the things she could remember or internalize, it had to be that?

"Virginity doesn't impact my worth." She nods, a smile on her lips as the air is knocked out of my body.

"What did you say?"

"I said virginity doesn't impact my worth."

"Where did you hear that?"

She thinks for a moment, squinting her eyes as she looks into the distance, trying to place it. "I don't know." She shrugs.

Maybe she's starting to remember.

I'm not sure if that's a good thing.

"Okay well, let's get you to bed," I tell her, pushing her back onto the bed. She lifts her arms, and I pull the dress over her body, grabbing one of my T-shirts from my bag. I leave her bra and underwear on, not wanting her to feel violated in the morning.

She turns over onto her side, and I roll her back before picking her up, walking her into the bathroom.

"What are you doing?" she asks groggily.

"I'm washing your face."

Placing her on the bathroom counter, I reach for the clean washcloth, wetting it before rubbing the bar of soap on it. I know most women would kill me for using bar soap, but it's better than nothing, right?

When it's lathered, I bring it to her face. "Close your

eyes," I command softly, but she opens them wider, terrifying me.

"Amelia," I chuckle, a grin on my face.

She smiles, doing as I asked. I wipe the makeup away before rinsing the cloth and doing it once more, making sure she's clean.

She's said she doesn't normally drink, and we're in a new place, sharing a bed. I'm not going to be sleeping on the floor tonight, absolutely the fuck not. I don't want her waking up uncomfortable.

When I'm done, she slumps into me, falling asleep. I take one of her hair clips from her bag, gathering her hair in my hand and twisting until I can clip it to the back of her head so she doesn't roll over on it in the night.

I carry her back to bed, tucking her in and kissing her forehead.

I change out of my clothes and am about to climb into bed myself when I hear something outside the door. I bristle at the noise, heading over to it. There's another scratch. I open it a touch, peering out to find Cooper standing in front of it, looking up at me with his large puppy eyes.

"Oh thank God it's just you," I say, scratching my forehead. I let him in, and he immediately runs to the bed, jumping up and curling up with Amelia, taking my spot.

I scoot him over, turn off the light, and fall asleep next to her as she snuggles up to me, nuzzling into my neck.

I wish it could stay like this forever.

TWENTY

AMELIA

There's nothing like a hangover to remind you of why you don't drink.

I've never felt so sick in my entire life.

"You had quite a few rum and cokes," Luisa tells me, handing me the bowl of scrambled eggs. The smell makes me want to vomit, and I hand them back to her. Absolutely the fuck not.

"You had fun though! You let loose! Got that stick out of your ass!" Jerry exclaims from the end of the table, taking a drag from her cigarette before stuffing a strip of bacon into her mouth.

I heave, wanting nothing more than to get away from the smells in this room.

I woke up this morning to Damon already gone. He left a note on the counter that said he was on a mission to find the gym Zach had mentioned is in the building the night prior. That was well and good for me, considering I'm not even sure what I'd say to him this morning.

I don't remember anything I told him, but I can just imagine it was something terribly embarrassing. I want to shrink into my chair and become invisible. There's a reason I don't drink, and most of that reason has nothing to do with not being in control, and everything to do with being absolutely simply terrible at handling liquor.

"Anyways," Jerry slams a hand onto the table, her mouth half full of bacon still. "We all are doing a little shopping today. We have the masquerade tonight and we need to look like we belong. You," she points her finger at me, "need to get it the fuck together so you don't pass out on us."

I shoot her a thumbs up, burying my face in my arms.

**

"I think that looks perfect on you," Luisa tells Elena as she tries on the most beautiful silver dress. Its off-the-shoulder cut looks beautiful against her deep skin tone.

She looks down at herself, smiling. "I have these long silver earrings, too. And silver heels. It'll be perfect."

"If you want to stand out like a sore thumb." Jerry rolls her eyes.

Elena flips her off. "Blow me."

Jerry puts her hands up, backing away. "I'm just sayin'."

"You're not even going Jer."

"Doesn't mean I can't have opinions."

What I have learned from this outing is that Jerry is one of the most annoying, argumentative people I've ever met. It would be endearing if it weren't so incredibly grating. I'm not entirely sure how the others do it.

"Okay, well," I say, slapping my hands to my thighs and standing up, grabbing my dress of choice. "We've all made our choices, are we ready to go?"

Luisa looks at the other three women expectantly, hoping they'll chime in and direct us where to go next.

"Thank fuck," Jerry mutters, already five steps ahead of me. She's halfway out the door, a cigarette already in her mouth when she peeks her head back into the store. "I'm fucking hungry. Let's go."

I really hope that doesn't mean we're going to be out for even longer, forced to get something to eat, but I just know that's going to be the case, anyways.

I want to get home and talk to Damon.

He never appeared this morning, and I'm worried about him. I'm not sure if I said something last night to spook him or what, but I'm overwhelmed with a need to ensure he's okay.

We pay for our dresses and shoes before walking out, finding Jerry leaning against the brick exterior smoking. "We're going to the diner." She doesn't look up.

"And where is the diner?" I try not to let my exasperation show, but I can tell from the look in her eye she heard it.

Pushing off the wall, Jerry flicks the cigarette to the ground, shooting me a glare. "Just around the corner," she says with a shrug as she walks off, the others following her dutifully.

I catch Luisa's hand. "I hate this so much," I whisper.

She looks at me, rolling her eyes. "Chill out, you're fine. She's funny."

She's *not*.

We make our way to the diner in silence. It's about a five-minute walk, and when we get there, we're sat immediately.

I can only hope this is fast.

We put in our orders and sit around in near silence, not knowing what to discuss. We can't exactly talk about what we do in the open like this.

"So Jerry, what's been going on with you? How's work?" I ask, seeing what she'll come up with.

She eyes me warily before taking her coffee from the waitress. Taking a long sip, she watches me over the brim, her eyes narrowed. "It's been okay," she places her cup down on the table.

"What do you guys do around here?" I ask Elena, genuinely curious.

Elena looks around, trying to see how much she has to hide. "We've been extremely busy, especially with the election coming up. There's so much to do and making sure these people aren't breaking laws is like dealing with toddlers."

"Oh, are you guys staffers?" the waitress asks as she comes up behind me, refilling my water.

Elena smiles at her. "I am! I love it."

"My uncle is a politician. And trust me, you can't trust any of 'em." She shakes her head before walking off, taking the water pitcher with her.

Elena throws me a knowing smile.

"It's a lot for sure, but I really love it here anyways. It keeps us busy. On our toes. And there's a ton of events. We were going to the masquerade tonight regardless of whether you came along."

I nod, excited to see my food heading our way. I hadn't eaten breakfast because of my hangover.

"It's pretty slow back home in Seattle. I love it, don't get me wrong. I wouldn't trade it for the world, but there's a lot of sitting around."

"That probably makes your boyfriend a little crazy," Jerry smirks.

I choke on the bite I just took, reaching for my water to wash it down. "He's not my boyfriend," I sputter half-heartedly.

"Yeah whatever," she replies, going back to her own food.

I look to Elena and Kim, who both give me sheepish looks before launching into a conversation about an event they have to attend next month. Meanwhile, Luisa tries to hide her snickers next to me unsuccessfully, and I glare at her.

"What?" she asks. "I like her. And we all know something is going on."

The only thing I can do is roll my eyes.

TWENTY-ONE

DAMON

A firm knock on my door wakes me from my daydreams as I pull on a fresh pair of pants and a T-shirt after my shower. It's only been a couple of hours since I got up, and I was told by the other guys that all the women went dress shopping for tonight. I was then informed that I wasn't going to be attending with them and that Amelia seemed fine with it. She never told me.

I know that she's survived six years without me, and I *understand* that the last person she needs to protect her is me. But there's something about knowing she's going to an event where someone who wants to kill her might be attending that makes me angry, and not being able to be there to help is even more annoying. Plus, what if it's someone I recognize?

I just wish she told me first.

I dry off my hair once more before throwing the towel onto a hook, heading for the door.

"Yeah?" I ask as I open it, but I'm shocked to find Amare.

I open the door wider, crossing my arms over my chest. I

like Amare, I do, but I won't lie and say that I completely trust that he actually likes me now.

"Hey, I wanted to run something by you," he says, walking into the room. I close the door behind him and lean against the wall, waiting for him to get on with it.

He takes a deep breath. "I think you should go tonight instead of me. Which is insane for me to say, but I think out of everyone you seem to know the most about her old life. Since we can all agree it probably has some connection to that, I just think you should be the one to go," he rambles, practically pulling his hair out.

I arch a brow, entertained. "This is taking a lot for you to admit, isn't it?" I ask with a grin.

"Don't be a dick," he smiles. "I just want to make sure that we get this over with. I want to go home, man. My back can't take these beds."

I sigh, pushing off of the wall and heading toward the bed myself. "Yeah actually, they really do suck."

He smiles, heading back to the door. "I have things I have to do, but I just wanted to run it by you. Is that okay?"

I pretend to think about it for a moment, not wanting to give him the satisfaction of seeing how happy it made me.

After the appropriate amount of time passes, I nod my head simply. "Yeah of course."

"Good. The guys are looking at tuxes in the room downstairs. You should go and grab one." He pats the doorframe once before turning, heading back downstairs.

I shake my head, trying to understand the weird interaction. I'm not sure I can crack him.

Heading downstairs, I find the rest of the guys in one of the bedrooms going through suits. Ronan is the first one to see me, waving me over.

"Amare said you'd be down. We're just picking whatever we want. Let me know. They're all up for grabs."

I nod in thanks, heading over to take a look for myself.

Dozens of suits hang from a closet, all different colors. I haven't worn a suit that isn't black before, and I'm not sure I want to take a chance now. I grab a simple black tux, pulling it off the hanger and putting the jacket on over my shirt. It fits, and the pants are about my size.

"I think I'm going to go purple, guys," Brandon says, smiling ear to ear.

"Purple is an absolutely insane choice bro," Zach tells him, eyeing it. "But I support it. Do it."

I smile. These guys are really cool. If they weren't working for the CIA and could literally kill me at any second, I think I would want to be friends with them.

"Are there more of you guys here?" I ask them, taking a seat in one of the chairs on the other side of the room.

"Nah. It's just us six. Which isn't much for the work we do, but we have a pretty steady stream of guests that come through and help. It's good to have new faces," Ronan informs me, trying on his tux. "All in all, there are usually at least eight people here most days of the week."

That's not terrible. "It's a big place. I'm sure that's nice."

"It is. Sometimes we get sick of each other."

"He's lying!" Brandon calls from the bathroom, and Ronan rolls his eyes.

"But I don't think I would want to be anywhere else. I love it here."

I smile. I never had siblings. It was always just my parents and me, and then it was just my mom. I was never super social growing up, and during college when everyone was out partying, I was studying my butt off to get into the Academy, only to blow it on my first job.

I have a lot of regrets in my life, but quitting the FBI is not one of them.

Half an hour later, I'm in my room when I hear the large doors to the warehouse open, a car driving in. I peek out the door, watching as the women climb out, bags in hand. Cooper and Maverick greet them, and I quickly retreat, waiting to see if Amelia will come up and talk to me or not.

About five minutes later, the door opens, and she steps inside.

"You guys were out for a while," I say, crossing my leg over the other.

She jumps, not having seen me.

"You're going to give me a heart attack, I swear." She holds her hand over her heart, bending over as she tries to catch her breath.

"Apparently."

She looks up, confused. "Why are you acting strange?"

I look at my hands before I glance back up at her, keeping my gaze low. "I don't know. I just think it's funny that you didn't tell me I wasn't going to the event tonight."

Her face pales as she drops her bags.

"How long did you know?" I want to see how far I can push, but I'm not sure if I have the upper hand or if she's *letting* me have it.

"Since yesterday." Her shoulders draw back as she levels me with a steely glare.

"But you knew I'd be upset."

She shrugs unapologetically, and I rise from my seat, taking a step toward her, my hands buried deep in the pockets of my jeans. I keep my head hung low, her eyes blazing into mine.

She takes a step back, almost tripping over one of her bags as her breath catches. I take another step forward, a small smirk growing across my face.

I like this.

Bringing this powerful, beautiful woman to her knees

sends a shiver down my spine as I lick my lips, taking another slow, steady step toward her.

Her chest heaves as her eyes narrow at me, her mouth opening as if to say something, but not a word making it past her pretty little lips. Her eyes flash as I get closer, clearly surprised at this shift of power.

She clenches her jaw as I step up to her, and while she takes one more step back, bumping against the wall, I cage her in my arms, bringing my lips just inches above hers.

"You knew I'd want to be there for you, didn't you." She nods, her eyes locked on mine. "When were you going to tell me?" I whisper, brushing my lips against hers. Her back arches as her eyes grow heavy.

"Today," she whispers simply.

"Mmm." I run a finger along my lips before placing my hand on her shoulder, slowly moving it along her skin until I can grasp the back of her neck.

"You said you want to know how it feels to be out of control?" I can feel her heart thudding in her chest as she pushes against mine, and as her vanilla scent wafts over me and she nods, I lose control.

Shifting, I spin her small frame until she falls back on the bed, and she props herself up on her elbows to watch me. I grab the tie I took from the closet downstairs from the dresser, bringing it to her.

"Wrists out," I demand, and the scowl on her face proves to me that she's going to fight this. No matter how good it feels, she's going to fight me. Because that's her. "Do it."

After a long moment of searching my eyes, she puts them out hesitantly, questions in her eyes. I place them together, wrapping the tie around them. Once her wrists are secured, I place them behind her head as I avoid her heated gaze.

When I'm happy, I cup her jaw as I bend down to look into her eyes. They shut, and I grab a little harder. "Keep them open, Sweetheart," I whisper. "I want to see every inch of you come undone."

"What are you going to do?"

I don't answer her. Instead, I back away, waiting a moment for her to let her guard down before reaching for her leg, lifting it. She falls back on the bed with a grunt, and I drag her around the mattress and to the side where I'll have more room.

Unbuttoning her jeans, I slide them off, watching her the entire time. She squirms, uncomfortable with the situation.

"I'm not going to do anything if you don't want me to," I tell her as I stand, my head tilted as I look at her beautiful body. Her sage green thong makes my mouth water, but I'd gladly put her jeans back on if she doesn't want this.

"I want this." She nods, and I smile, bending down to meet her.

I've been dreaming about the sight in front of me since a couple months into my mission, and her arousal only makes it that much more thrilling.

"You're already so ready for me," I murmur, running my finger over her as I watch her throw her head back, a small moan escaping her.

"How many times have you pictured someone touching you like this?"

She shakes her head.

"Tell me."

"I—I haven't really," she whispers.

"Have you thought about me touching you?" Her eyes squeeze together, and when she opens them, I can see the shame. I pull back.

"There's no shame in any of this, Amelia. Let go."

She nods, licking her lips. "I've thought of you a lot," she forces out.

I smile.

I run the pads of my fingers over her thighs, watching as

she squirms. When she settles, I watch her eyelids grow heavy as I run my fingers along the crease of the drenched fabric. Her body arches as her eyes snap to mine, darkening before rolling back into her head.

"Damon please," she moans, but I don't listen. Instead, I continue to run my fingers over her, experimenting with different pressures as I watch how her body reacts to me.

It's delicious.

"Damon," she says, mumbling incoherent words as I press harder.

"Use your words, Sweetheart."

"Please."

"Please what?"

Her eyes shut as her brows furrow in frustration. "I want you. Please."

She doesn't have to ask me twice.

I tug on her underwear, and it bites into her skin before snapping. It doesn't go unnoticed how her eyes roll back despite the pain.

"See? That's not so hard." I smile, watching as her eyes open, a snarl on her lips.

I use two fingers to spread her open, slipping another inside easily. I feel her clench around me, and I pump into her, circling her clit as I watch her writhing at every flick.

"You're being such a good girl for me, Amelia. Are you going to come on my fingers?"

Her face looks pained as she looks at me, but I keep going, knowing she'd tell me if she wanted me to stop.

"Damon," she breathes, and for a moment, I think it's here. I continue pumping my fingers in and out, but her release doesn't seem to come.

"What do you need, Amelia?" I ask, my voice low.

"I just, I need…"

"Never feel embarrassed with me. Tell me what you want."

She seals her eyes shut once more before turning her head to the side, refusing to look at me. "I need pain."

Without judgment, I understand.

In one swift movement, I flip her over. With her hands tied behind her back, she falls over, her shoulders propped against the bed, her ass in the air, her pussy bared for me.

Without her having to beg, I bury my tongue inside of her, finally getting a taste of her after all those years. The sweetness invades my senses, heating my body to its core. I feel my dick stiffen even more if that's possible, and I have to remind myself that right now is about her. That can wait.

"Fuck!" she moans, her mouth hanging open as she pants.

I bring my palm down on her ass as I lap at her, feeling her still in my grasp. I bury two fingers back inside of her as I continue to taste her deeper.

"Damon I—" But I know what she wants. I spank her again, harder this time, and she comes undone at my touch, her moan muffled by her face in the blanket.

I keep going until she shakes, her body caving in as she flattens herself against the bed.

And I've never felt more sure that this woman was made for me. She was made for me in her past life, this life, and every single fucking life to come.

TWENTY-TWO

AMELIA

It takes me longer than I'd like to admit to gather my thoughts as Damon unties my hands, helping me sit up. My shirt is askew, my hair messy, and I feel a haze setting over me.

And he hadn't even actually fucked me.

Settling between my legs, he sinks down until he's eye-level with me, running his thumb along my lips before gripping my chin. "Are you okay?"

I nod, not knowing what more I can say.

"I need you to use your words, Sweetheart."

"Yes, I'm okay," I whisper, hoping he understands that I really am.

It's not as if I haven't touched myself in six years. I have. I've learned a lot about my body, and I've known that I need a little bit of pain to come. A little bit of sting. But for some reason, that fact sends shame thundering through me.

I look him over. "Do you want—do you need help?" I ask him, my eyes drifting down.

He shakes his head, a small smile gracing his perfect lips. "No. That was all about you." He kisses me, his tongue gliding over mine as his hand cradles the back of my neck, squeezing lightly, the taste of myself on his lips feeling so sensual and so goddamn sexy I almost want to ask him to just throw me back and fuck me.

"What got into you?" I ask as I pull away, watching him stand and straighten out his tie.

"I was pissed off at you and figured I'd try to see how you'd take letting go of some control," he shrugs as if it's the most normal answer in the world.

"Was that supposed to be a punishment?" I smirk, quirking a brow.

He looks me over, and my nipples harden. "Sure," he says simply, turning to retrieve something from the closet.

"That was, that was *some* punishment. Wow. It was awful. Would really, *really* hate to ever experience that again." I rub my forehead, smiling as I look at the ground, avoiding his eyes.

He chuckles, and a small rustling snaps me out of my daze. He holds a tux in his hand, a satisfied smile spreading across his face as I process.

"Get dressed, Sweetheart. We need to be ready for the masquerade in an hour."

My mouth hangs open, and although I want to ask him how he's going, he walks past me and out the door before I can, leaving me half naked on the bed, wondering what the fuck is happening.

An hour later on the dot, I grab my earrings, throwing them on as fast as I can before heading out the door, meeting the girls downstairs.

The second I step through my door, I feel heat flow

through me, instantly wanting nothing more than to be taken back into the room and stripped by Damon.

I search the room, finding him almost instantly, his eyes searing into mine as he watches me struggle to walk down these awful steps in my heels. I really should have put them on when I got downstairs, but it's too late now.

When I reach the bottom, his mouth is agape as I reach out, taking his hand. "Do you like it?" I ask shyly, unsure who this new person is invading my body.

"You look so fucking beautiful," he tells me as he tucks hair behind my ear, grinning. I look down at my dark green gown. I was a little nervous about the low scoop of the neckline, but Luisa said it looked perfectly fine, and that I had to get the stick out of my ass, which only allowed for Jerry to insult me more.

I'm getting really tired of that insult.

But it's the slit up my thigh that I love the most. And the *pockets*. I stick my hands in them, spinning as Luisa grins at me. "I fucking told you that was the right pick."

"You guys ready to go?" Jerry asks, interrupting us as she steps out of her room in a tuxedo, making her way downstairs.

"I thought you weren't going." My head tilts in confusion.

"I'm not. I'm your driver." She rolls her eyes as if she's never heard a more idiotic comment in her life. "Let's go people, we don't have all fucking night." She takes out a pack of cigarettes, sticking one in her mouth before bringing us through the front doors.

Around the corner sits a giant limousine. One that I'm absolutely certain wasn't here the other day.

"Where did this thing come from?" I ask as I eye its chrome detailing.

"Stole it earlier."

She says it as if it's completely normal to steal a car in broad daylight on a whim.

She opens the door, making a show of directing the women in as the lit cigarette hangs from her mouth. When it's my turn, she lets go of the door, rounding the front. I roll my eyes as I climb in, feeling Damon right behind me.

Even with four of us, the vehicle has plenty of space. While Elena and Luisa space out, I stay where I am, feeling comfort in Damon's body heat next to me.

"Look in the cubby on the right-hand side, right next to the champagne," Jerry instructs, and Elena moves toward it, pulling out a small box. She opens it, taking out a small circular object.

"They're earpieces. They won't be detected by the metal detectors they're making everyone step through. Put them in. They're already on the right channel. I'll be outside keeping watch, making sure nothing goes awry."

I can say what I want about Jerry, but at least she comes prepared. Stolen limo and all.

Elena hands out the earpieces, and I fit mine in. It sits snugly deep within my ear, and I decide I'll worry about how we should get them out later.

"They work just fine in the building; I tested them the other day while I was scoping it out. But since they have to be made of materials that won't be picked up, they're not as powerful as most. Stay away from any basements or closed rooms, as it'll interrupt the signal."

We nod, and I feel Damon's finger brush over mine, heat moving up my fingers and arms, spreading across my chest.

I want to embrace him, but I know I can't. Not right now. We have a mission to do, and I can't let anything emotional hurt the mission.

That's what I've been so scared of.

We arrive thirty minutes later, the large building in front of us done up to the nines, a beautiful red carpet leading up the stairs and through the doors. Elena hands us our tickets and makes sure to remind Damon that his name is Amare tonight.

Which reminds me that I have to have a little talk with my dear friend. On the other hand, I'm positive that Damon being here tonight means that the men have moved past whatever weird issue hung between them.

"Do you guys know what you're doing tonight?" Jerry asks from the front.

"We're getting in, gathering information, and getting out," I tell her.

"What information?"

"Seeing if there is any information about the secret society or anyone we recognize."

She nods. "If anyone acts even a little odd around Amelia, you mark them down as suspicious, got it?" she asks.

I shoot her a thumbs up, and she sneers at me, letting us out of the car.

"Put your masks on for fucks sake," she hisses before pulling away.

Heading up the stairs, we're greeted by large men with guns, watching over all the guests. There are so many gorgeous dresses around us, and for once I wish I had to dress up more for work. It was fun today.

Damon's hand comes to rest on the small of my back, and I smile at the touch, looking over at him. He looks ahead of us, a serious look in his eye. Someone is in protective mode.

I focus ahead of me, coming up to the ticket holders.

When we're finally in the building, I look around. Although I think coming here is a good idea, I'm not sure how we're supposed to tell anyone apart from others. Everyone wears a mask, and without the full picture, I don't think anyone will recognize one damn person.

"Jesus this is going to be a long night," I mutter. Luisa rubs at my arm, taking my hand and leading me to the bar.

I order an amaretto sour, my go-to drink for on jobs. There's not enough alcohol to cause any issues, *and* it tastes good. Luisa orders wine, holding the stem gingerly between her fingers. Elena grabs her espresso martini, taking a sip with a smile.

"Old fashioned please," Damon asks beside me, and I can't help but smile. I'm not sure why I expected anything different.

We stand to the side for a couple of moments, looking around, seeing if we can possibly spot anyone. When Damon decides we can't, he takes my hand, leading me to the dance floor.

We don't say a word as he wraps one arm around my waist as the other holds my hand. He spins me, our bodies swaying to the music.

I can't say anything without the others hearing, but I try as hard as I can to convey what I'm feeling through my eyes. They lock onto his, and I bite my lip, tasting my strawberry lip gloss as I do.

"You look stunning tonight," he murmurs gently against my ear, sending shivers down my spine.

"You two just need to fuck already," comes a voice in our ear, way too loud. I cringe, trying as hard as I can not to grab my ear.

"There's something wrong with these," I whisper, hoping she can pick up on it.

"There's nothing wrong with them. Don't take them out."
Whatever.

I bite my lip, my eyes never wavering from his. "I hope your parents don't kick my ass for putting you in so much danger."

The corner of his lips twitch as he lets out a small chuckle. "My parents are both dead. I promise you're good."

It feels like a punch to my gut. "Oh, I'm so sorry Damon, I didn't mean—"

"Really, Amelia, it's fine," he says softly.

A chuckle rings out in my ear.

"I'm sure they were really good people." I use my moment of embarrassment to start checking out the others in attendance.

"They were. My dad was the reason I went to the Academy. Died on a job. My mom died a couple of years ago. Two years after, well," he pauses, and my eyes flash to his. "Four years ago." He winces, looking around.

I change the subject. "I can't tell what anyone looks like," I say as I scour the room for anyone who looks even remotely suspicious. Anyone whose eyes linger on me for a little longer than necessary, anyone who looks like they may be doing the same as we are. But I can't tell while everyone is cloaked by masks. "We need to move around. The others are talking to people at the perimeter."

"Luisa doesn't know these people."

"No, but she's a socializer." I smile. I really do adore my friend.

Damon pulls me from the dance floor, and I bump into a large man. He drops his drink down my front, and I gasp in surprise, feeling the liquid on my skin.

"I'm so sorry my dear, here," he hands me a napkin, turning back to his partner without a care in the world. Damon's hands fist by his side, but I put a hand up to stop him. The very last thing we need is to get kicked out of this place tonight.

Instead, shooting the man a glare, I drag Damon in the direction of the bathrooms.

"What just happened?" Jerry's voice booms through my ear, shaking my brain.

"Jesus Jerry I'm going to get a fucking headache if you keep this up."

"What happened?" she repeats.

"A guy spilled his drink on me. It's fine."

I leave Damon at the entrance to the bathroom as I head inside, blotting at my dress at the sink. I take my mask off so I can see better, and a woman steps out of a stall, walking up to the sinks to wash her hands. She has pretty blonde hair and green eyes, highlighted by a glittery purple shadow. Her dress is black satin, hugging every curve.

Her eyes meet mine.

"Your dress is gorgeous," I smile at her.

"Thank you, yours is too," she replies, grinning at me, her eyes flashing with something I can't quite place.

"How long have you been planning for tonight?" She grabs a paper towel.

"It's been a while," I tell her, putting my own towel down, giving up.

"Same. It's always one of the best nights."

She waves at me before heading out of the room, telling me to have fun.

Returning to the hallway, I hear a crackle in my ear before Jerry's voice calls out to me again. Damon rolls his eyes, pulling me down the hall another couple of steps before opening a door and shoving me inside.

"What—" I begin to ask, but he shuts me up with his lips, immediately slipping his tongue inside to deepen it. Pushing me back into the wall, what feels like a broom pokes into my back. The pads of his fingers sweep up the slit in my dress, his touch like fire on my skin. I moan into his mouth, understanding why he pulled me in here.

For a moment of *quiet.*

Normally I would never be so reckless. So humanly reckless.

But in this moment, I don't care.

His hands move up my waist, lingering for a moment

before moving higher. He's hesitant. Careful. I grab his hands, tightening his grip on my chest as I let out a guttural moan.

"You like that?" he asks, nipping my lip. I nod, and he pinches my nipple harder, adding more pressure.

It's sheer ecstasy. The most thrilling thing I've ever felt in my entire life.

"God, I want you," I tell him, wrapping my leg around his.

"Not here, Sweetheart. But when we get home, I'm ripping that fucking dress off of you the second I get you in that bedroom," he promises as he trails hot kisses along my collarbone and up my neck, sucking at the sensitive skin at my ear. My eyes roll back, my breath shallow.

About five minutes later, we've got it out of our systems. Taking a second to make sure we look presentable, we smile at each other, grab our masks off the floor, and slip out of the room, instantly hearing Jerry in our ear, pissed that we both disappeared.

"We were just in the bathrooms fixing my dress Jerry, chill," I tell her.

"The other two are off talking to people and you idiots just disappear?" she asks, and I make a face, looping my arm through Damon's as he leads us back into the main room. I look at him, taking in the way his eyes are lit up when they suddenly sober, a mixture of surprise and horror taking over as he turns me, forcing me to put up my mask.

"What are you doing?" I ask, all of a sudden a little pissed.

"You guys okay over here?" a man asks as he walks over with a woman. The same woman who I spoke to in the bathroom.

"Yeah, we're doing great, thank you." I smile at him, but his face twists, his thick, unruly brows coming together.

"Do I know you?" he asks, turning to the woman by his side.

"Probably not, we're not from around here," I smile, feeling Damon stiffen next to me, his face hard.

"You both just look so familiar," he says, and I start to get worried.

"Who is that?" Jerry asks.

"Anyways, nice to meet you both," he extends a meaty hand, and I take it. The woman was so nice earlier, surely the man on her arm can't be too terrible. Maybe they know something, and this is our in.

I can feel Damon holding in a breath by the way he freezes.

At the last possible second, I decide to make a choice. One that may make finding who wants to kill me go faster but could also cost me everything.

"I'm Ellie," I tell him with a smile.

And that's when everything goes to shit.

TWENTY-THREE

DAMON

I'm not sure what to do in the situation. The only thing I *can* do is hold my breath, praying to God that she doesn't make a wrong move.

But of course, this is Amelia, and nothing she does is predictable.

If I'm honest, I saw this move coming from a mile away. She's great at what she does, but when she doesn't want to do something, she tries to take shortcuts, not caring if it puts her at a greater risk of danger.

This is one of those moments. She'd rather be home but being home requires us to have information. Information that is incredibly hard to get here.

I just wish we hadn't taken off our masks, or we could have avoided this entire conversation.

The man bristles, his wife looking up at him in shock.

"What is this, Burnard?" she asks.

He looks down at her before his eyes make their way back to Amelia's, whose eyes drift to mine in confusion. Burnard then glances at me, realization dawning on him. His face hardens as he takes us both in.

"What the *fuck* is going on here?" he spits, his hands fisted at his sides, shaking in rage.

"I don't understand," Amelia says, but I can tell it's starting to register. Something is very wrong.

"What is happening?" Jerry screams in my ear.

I can't answer her without tipping Senator Huxley off.

"Senator Huxley, it's nice to see you again," I say, my voice hard as steel.

His jaw clenches as his wife grasps his arm. "I thought you said your daughter was dead," she starts, but he cuts her off.

"I don't know what you're talking about," Amelia says, her voice calm and collected as she tries not to freak out.

The Senator spits. "What did you do?" he asks me, fury in his eyes as he shoots daggers at me.

"I don't know what you mean, Senator Huxley," I repeat, trying to mimic Amelia, but falling a little short.

"You know damn fucking well what's going on," he growls.

"I think you're mistaken," I say as I grab Amelia's arm, leading her away.

"Are you guys away from him?" Jerry asks, quieter this time.

"Yes," I say softly as Amelia starts to shake in my hands, likely going into shock. I need to get her out of here this second.

We're almost to the door when a waiter comes out, placing a hand on my arm as he escorts us into the dining hall. "Dinner is being served, this way please."

I try to break free but can't. Instead, we're led into a large, golden room with a large table at the center, decorated with white flowers, and gaudy golden plates. I walk Amelia down to the end, finding our names next to Luisa and Elena. They look up at us, concern in their eyes. I shake my head just a touch, pulling out Amelia's seat and helping her sit. She's stiff, barely managing to bend her legs to sit.

Her back is rigid as she stares in front of her.

The seats in front of us are empty, and I pray to God that Senator Huxley has already found a seat. But I've learned that God doesn't exactly answer my prayers long ago.

The large man takes his seat directly across from me as his wife struggles to pull the large, heavy chair out for herself. When she's able to, she makes herself comfortable, a scowl on her face as she watches Amelia, who still stares directly in front of her. I knock her leg, hoping she snaps out of her trance. I don't need Mrs. Huxley thinking she's staring at her the entire dinner.

"Where are you all?" Jerry seethes into our ears.

"This is such a nice dining room," Luisa says, looking around. "I'm really excited for this dinner, aren't you, Amelia?"

My eyes widen as she looks at me, and hers widen in return.

"You ready for dinner, Ellie?" I ask, my eyes flickering to Luisa's in hopes that she gets the hint. I also hope that Senator Huxley thinks Luisa was talking to someone else.

"This is getting so fucking confusing," Jerry complains.

Amelia looks at me, a small smile on her lips.

"Well, you were able to get that stain out of your dress!" the woman across from her states, flashing a white smile.

"Yes, thankfully," Amelia swallows. "What's your name?"

The woman takes her napkin and places it on her lap as food is brought out. "My name is Naomi."

"Nice to meet you,"

"Likewise."

An awkward silence fills the air as the Senator eyes me.

As soon as the food is placed in front of us, someone at the other end of the table clinks their knife against their wine glass, getting everyone's attention.

A tall, skinny man stands at the head of the table, his gray, thinning hair slicked back. "I want to thank each and every one of you for being here," he tells us with a nod, placing his glass back down. "This is one of my favorite events of the year, and I'm so thrilled to let you know we've made over one million dollars for the charity of Senator Burnard Huxley's choice!"

Everyone around the table claps, and I look at him. His eyes are still locked on mine as he nods, a strained smile on his lips.

"It's so great to have you all here! Please enjoy dinner and drinks afterward!" He sits down, picks up his fork, and stabs it into his salad. I look down at my plate and do the same, pretending the man in front of us isn't there.

"You ready to eat, Sweetheart?" I ask Amelia as I look over her. Luisa does the same, watching her like a hawk to ensure she doesn't freeze up. There's probably a lot going through her brain right now, and I want to keep her from going into shock until we're home.

"Yeah, I'm not super hungry though, I ate a lot earlier." She picks up the glass of wine in front of her and takes a sip. She winces, possibly remembering last night, and puts it back down. She eyes her salad for a moment before picking up her fork, sighing, and stabbing a piece of lettuce.

My eyes flash to Luisa, our gazes meeting for just a moment. Elena looks up for a moment as well, concern flashing in her eyes.

"Are you feeling unwell, dear?" Naomi asks, putting her fork down and taking a sip of water.

Amelia shakes her head, plastering a smile on her face. "No, I'm okay, thank you for asking." Her eyes flash to her father as he watches her, sweat beading on his forehead. "I hope you guys have had a wonderful night." She smiles.

"We have. What have you been up to all these years?" Naomi asks, her head tilted. Huxley looks like he's about to pass out.

Amelia takes a moment to think about what to say. "I've been on some research missions," she says, and I run my fingers along her thigh, hoping to relax her stiff shoulders.

It works, but just a touch.

"I really could have sworn I was told—" She's cut off by Huxley, who clears his throat, scowling at her.

"What I would give to be a fly on this wall right now," Jerry says quietly in our ear, and I hate that I can't remind her that she basically is a fly on the wall at the moment. The only thing she can't do is see.

We slip into an awkward silence as we eat our meals, and I just hope it goes quickly so we can get out of here.

"I'm at the front. Get her out," Jerry calls into our ears after dinner.

I nod as if she can see me as I make my way past the guards, putting on a smile, pretending like nothing is wrong, even though the world is crashing down on us.

Luisa is at my side, and we quickly make our way down the stairs, slipping into the limo along with Elena.

"What the actual fuck was that?" Jerry immediately berates us.

"What happened?" Luisa asks, grabbing Amelia's arm, but she doesn't respond. She doesn't say anything. Instead, she sits there, staring off into space, shaking ever so slightly.

"The man at the table with us? That was her father," I say, dropping the bomb. I'm not sure how much the D.C. Fallen Angels know about her father.

"I—" Amelia makes a sound but doesn't continue, instead looking at her hands, her expression vacant. She's been silent since we stopped talking to the others at dinner. We slipped away afterward unscathed, right before Naomi was about to ask for a hug.

I grasp her hand, squeezing it in mine as I just try to be there for her.

"Amelia?" She doesn't answer. "Get her home. I'll give her a bath; she needs to relax and process," I tell the others.

"Did we learn fucking *anything?*" Jerry yells, livid. "We don't fuck around here, Damon. That was one of our only chances of getting you guys help. Don't fucking waste our time."

"Can you just shut the fuck *up* for a second?" I bellow, practically shaking the car. Everyone falls silent, looking at me.

"He didn't fucking know her. It was clear he had no fucking clue she was alive." I turn to Luisa. "I fucking told you he wouldn't care enough to come after her. You guys questioned me. I was right. The man doesn't give a shit. He was more upset he had no idea what was happening."

Luisa folds into herself, and I feel bad. I do. I didn't mean to be that hard on her, but I was right.

"Just get her back to the warehouse," I snap, holding her to me.

———

The second we pull up to the warehouse, Amare is pulling open the door, trying to yank her out.

"Get the fuck off of her," I growl, shoving his chest.

"Who the fuck are you to tell me what to do?" he screams at me, and I can see it in his eyes that I'm about to get laid out on my ass.

"She's in shock, Amare. Let her fucking be. She needs space."

"From you?" he seethes.

"Not from me." I shake my head. "I'm the one fucking person here who knows exactly what she went through that day. She just came face to face with her father. You know what happened. She's going to want answers. Back off."

"Don't fucking speak for me," comes the voice from behind me as her face twists in a snarl, her body shaking as she makes a move to head inside.

"Amelia—" I call, trying to grab her, but she shakes from my grasp. "Don't you dare speak for me again, Damon." She spins, heading inside as Amare and I stare at each other, fuming.

The second we hear the large doors slam closed; his eyes soften just a touch as he gestures behind him.

"Go get her," he whispers, letting down his guard, realizing how stupid he looked.

But I did, too.

I nod, looking around at the others all standing around watching. Shaking my head, I jog inside, running up the steps, ripping our door open to find her sitting on the edge of the bed looking lost.

"Tell me everything," she says.

And I do.

Six years and two days ago

My phone has been ringing off the hook, but I can't focus on anything other than the punching bag in front of me. Sweat falls into my eyes as I take all my anger and frustration out on it, trying not to tear my own heart out.

I should have told her sooner. I should have fucking told her sooner. I know that now.

Two days ago, I told Ellie about the mission. Told her that I had befriended her under false pretenses. That it wasn't just fate.

She took it as horribly as I thought she would.

Over the past year, we've become close. I've learned so much about her life and what a piece of shit her father is. I've wanted nothing more than to take her away from here, run away with her to somewhere far away, making sure she never feels unloved a single day of the rest of her life. But that's not realistic. Things like that don't just happen for people. And it doesn't happen for me, that's for damn sure.

My phone rings again, and I groan, wiping my forehead with my arm. I grab it from the stool, flipping it open.

"What do you want?" I spit, rage sweeping through me once again.

"She's in trouble," my contact rushes out, breathless, and I feel as though a bucket of ice water was dumped over me.

"What do you mean she's in trouble?" I'm already throwing my shit in my bag, heading out.

"I mean that her father is waving a fucking gun around in their home."

Fuck.

I knew he was unstable. I was told ahead of time that there would be some information coming out about him soon, and that it wouldn't be good. They were things that could ruin his entire life, Ellie's too.

"How long do you think I have?" I ask.

"I don't know. I don't know if he's even going to do anything. Damon, you need to get there."

We had listening devices planted around her home since her father kicked me out that day months ago. He hated that I threatened his power over her. That she loved me and didn't want to marry his sleazeball friend.

He wanted to use her, while I wanted to save her from him.

Ellie wasn't the fragile girl she seemed to be when I first met her. She has spirit, that's for sure. And she'll fight for herself. But no person can outfight a gun.

I don't bother changing or grabbing anything else from my house. I have my keys and the gun I keep by the door.

Flinging my car door open, I don't bother to put on my seatbelt *as I fly down the road, counting the minutes that tick by, hoping I don't get a call to tell me something has happened.*

I'm so, so close.

But the second I pull into her driveway, my phone lights up.

"What?" I ask as I get out.

My contact's voice is shaking. "Are you there?"

"Yes. What do you need?" I'm running inside.

"Damon don't go—" But I don't listen. Not with the scene in front of me.

Blood is spattered everywhere, but I don't see any bodies.

"Ellie!" I scream, not recognizing my own voice over the ringing in my ears.

I run through the hall and into the dining room, and the second I see it, I know the sight will be scarred in my mind for the rest of my life.

Senator Huxley sits in his chair at the head of the table, his head in his hands. He doesn't cry, he doesn't even seem to be breathing. He just… is.

At his feet are his wife, his son, and his daughter, Ellie. All with bullet holes through them.

His wife gasps, her neck bloody as she looks at me, using the last bit of energy she has to look at her daughter, a tear slipping down her bloodied face.

Agony rips through me as I make my way to Ellie, feeling as if I'm a ghost in this home. This isn't real. None of it is. This is a dream. An out-of-body experience. I'm not here, and neither is she.

Kneeling next to her, I grab her hand, shaking her.

"She's dead," Huxley says, and my gaze lifts to him, and I see nothing but red.

I black out in the moment, pushing him out of his chair and onto the ground, screaming. The next thing I know, I'm restrained, my body pushed to the table as two agents try to restrain me. I break out of their hold, trying to punch him, but they push me back, one of them punching my face, sending me reeling back. I land against the table, splitting my forehead open.

There's so much fucking blood. It's everywhere. And it's my fault.

If I had just been here. If I hadn't allowed her to push me away...

I wish with everything in me that I fought harder.

"I'm so fucking sorry," I whisper as I hold her to me, her body quaking.

"What happened to him after?" she croaks.

"He was taken in for questioning. We had so much on him. So much. But somehow, he was let off. I was so angry. The justice system failed. Three innocent lives were taken, and yet he got off free." I scoff, looking down in disgust.

"Did you see what happened to me?" she asks quietly.

I nod. "It still feels like a fever dream. I was in therapy for a long time after that day trying to process everything. You, your brother; I just couldn't take it." I take a deep breath. "The second I settled down they let me see you. You were just lying there, lifeless, and I couldn't do anything about it. I couldn't save you."

Tears slip from my own eyes.

"The EMT's got there and took you. Said if your heart had stopped a little before they got there, they had a chance to bring you back. Your mother, too. Your brother had no chance." I want nothing more than to be swallowed whole. I don't want to tell her all of this, but I have to. She asked. I promised I'd tell her if she asked.

"They took you to the hospital, but it was too late." I let the sob escape me as I hold her head to my chest, rocking her back and forth. "For six years I prayed I could go back in time and fix it. To bring you back. I fell in love with you, Amelia. You were my first and only love, and I spent six years trying to heal from what happened that day."

"And then you found out I was alive," she says meekly.

I kiss her forehead. "And then I found out you were alive."

A heavy silence falls between us as her breathing evens out. She rubs her eyes, smearing her makeup even more.

"I still don't remember," she starts, her voice small. "I know I had people who loved me. I do. But I've never felt that." She sighs, and I shift on the bed, my lips against her temple.

"I want to feel loved for the first time. Please."

I pull away from her, looking into her eyes. "What are you asking?"

"You love me?" she asks.

I nod. I do. I always have. But I don't want the words to come now. Not because of this.

"I want you to show me. Please."

"Sweetheart," I start, wiping a tear away from her face. "A woman like you never has to beg me for it. Take whatever you want."

Her lips are on mine in an instant, and I fight with her for power, my teeth nipping at her sensitive, bruised lips. They clash with hers, our tongues mingling, fighting for the upper hand.

I push her back, my knee between her legs as I take her in.

There's nothing I want more than to give this woman everything she has ever wanted in her entire life.

TWENTY-FOUR

AMELIA

Damon looks at me as if I'm the only person on this earth, and it lights me on fire.

It's a feeling I've never known. A feeling I likely will never feel again if he's ever gone.

For the first time since he's been here, I don't picture him leaving. I don't know how it will work, but I think he'll stay with me until the very end.

I just want to feel loved.

I pull his tie, taking pleasure in how his body feels as it falls on top of mine. My hands grasp at his firm muscles as they flex under my touch.

I kiss up his neck, and he comes undone. Unzipping my dress, he peels it off, throwing it to the floor. I make quick work of my bra and underwear, and before I know it, I'm lying in front of him, baring it all.

I would be embarrassed if it were anyone else. But Damon feels like home. Comfort. Safety. My body aches for his adulation.

As much as I want him to show me how much he loves me, I want to show him how much I trust him. I've never felt love; not really, anyways. But if I were to label anything at all as love, it would be this.

Heat spreads over my body as he looks me over, biting the inside of his cheek as his eyes move from my core, up to my waist, and to my chest. Coming down on his forearms above me, he dips his head, taking my nipple into his mouth. He watches me as he does so, loving the way I squirm under him. I go to move my arms, but he grabs my wrists in one of his large hands, pinning them above my head. He uses his other hand to run his fingers softly over my over-sensitive nipples before squeezing, moving on to the other.

"Damon please," I plead, but it's no use.

"I'm busy," he says as he runs his tongue down my abs, leaving butterflies in my stomach as he reaches my center.

He's not careful this time. There is no lead-up. He simply devours me. Takes me whole. Leaves me ruined.

As his tongue dips inside of me, ravaging me, he reaches up, grabbing my breast in his hand and squeezing, making sure to capture my nipple between his fingers. I yell, loving the pain as pleasure sweeps through my body, leaving me speechless.

I come undone at his touch, and as he twists my nipple even more, another wave rips through me.

When he's done, he sheds his tux, whipping his tie off and sending it flying to the floor. His pants drop, and his cock springs free, hard, and ready. I admire it, ready for whatever he's about to bring.

"Are you on anything?" he asks me, bending over and holding my chin in his fingers.

I furrow my brows.

"What do you mean?"

"Are you on the pill or anything?"

Fear sweeps through me, and I don't know how to tell him I'm not without completely ruining the mood, upsetting him.

"Why are you looking at me like that?" he asks, searching my eyes. He's soft with me. Caring.

"I, Damon I—"

"Amelia, what's wrong?"

I look down, a tear falling from my eye. "They took that from me," I whisper.

"They took what from you?"

"Damon, I don't have a uterus. They took it. Before I woke up. They take them from us when we're initiated." They don't want us to have kids. Don't want the possibility of it happening.

We didn't have a choice.

Knowing what I know about the world now, I wouldn't want to bring someone into it, anyways. But it's always nice to have a fucking choice.

I watch as a range of emotions sweep over his face. From rage to heartache, back to sheer lividity, I don't know what to expect when he opens his mouth.

But he doesn't. Instead, he dips his head down to kiss me passionately. Lovingly. Drinking me in like I'm his only chance at survival.

"Damon," I start, but he shuts me up with a kiss.

"I love my name coming from your lips," he murmurs between kisses, and all my blood runs south once more.

He looks down, running a finger over my center. "Do you see what you're doing to me?" he asks, stroking himself with my come. My eyes fall back as I let his words ruin me.

"Look at me, Sweetheart, I want to see your eyes." I obey, wrapping my legs around him.

He looks around, looking concerned for a second. It doesn't take me long to realize why. He just doesn't know how to ask.

"You don't need one," I tell him, grabbing the back of his neck and bringing his mouth back down to mine.

"Are you sure? I haven't been with anyone in years," he murmurs. "I'm clean."

I nod. He already knows where I stand with that.

He doesn't need any other invitation.

He pushes into me, and I feel myself come undone before he's even all the way in. The feeling of him rips me apart, but the way he looks at me puts me back together once more.

I sink into his kiss as I run my hands across his muscles, following his tattoo up his arm as I dig my fingernails into his flesh. He moans into me, making me feel powerful. Unhinged. I'd choose him over the entire world every single chance I got.

I would burn this fucking world down for him.

"It's like you were fucking made for me," he whispers into my cheek as he nips at me, his hand fisting my hair, tugging on it. The bite makes a wave of pleasure sweep through me.

"You're being such a good girl, Amelia. You can take it for me, can't you?"

And I'm a goner.

I thought the last orgasm was the most intense I've ever experienced—which to be fair, doesn't mean a ton considering I only had myself to experiment with—but this?

I'm in heaven. I'm floating on cloud 9. I've never felt this before. Never in my life.

If I died now, I would be happy. Whole.

He pulls out, thrusting back into me, yanking on my hair as he does. I gasp, my head flinging back. "You're so fucking beautiful, Amelia. The way you take me, fuck."

I moan, and he takes my lips in his again, grabbing my throat as he cradles my head in his large palm.

My eyes flash open, and he doesn't miss the way my body responds. "You want this?" he asks as he tightens his grip around my neck, cutting off my air. I nod, my vision going blurry as he pumps into me harder and harder. I grab his hips, scratching at him, tearing into his flesh. I want him to squeeze harder, my head growing fuzzy.

My walls contract around him, rapture quaking through me. Damon tenses above me, letting go of my neck as his eyes close, his mouth hanging open.

It's the sexiest thing I've ever seen.

And I wish we could stay here in this moment for the rest of our lives.

We don't say much after. We don't need to.

Instead, we wash up before falling into each other's arms in bed, drifting to sleep.

TWENTY-FIVE

DAMON

I wake her up in the morning with my face between her legs, but she doesn't allow me to get very far. No.

She wants what she wants, and I'll give it to her every day, no matter what.

"Damon, I want to do this for you," she says, looking up at me with her giant brown eyes expectantly.

I nod, brushing her hair out of her face gently.

"Fine, but stop whenever you have to, okay?" I ask. She nods. Sliding out of bed, she sits on her heels on the floor, waiting for me to stand.

When I do, I brush my fingers over her face as I look over her. Her face is puffy from crying last night, and even though I washed her face for her before we went to bed, she still has some makeup smeared around her eyes.

She's breathtaking either way.

She looks at me expectantly as I drop my boxers. "I need you to use your words, Sweetheart, you look so goddamn perfect looking up at me like that." But in usual fashion, she doesn't do as I say, and I let her get away with it.

She grabs my dick in her hand the instant I'm in front of her, pumping it as she takes it into her warm, wet mouth. I sigh into her, closing my eyes as I let the feeling wash over me.

"That's my girl," I tell her as I gather her hair behind her, pumping into her. Her eyes drift up to mine, and I can't help but think of how lucky I am to have found her again. She's mine. Made for me, I'm sure of it. No other woman on this planet could ever compare. And no one would have to.

She tries as hard as she can to take me into the back of her throat, but it's clear she's putting on a brave face. Spit falls from her mouth as tears well in her eyes, and although it's one of the sexiest sights I've ever seen, it's not what I want her to deal with at the moment.

Instead, I pick her up, deciding I want to try something.

"Do you trust me?" I ask her, grabbing my belt. She eyes it suspiciously before her eyes return to mine and she nods.

"Good. Get on the bed." She does as she's told, thank God. "Get on your hands and knees, and bend over."

I loop the belt around her neck, holding either side of it in my hands firmly, giving her enough slack that she can breathe.

I can tell she likes certain things, and I have a feeling she'll love this, which is only confirmed as I feel her, dipping a finger inside of her before licking it.

I've waited for so long to taste her, and I'll be taking every single chance I have to keep doing so.

"Are you dripping for me, Sweetheart?" I ask, tugging on the belt, forcing her head up. She moans in answer, her ass wiggling in anticipation. I smack it once before pushing inside, my eyes rolling back in my head at how fucking good she feels.

"Fuck baby that's it," I tell her, running my hand over her

back. "Can you grab the headboard for me? That's it. Good girl."

She pushes into me as I keep a firm hold on the belt, forcing her head up as I palm her breasts with my other hand.

With one more smack to her ass, she quakes, her body collapsing as I immediately let up on the belt, pulling out of her.

I hook my arm around her, flipping her over so she's facing me, and I crash my lips to hers, taking a second to be in the moment, my lips devouring her.

When I'm ready, I enter her again, thrusting into her as I suck on her neck. She moans, and I twist her nipple between my fingers. "That's my girl. You can take it," I whisper, sending her over the edge.

And there's something about the way she comes undone beneath me that makes me think she's finally free.

"Where are the eggs?" I ask Zach as I peer into the fridge.

"We may be out. But we have bread. I made toast this morning," he tells me, pointing to the pantry.

I nod, finding the bread and bringing it to the counter. I take out a few slices and pop them into the toaster.

No one seems to be around today. They're either busy or avoiding us. I don't think they heard anything last night, as the rooms seem to be pretty soundproof through the foot or more of concrete, but I worry that I'll have to have a difficult conversation with them at some point here soon.

I want nothing more than to wake up with Amelia in my arms for the rest of my life. But I also know that I can't just live in their house without the CIA having a serious problem with it. I'm not stupid enough to think that this can be a normal relationship, and yet I'm not okay with giving it up. I won't.

No matter what, I'm here, and I'm not going anywhere.

A couple minutes later, Amelia makes her way down the stairs, a smile on her perfect face as she comes up to me, grabbing my arm and snuggling into me. I close my eyes, savoring the feeling.

This could be every morning in a perfect world.

"I spoke with Luisa earlier. I'm going to meet the girls somewhere this morning. I just need time out of here." She looks around, sighing. "Then we'll have to come up with a game plan tonight, okay?" she asks.

I nod, kissing her on the lips. "Whatever you need."

She beams up at me, running her fingers through her hair.

She disappears back upstairs, emerging a couple of minutes later with her hair up in a ponytail, mom jeans, and a sweater on.

She gives me one last kiss before she climbs into one of the cars, hits the button to open the large front doors, and drives off.

We also haven't spoken about what she told me last night. About how they took such an important part of her body from her. The more I think about it, the more I think it doesn't really matter. I don't need kids. I never even thought about having them, if I'm honest. Not if it wasn't with her.

She's perfect the way she is, and I'm never going to make her feel as though she's any less for something she doesn't have.

"I don't know, I just think that the Sequels were better." Brandon shrugs, sinking into the couch in front of me.

"And I think you're lying if you actually think that. Jesus Christ, how the hell do you think that they're better than the Prequels?" Ronan scoffs, disgusted at the mere thought.

"And I just can't believe that you fuckers aren't even

considering the Original trilogy. Really? Sand? He's scared of fucking *sand*? That's almost more pathetic than Superman's one and only weakness being a fucking rock," Zach spits.

Ronan squares his shoulders defensively. "He doesn't actually say he's scared of sand. He doesn't care about sand. It's not that big of an issue. He just doesn't like it."

"The acting is so bad."

"You take that back," Ronan seethes. "He was *amazing*. Was the acting good? No. But the writing was bad! It was a fantastic story, much better and more cohesive than the Sequels, that's for sure."

"I can't even argue that," Brandon's shoulders hang. "Rey was hot though."

They all nod, and I roll my eyes.

"I'm not sure why this is even a topic of conversation when the Clone Wars exists," I say, wanting to add to the conversation.

"That doesn't count," Ronan tells me, taking a sip of water. "That's not one of the movies."

I roll my eyes again.

I check my watch as they continue to bicker. It's been two hours, and I haven't heard from Amelia at all.

"Have you guys heard from any of the girls?" I ask suddenly, eyeing them all. It's not like I have a phone, but usually, she tries to get in contact somehow.

They shake their heads, looking around, worried.

The girls came home an hour ago. Amelia wasn't with them. She was never with them.

And I'm ready to burn down this entire fucking planet to find her.

Jerry stands in front of me, her hands on her hip as she

glares. "You need to calm the fuck down," she hisses, her eyes narrowing.

"She's out there somewhere and no one knows where. After yesterday. There has to be some way..." My voice trails off as I think. My heart rate has picked up, and I find it hard to breathe.

She's probably terrified, wherever she is.

I desperately need to find her, however, I can.

TWENTY-SIX

AMELIA

My head hurts. Actually, my entire body hurts.

I wake from my groggy haze with a pounding headache, my hands tied behind my back as I sit on a cold metal chair. I look around me, trying to understand what's going on.

I'm in a warehouse, but not the one the Fallen Angels are in. No, this one is different. Empty. Lifeless. Cold.

I'm so incredibly cold.

"Ellie, how nice of you to join us," the voice comes from in front of me, and my eyes snap to his. It's the man from the masquerade. My father.

"What is this?" I grit through my teeth, trying to keep them from chattering.

He shrugs, uncaring. He sits in his chair, his legs spread in front of him. He's breathing hard as sweat runs down his red face despite the cold temperature. His beady eyes bear into mine, and I want nothing more than to knock the smirk off of his face. "I want to know how you're alive. What you've been doing. This whole," he pauses, "thing you have going on." He pats his knee, his head tilting as he takes me in. "You were much prettier as a blonde."

I gag, trying my hardest not to throw up. "I'm sure you'd think that," I spit, my nails digging into the plastic securing my wrists, trying to get out of the ties.

"What do you remember of that day?" he asks suddenly, standing from his chair and walking over to a table. My eyes grow wide as I see a large knife sitting on top of it, glistening in the moonlight. I've been out for a long time. It was around eleven in the morning when I left, on my way to meet the girls out. I was looking forward to looking around the city and spending time with them.

I just needed to get out of there. The place is beautiful, but I needed fresh air and some quality time with friends.

I eye him as he runs his finger along the blade, and I can't help but feel as though I'm not going to make it out of this one alive. I really hope Damon knows I love him. I just hope he'll be okay with knowing that. That he's gotten some sense of closure. He can't save me from this. Not this time. This is all my fault.

"Why did you murder your family?" I ask him instead.

He looks me over, picking up the knife. "I'm the one asking questions right now," he growls, turning to me.

"I think you owe me an answer." I hold firm.

"You were all in my way," he says simply, holding the blade up to the moonlight. "It just made sense. A shame it didn't work, though. I really thought you were dead all these years. It was peaceful."

"I was a child."

"You were a twenty-one-year-old brat who thought she knew better than me," he spits, walking over to me with a limp in his step, his breathing ragged. "You were going to take everything from me. Running against your own father? Threatening to take away what was his? What the fuck is wrong with you."

I don't remember any of that, and Damon never told me. Maybe he didn't know.

"I wanted you to be the perfect wife. You would marry my business partner, have his kids, and be his bitch. You'd be taken care of for life." He chuckles evilly. "But you had to be ambitious. The perfect daughter. Did you know they called you that? Can you remember that? They called you the Perfect Daughter. You made headlines. You were my little girl. But what kind of girl goes and fucks me over that way? You would have sunk me. I couldn't let you do that."

I don't think he knows that I don't remember any of it, so I pause, pursing my lips before continuing. "I don't remember," I stick with, "What did I do?"

"You don't remember? I put you through community college to keep you around. To let you date William. But you had to go behind my back and apply to Harvard. Did you know when I learned that you were accepted? With everyone else. I found out online. I knew I couldn't let you go. It would have been easy. I just wouldn't pay for it. But then you had to get a scholarship."

"How would that ruin your career?" I grit as my nail falls from the plastic, digging into my skin.

"You were going to run. Against me. Your own father. You didn't like how I was running the state. Didn't like the laws I was helping to pass. You said I was running it to the ground." He scoffs, rolling his eyes. "I might be. But it all serves a higher purpose," he says, a sick smile on his lips.

"I don't understand," I say, my brows furrowing.

He limps over to me, his teeth bared as he slaps me across the face. "What is there to not understand? God, you really are so stupid, aren't you? To think that you were going away to that school. To think that anyone would vote for you."

"So, I was trying to run against you?"

He eyes me, his gaze burning a hole into my skull. "You were going to tear everything down. Expose me for what I was doing. For what the Society was doing. We wanted to make the country a better place, but that meant destabilizing it. Taking over. You were going to expose every single one of us, and I couldn't have that now, could I?" He sneers at me, his teeth dark against his pale, purple skin.

"No, we really can't," I add with a sigh.

"The others, I feel bad about. I even mourned. But you? You were a headache. A disease to my name. I would do it again if I could." He pauses, a smile on his face. "Funny how things work out, right?"

TWENTY-SEVEN

DAMON

"Get me a fucking phone!" I scream at them, losing my fucking mind.

Luisa rushes up, a phone number already dialed in. "It's Stella. She can help. She wants to help, Damon. Please listen to her."

I've been a little bit problematic the last couple of hours.

Okay, a lot problematic.

I haven't wanted anyone to help me. I've been screaming at everyone. I've been pushing everyone away.

But what else am I supposed to do when the one person I'm here for, the one person I sacrificed everything to help, is out there somewhere, and we can't find her?

I haven't wanted to listen to anyone. No one can find her. There's no tracking they have that can help, and Jerry has been obnoxious about it. Every single time I demand to see their tech, she turns me down.

"We don't have that type of tech here, Damon. Get the fuck away from me."

ANNA NOEL

"Hello?" Stella asks as I put the phone to my ear.

"Do you have any way of finding her?" My voice is pleading, pathetic even. But I don't care. Not when it comes to finding her. Not when it comes to saving her. I just want to make sure she's okay. Alive.

She doesn't answer, instead typing away at her keyboard. I take a steady breath in, trying to keep my cool.

When I find out who did this, I will make sure they regret every single day they've ever been alive.

"I'm hacking into security cameras around the area right now. I have our system locating her face. I'll call you back soon if I get a hit. In the meantime, I'll try a few other things, okay?"

I grunt into the phone.

"Damon? She's going to be okay."

It's been two hours, and my attitude has only gotten worse. She could be dead by now. I would be out burning down every fucking building if I could be right now.

Jerry sits across from me at her chess set, moving her Queen. I move a pawn.

"Chess is relaxing, isn't it?" She shoots me a smile, and I almost want to return it, if only for the fact that I don't think Jerry usually smiles. Ever, really. I don't believe it.

But it just makes me feel worse. She's showing me sympathy. This woman who doesn't care about anything, who's tough and demeaning, is showing me sympathy.

I don't think she believes we're going to find her.

For my own sake, I have to believe. I have to believe it with every fiber of my being. If I don't, I don't know what I'll do.

"It's not, but thanks for trying," I shoot back, moving another piece.

She slouches back in her chair, puffing out her cheeks before making another move.

"So how did you end up here?" I ask her flatly, watching her every move. I used to be in chess club as a kid, and I'd like to think I'm good, but Jerry is giving me a run for my money.

"Well, for starters, I do, unfortunately, remember everything," she tells me, and I look up, my brows furrowing. Luisa said that she remembers everything and it's a punishment. I wonder if that's part of why Jerry is... the way she is.

"How did you die?" I ask, not caring if she would consider the question rude.

Her eyes flicker to mine before drifting back down to the board, studying where my pieces are. "I didn't die. I just had no one."

"What does that mean?"

"It means that I was abandoned as a kid. My parents gave me up, but kept my twin apparently, from what I hear. I was bounced from foster home to foster home."

My shoulders sink, my mood getting worse. "I'm sorry you had to go through that," I tell her, and I'm being honest. I feel terrible.

She shrugs, grabbing a cigarette. She takes her lighter out of her pocket, flicks it on, and holds it to the object between her teeth. I watch as the paper burns.

She pockets the lighter, bringing her hand back up to grip the cigarette between her fingers, taking a long drag before blowing it out.

I've never liked cigarettes. I've had too many family members die from smoking, so you could say that I even had a little bit of a hatred for them. But there's something about Jerry that makes it look so natural. Like she was made to have one between her lips at all times. It was just part of her.

"How did you end up here?" I ask her.

She lets out a quick laugh, her lips pulling at the corners.

"I was starving on the streets. Left home. Didn't have anywhere else to go. Found Ronan and he brought me in. I had no one, so they initiated me."

"Oh, how old are you?" I ask her.

"Twenty-eight," she grins, her queen taking another pawn.

She looks so much older, and I don't understand how.

"Have you talked to your twin at all?"

Something lights up in her eyes, and she narrows them at me before smirking a little. "Not yet."

"What does that mean?"

"It means I haven't talked to her yet. Doesn't mean I won't."

I nod, pretending I understand.

"If you were initiated here, does that mean they," I pause. I'm not sure if Amelia would want me to mention the hysterectomy. It's personal, even if they do it to all of them. But I decide to ask anyways. If there's one person I *could* ask without offending, it's Jerry. "Did they perform a hysterectomy on you?"

"Yep," she says without skipping a beat. "Sure as fuck did."

My bishop dies.

"Do the men usually get the same treatment?" Her eyes flicker to mine again and she nods.

"Why do you want to know?" her voice is harsh as she sits back in her seat, looking me up and down. "You want to join?"

I shake my head. "No, I was just wondering. Amelia had mentioned it and I just, I don't know. I don't know a ton about it or how people are initiated, and I wanted to know if they did that to everyone everywhere."

Jerry eyes me for another moment before her focus drifts back to the chessboard. "Well to answer your questions, they do it for both men and women. Don't need anyone getting knocked up when you have a job to do, you know? It's a requirement for initiation."

"If someone is saved but doesn't want to be initiated, what happens?" I ask her. It's a question that's been on my mind for a long time now, and I'm desperate to have an answer.

"They knock them out and drug them. They'll do that however many times they need to in order to get the answer they want."

The way she says it sends shivers down my spine, and I want to vomit. I can't imagine that.

Sure, these people get a second chance at life. That's impressive. Negating the ethical issue of it, it's cool that we have the technology to save people on the brink of death, or in Amelia's case, already dead. But it's insane that they could just force people to do something that they don't want to do. That they can be brainwashed.

But the Agency has done worse throughout history, that's for sure, so I'm not sure why I should be surprised.

It's something I've grappled with since I first learned what this was. What they do. I'm not sure how I feel about it. Whether I'd want to take them up on the offer if it ever happened to me. I understand the need for someone on the inside to make sure that the country is running smoothly and that no one is fucking everything up. I get it. I, more than anyone, completely understand it. I watched as a man who admitted to killing his wife, son, and daughter in cold blood walk away with just a slap on his wrist. It didn't even hurt his political career.

It was played off like a tragic accident. He gained sympathy from most of the country and was able to retain his seat.

The law didn't matter to a lot of people. Sometimes there needs to be a balance of power, and Project Fallen Angel seems to be that balance. But they're also run by the CIA, which is a problem all in itself.

I'm not sure I would agree to it.

But if they brainwashed me? I'm not sure. I wonder how fast I would crack.

The phone in my lap rings, Stella's name flashing on it.

"Please tell me you have good fucking news," I snap, instantly feeling a little bad.

"I have her at a warehouse. It's about twenty minutes away from you. I'm sending you the address now."

The second it's through, I hang up, informing everyone of the situation. They run to their cars without a single question.

We're getting her back.

TWENTY-EIGHT

AMELIA

Tears pour down my face as pain rips through me. The dagger sticks from my leg, and each time I don't give him an answer, my father moves it, digging it deeper, splitting me open.

"I want to know who you're working for. You tell me, I won't kill that West boy," he says his name with such disdain that I believe Damon when he says he hated him.

"I don't have anything to tell you," I cry out, choking on a sob.

I may not feel that much loyalty to the Agency, but that doesn't mean I'm going to secure my friends' deaths. The second he knows about the project is the second everything crumbles. The second every single person I care about dies. Because of me.

I'd rather die in their place. The secret can die with me. They can go back home, safe and sound.

The one thing in the back of my mind... who put the hit

out on me? It wasn't him, if he didn't know that I was even alive, who the fuck put the hit out on me?

Yanking the dagger from my leg, my father holds it to my neck, staring down at me with authority he only wishes he had. I breathe in, trying to keep my body from shaking.

He backhands me, and I go flying to the ground, landing on my side with a huff, something in my arm snapping as my head hits the ground. He lifts my chair back up before lifting his hand again, but someone walks in behind me. His gaze lifts, his eyes softening.

"What are you doing here?"

BOOM

Blood is everywhere as a bullet flies through my father's forehead, his lifeless eyes looking at me once more before he falls to the ground, a pool of blood puddling around him.

I scream, kicking, trying to get away.

Maybe it was Damon. Maybe Damon is here to save me.

I was convinced I could get out of here myself, but I can't. I'm so tired of fighting...

But it's not Damon.

Naomi walks around me, and for a second, I think she's here to save me. Maybe she knows how awful my father is and wanted to take him out. The smirk on her face tells me otherwise, however, and a chill runs down my spine. I don't trust her. Not at all.

She comes to a stop behind him, kicking him with her shoe.

"Ellie, how are you?" she asks me, the American accent she had at the masquerade replaced with a German one.

I shrink back. This can't be good.

"What? Cat got your tongue?" She smiles, looking around the building. "This place is such a dump. I'm not sure why he brings people out here."

"Who are you?" I ask quietly, shaking as I slowly bleed out.

She cocks her head to the side, tapping her gun to her lips. "I'm someone who has a large interest in you," she starts. "A very large interest. In fact, we have for a while."

"Tell me who you are," I demand again, narrowing my eyes. Sweat beads at my forehead as I try to keep my thoughts together. I can't drift off now. I can't let everything go to waste. For the first time in so long, I don't actually want to die.

"Oh, sweetie, you have no idea what real spying is, do you?" She cocks her head, giving me a sympathetic look. "Look. You'll be dead in a few, so let me fill you in. Give you some pointers. You want to make real change happen in this world? You go to a country and destabilize it. How do you do that? Marry a Senator. One you know is a piece of shit. A sheep. One you can convince to do whatever you want. Maybe even one in a secret society that wants to see their own government crumble."

I think about what she said. She's a German spy. But what does she want with me? I'm not naïve. I know there are spies everywhere. American spies are stationed in almost every single country. It would be insane to think that there are none from those countries here. Especially with how complicated things can be here.

"So, you knew about what he did before you came here?"

She looks me over, sitting in the chair my father had set up in front of me. "I did. I knew all about you. That was part of my case. The beloved daughter who died but was seen elsewhere by our spies. God, it's so easy to spy on you Fallen Angels. I mean everywhere. The CIA really don't know how to be slick."

She has a point, but I don't feel like telling her that is going to do me any good.

"You put the hit out on me?" I ask her, my mouth dry. The only thing I can smell is iron, and I just want to get my death over with at this point.

"It wasn't hard to find you. In fact, it was so easy. I was shocked. Honestly. God, I almost wish it was harder. I knew others had seen you, but I didn't believe them. All I had to do was run some tests through our database to find out that a surprisingly odd amount of people were just, well, alive despite being ruled dead. All with different names. It was so easy to see that the Agency was up to something.

She taps her gun to her lips, crossing her arms over her chest.

"Why did you put my old name on the hit?" I ask her, my eyes fluttering closed just a bit. I'm so tired.

"Because I knew it would get to your father someway. It would get you out of hiding. It would have that boy on a mission to find you. There are so many reasons I did it, really. And they're all so smart of me if I do say so myself. Honestly. I want to give myself a pat on the back for that one. He led you right to me! Can you imagine that?"

I don't want to rain on her parade and let her know that he did no such thing. It was me who pulled him along with me, but I understand what she's getting at. I do.

"One person can't take down an entire established agency, but they can take out the one person in that agency who risks bringing everything down on top of you," she tells me, her lips tight as she looks at the gun in her hand.

"I don't remember anything from before," I tell her, my throat closing up on itself. "I promise. I wouldn't have known he was my dad. There are so many people with my last name, I wouldn't have known if you hadn't brought us together."

She shrugs, a smile on her lips. "Oops, that's a shame." She bends down, eye level with me. "One life for many, as they say, right?"

"You're a German spy?" I ask, coughing up blood.

"I feel like you know the only reason I'm telling you this is because you're dying in a couple of minutes, and if you don't know, I just informed you. But yes, I work for the German government. We've been eying your government for quite some time, ready to tear it down when we can. We're still a long way out, but we're getting there."

"Then why were you coming after me?" I ask. "I wasn't doing anything."

"You killed my business associate," she hisses, getting into my face.

I roll my eyes. "I've killed many people. Which one was this?"

She bares her teeth. "Carl."

Oh, the man who led me to the man I killed that day in the basement. The one with a weird desire for hookers. That Carl.

"He was a German asset?" I ask, confused.

"There's more of us than you think."

I nod, even more confused than before.

"Who was he to you?"

She eyes me, a permanent frown on her pouty lips. "I came here with him. Trained with him. We were close, and you killed him. Just took him out like he was nothing."

"Well, now I'm extra glad I did. Damn. I did really good with that one." Before she can say anything, I add, "Tell me why you were coming after me. The real reason. There has to be more than that."

"You were so close to finding out more about the secret society. They were all a part of it. You cracked the case you were working on with Carl, you find out about the Secret Society, everything comes crumbling down. It's so easy, marrying a Senator and having him do the dirty work for you. They wanted to destabilize the country. I wouldn't have had to lift a finger."

"Then why would you shoot him tonight?" I look down at my father, the pool of blood reflecting in the moonlight coming in from the windows.

"He got messy. Wasn't listening to me." She shrugs.

Prowling over to me, she puts her hand up as if to smack me, but before she can, the doors burst open, light pouring in as the roar of car engines echo throughout the warehouse. The woman in front of me gapes at them, and I can see the wheels turning. She doesn't know what to do.

A car comes to a stop in front of us, Damon jumping out, the gun in his hand pointed directly at Naomi. My step-mother. The German spy. Apparently.

"Drop the fucking gun," he threatens, but she looks around, taking everything in.

"You know we're going to get our way no matter what, right? If I'm dead, someone will take my place. They'll send however many people they need to in order to get the job done."

"Drop. The. Gun," Amare demands, coming up behind her. But she just smiles, points her gun at me, and shoots.

———

The bright lights are too much for me. I can't feel half of my body, but I can feel the person next to me.

I use almost all of my energy to turn my head, finding Jerry. If I thought I had died and gone to heaven, this would be my wake-up call. I can only be in hell or still living. She's the last person I wanted to see.

"Good. You're awake. I can leave and smoke a fucking cigarette." She rolls her eyes.

The soft beeping sends panic down my spine. "Where is everyone?" I ask.

"Damon is in critical care. Getting some bullets pulled out of him. Your other little friends are currently in a meeting with some chick named Veronica. I don't know. Don't give a fuck."

My pulse quickens, and I can feel the rush of my blood in my ears.

"Is he okay?" I ask her, panicked. I can't breathe well, and I choke.

"Chill out, Jesus. He's doing okay from what I know. Now get some rest. All this panicking isn't doing no one any good."

I drift out once more.

I wake up once more, again annoyed that I'm actually living.

Until I remember Damon.

Damon.

The only thing I want is for him to hold me. For him to touch me. For him to tell me everything is going to be okay.

The beeping sobers me as I look around, trying to find anyone to help me. Anyone to tell me everything is going to be okay. Someone to tell me that Damon is okay.

"Amelia you're awake!" Luisa says as she walks through the door to my room. I look around, taking everything in. "We weren't sure when you'd wake up."

"How long was I out?" I ask her. "You've been in and out for the past twenty-four hours."

"Where did Jerry go?"

"She went home. She had to deal with," she pauses, making a face, "something that came up,"

I make a mental note to ask her what that's about after I'm out of here.

"What happened?"

"Well, you had lost a lot of blood by the time we got to you. You were already half out of it. But we got to you and Naomi didn't seem to care the guns pointed toward her head—"

"How many of you came?" I ask, my brows furrowed.

ANNA NOEL

"All of us. Why wouldn't we all come?"

I didn't think they cared about me that much for all of them to put their lives on the line to rescue me. They didn't know what they would be walking into. Had no idea who had me and how many people would be there with guns.

"Anyways," she continues, "she pulls the trigger, and Damon shot her. Amare had knocked you out the of way of the bullet, but it sent you into the floor and you hit your head pretty hard. That idiot. Jesus, I thought I was going to die when he did it. There was a time there that I didn't think either of you were going to live if I'm honest."

"He got shot?"

"Oh yeah. Had several bullets in him. You hit your head really hard on the ground. It knocked you out pretty good. He came over to you without checking if the bitch was dead. She wasn't."

"Who killed her?"

"Amare took her out. He was right behind Damon. The second she pulled the trigger, Amare did too. He made sure the bitch was dead before he freaked out over you and Damon." She sees my look. "Yes, he was concerned over Damon. Those two seem to be friends now. I don't know. Men are complicated sometimes."

I chuckle, rolling my eyes.

"Damon is okay?"

"He's been in a coma, but he's okay. He's expected to make a full recovery. We're not sure when, but at some point, he'll be back to his usual, disgustingly positive self."

I smile, leaning back into my pillow. "Have you heard about when I'll be able to get up and move around?"

She shakes her head. "No, you're not going to be able to do that for a day or two at least. I promise Damon is okay. Amare is with him right now, watching over him. We're not going anywhere, okay? Relax."

I nod.

"Do you need anything?" she asks me, her eyes warm.

I think for a moment. "Can you bring me a book?" I ask with a smile. I need something to pass the time. If I can focus on it. I'm not sure how my brain is going to treat reading.

"On it."

TWENTY-NINE

Damon

Two months later

She's been sitting with me every single day for the last week. Probably longer than that, but that's all I can remember. I feel her touch against my hand, the brush of her pinky through mine. I know it's her.

She feels like home.

I feel stronger with each day that passes, but I do think a lot about death.

Death is a fickle thing. It's beautiful and tragic, terrible and lonely. At one point in our lives, we probably wish for it. Beg for it. For it to be simple.

For it to be quick.

But it doesn't take much to know that finding something to live for changes everything. Suddenly, you have someone there hoping for you. Wishing for you. Looking after you. Rooting for you.

Desiring you.

And that can make all the difference.

"Damon, I love you. I just really hope you know that." She squeezes my hand, and I smile.

"Did his lip just twitch?" she asks. Did it?

If I had to go back and replay that day, I wouldn't do a single thing differently. The German spy was about to shoot Amelia, and I shot her first, sending her to the ground as Amare knocked Amelia out of the way. She knocked her head on the ground pretty hard, and I went to her, praying she was okay.

But I wasn't looking, and I should have made sure the bitch was dead.

Four bullets later, I'm in limbo. Floating around, able to hear the love of my life but not see her. Able to feel her touch, but unable to touch her myself.

I just want to tell her "I love you too."

"What?" she asks, gasping. "Damon, did you just talk?"

I peel my eyes open, the bright lights hurting them. I shield my face, flinching.

"Get Veronica in here."

"On it."

She grips my wrist, shaking me.

"You came back to me," she sobs, shaking as she hugs me.

"I love you, Amelia," I tell her, trying to pick up my hand. I can't.

"I love you too Damon. You idiot. Why would you do that, huh?"

She grabs me, her beautiful face a mask for fury before it melts.

A woman walks through the door, tossing her hair over her shoulder. "Oh good, Damon, you're awake. We have some things to speak about."

"You told her to go fuck herself?" Luisa asks, her eyes wide.

"Yeah, wouldn't you if you got the chance to do it again?"

She considers this for a second, her head tilted to the side as her eyes narrow. "Yeah, actually, I think I would now that I think about it."

I sit back on the couch, my hands behind my head. "Exactly."

"But you're still here."

But I'm still here.

I was released from the hospital a week later. After telling Veronica to go fuck herself, I did eventually agree to be initiated into the Fallen Angels. I only had a few stipulations.

Those stipulations didn't end up mattering, however, when I wasn't physically cleared to even go on any jobs. Veronica and I are discussing other things I can help with.

Despite my hatred for the project and what they did to Amelia, I saw it as my only option if I wanted to be with her. She also saw it as the only option, which is why Veronica was there in the first place.

She somehow knew I would cave.

When it comes to her, I'm a weak man.

I wouldn't have it any other way.

We've spent the last week living in the Seattle compound, but eventually, we've been discussing buying a house nearby. Amelia is also on medical leave for a bit, but Veronica is trying to pull some strings to make it a little more permanent considering we *did* uncover a giant conspiracy.

We didn't *end* the conspiracy, but at least they know about it now. At least it's out in the open.

We heard from Jerry once, but she's been having some family issues from what I can tell? I'm not sure what that means, but maybe she reached out to her sister. She seemed to be in a particularly foul mood on the phone with Amelia the other day, but she *has* called to ask how we're doing, and I think that counts as love, right?

I've loved taking Cooper for walks with Amelia. The property around the compound is gorgeous, but I've had to refrain from asking her how many bodies are buried in the woods. I really want to know in theory, but I know once I know I'll stress about it until I block it from my mind.

I'm not a killer, and I'm not even going to pretend to be.

Which brings me to one of the last negatives of living in this house with them. The basement. The fucking basement. I've been here for a week, and I've heard voices yelling twice as I walked by the door. Every time I look at Luisa or Amare, they avert their eyes, not wanting to tell me what's going on down there.

I could look for myself, but something tells me I don't want to.

Despite the dead bodies and prisoners, life here is great, and having Amelia all to myself makes it all the better.

"You guys ready?" Amelia asks as she steps into the family room. She's wearing tight jeans and a green T-shirt, one of my favorite outfits on her.

"Finally," Amare whispers under his breath with an eye roll, taking his feet off the coffee table and standing. I get up, heading over to her. I wrap my arms around her waist, pulling her into me and kissing the top of her head.

"Is Coop coming with us?" I ask.

She looks at him, considering it.

"I think it should just be us today," she says finally.

"Who's driving?" Luisa asks.

"I think you should," Amare tells her.

"I drove last time,"

I look between the three as they bicker, feeling joy in my heart at this little family I've created.

For Luisa's infectious smile, and Amare's brotherly words. For Amelia's heart, and for Cooper.

I'm just thankful to be here at all.

I have everything I could ever need.

EPILOGUE

TEN YEARS *later*

Time changes us all. I'm just thankful I got more of it. More time to feel the breeze against my skin, and more time with Amelia.

"Sweetheart, come to bed," I call, interrupting her reading time. She glares at me, tired of my bullshit. I just want to get her back into bed.

"We have an early morning," she reminds me, looking at me suspiciously.

"I know. Still. I want you here."

It's been a long time since I woke up from my coma. It turns out, we both sustained some pretty traumatic injuries that day. Since then, they've found everyone responsible for the conspiracy, taking out the threat.

It took a long time.

But for the help, Amelia and I have been largely left alone.

We still live in Seattle, and we regularly visit Amare and Luisa, but we have our own home here, working with Veronica to make life a little bit better for agents coming in.

ANNA NOEL

Amelia's case was extreme, but the need for therapy and a more sensitive entrance to the Project was established.

Amelia has never been so happy.

Speaking of Amare and Luisa, they're still active in the project. They liked the direction they started to go in, and they like making a difference. We do too, and we're grateful for them. Luisa has talked about retiring soon and adopting. I'm not sure I believe her though, so we'll see.

Amare hasn't spoken of retiring at all, but I'm hoping he does. I'd like someone who can go golfing with me whenever I want. And someone to work on cars with me. I just want my best friend around all the time. Retired life isn't so bad, but it can be boring.

The DC Fallen Angels still keep in contact with us. After that day, Jerry had some, well, some issues to attend to back at the warehouse. The others say she was in a foul mood for months after, but it wasn't because of us.

I can't imagine what it was like to be around her during that time.

We lost Cooper a year ago now, and it broke Amelia. I think she was more heartbroken over his loss than learning about her past. I was too. He was my best friend.

I've been trying to convince her to get a new pet, but she still complains that the loss is too fresh. She can't bear it. I just want to make things easier for her. To make her happy.

Which is why tomorrow, against her wishes, I'm bringing home a new Dalmatian. I know she'll forgive me someday.

"You know, a good husband would let his wife read." She smiles up at me, snuggling into bed.

"I know. But good husbands also do other things to make up for it," I tease, my hand running down her thigh.

"What kind of things?" Her eyes flicker with mischief, and I grin. It's taken a long time, but she's been able to let loose a little more. She's gotten some of her personality back, and I cherish it every single day.

320

I swing my leg over her body, pressing myself into her as I take her lips in mine. "I can think of some things," I tell her.

"Oh yeah? You want to show me?"

I don't know. I like knowing I can make a difference while living peacefully with the one person I care about most in this world.

I wouldn't have it any other way.

Five years later

We walk along the path, pointing out butterflies as they fly around us. Olivia wobbles next to Amelia while Elijah runs around, a stick in his small hands.

"What's that?" Olivia asks, pointing to a tree. I pick her up just as Elijah is about to hit her, and he whacks my legs instead.

"Elijah!" Amelia snaps as I suck in a breath.

"What mom?" He looks up at her with his beautiful blue eyes.

We decided we wanted to adopt a few kids three years ago when the Agency finally handed us our papers, letting us know we're free. My name was never changed, as I worked with them indirectly and didn't need to. I never actually died. There was no reason for a cover up.

Amelia is now Amelia West, and every single time I see the ring glistening on her finger, I smile knowing we have an entire life ahead of us. One that doesn't involve killing people, locking people up, or torture.

We've been happy. Excited to have this piece of happiness to ourselves.

And we love Seattle. Amelia recently discovered a certain vampire movie and has forced us to explore more of the state, but I'd gladly follow her anywhere.

We adopted Elijah and Olivia after hours of discussion, ensuring it was what we really wanted. We never really thought of ourselves as parents, but after what we've seen of the world, we wanted to protect the kids we can. I want to make sure they know they're loved every single day.

"Guys, wait up!" Luisa calls from behind us. I look back, watching her attempt to catch up, Mila in her arms.

Luisa retired two years ago, and it was the best day of her life. To say that she peaked would be an understatement. It was like she was twenty-one again. For about three months, she lived out her wild child dreams before settling down, determined to find a nice man.

She found one.

They adopted Mila a year later.

We stay in our small bubble of peace, protecting our kids as we shield them from the evils of the world. I want to make sure none of them ever have to experience what Amelia did.

"Marshall!" Amelia calls ahead of us. A second later, a Dalmation rounds the corner, bounding up to us as his ears flop, his tongue hanging from his mouth.

Apparently, if you get someone you love a puppy before they're ready to have one, they claim sole naming rights.

It just so happened that in her boredom at the time, she took a specific liking to a certain sitcom character from Minnesota.

"He looks really tall," she had said, hearts in her eyes.

"The actor is an inch shorter than me," I had informed her.

"What does that matter? His Midwestern accent is cool."

"Sweetheart, he grew up in California."

She rolled her eyes at me, waving me off.

Life seems incredibly boring compared to how it was, but is that really such a bad thing?

"Mom, I think I need the Lego set Caden has," Elijah says for the tenth time. He hasn't shut up about it in weeks.

"We'll see my love," Amelia tells him, running her fingers through his hair.

She smiles at me, gorgeous as ever. Her hair is shorter, her worry lines more prominent. Despite what society tells us every time we turn on the TV or look at a newspaper, neither of us cares about signs of aging.

It's physical proof that we have more time left. That we're alive, making the best of this life.

And that's all we can really ask for, right?

SNEAK PEEK

Here is your first look at Project Fallen Angel book two,
Harbinger.

**Subject to change

CHAPTER ONE

Sydney

One of the only things I remember from my childhood is my father murdering a man in cold blood right in front of my eyes. I knew at that moment that I needed to get out.

I was seven.

It didn't take me long to realize my parents weren't good people. Pain and suffering followed them. Followed me. I spent most of my teen years away, and eventually, they stopped calling. Stopped expecting anything of me.

Eventually, I escaped.

So when I got the call on Wednesday that they had died in a tragic accident, I didn't feel anything. I still don't, despite the fake tears running down my face and the perturbation in my heart as old family acquaintances approach me, asking me how I've been.

I've been good. I've been doing fine on my own. I never missed them. Maybe the world will be better now that they're gone. Do you know what they've done? Do you know how many innocents they've killed?

I want to scream. To run away from here. To go back

home, curl up under my covers, and only emerge when this is over.

"Are you okay?" Adam asks, his hand on my upper back.

I nod, running my fingers through my hair, desperately wanting to put it up after an older woman I didn't recognize told me I look so much like my mother. We always had the same flaming red hair, the same green eyes.

"We're definitely going out after this," he tells me, looking around at the hundreds of people who showed up to celebrate my parents' lives. I wonder how many of them are secretly glad they're dead, too.

"I'm going to need a drink for sure," I say, picking up my bag. "I need a second, I'll be in the bathroom."

Adam nods, walking away toward a group of women, a large, charming smile plastered on his face as they look him over. I roll my eyes, shaking my head as I turn the corner toward the hallway, only to recache off of a wide, solid chest.

"Oh I'm so sorry," a deep voice tells me as large, powerful hands steady me.

I give a meek smile as I brush myself off. "It's fine," I start as I finally meet his eyes… and stop.

This man is the definition of tall, dark, and handsome.

He smiles, but it doesn't quite reach his beautiful brown eyes.

There's a moment of silence before he extends his hand, reaching for mine to shake. "Jeremy," he introduces himself as his large hand envelopes mine.

I shakily return the smile, a little suspicious. "Sydney," I tell him, not breaking eye contact for even a second.

Dropping my hand, Jeremy places his in the pockets of his grey slacks, looking around the room. "Nice night, eh?"

My eyebrows shoot up. "If you mean a nice night for my parent's funeral, then yeah, I guess."

His full lips smirk as he meets my eyes once more.

Fucker.

"Now if you excuse me, I was just on my way to the bathroom," I tell him, attempting to get around him, but he steps into my path again, blocking me.

"Get a drink with me later." His hand grabs my arm, and I eye it before my gaze makes its way to his face.

"I don't think so."

"I want to apologize for my comment about tonight. Please. We can just go right next door."

I think about it for a second. I have backup here. Adam has been my trusty sidekick for what feels like ages. One text to him, I'm out. Besides, who could turn down a free drink?

Certainly not me.

I smile, tossing my hair behind my back before looking up at him with my most angelic smile. "Sure, handsome. That sounds great."

———

"I don't know, I just think whales are really cool," I say, taking another sip of my bourbon.

"They are interesting," Jeremy smiles, looking at me over the rim of his glass.

"So what about you?"

"There's not much interesting about me," he starts, looking me up and down once more.

I'm not a stupid girl. I know he's trying to get me drunk. For what reason, I'm not sure. I know there's a possibility of being in danger right now.

Which is why Adam is right across the room, his eyes on me as a woman tosses her hair over her back, grinding into him on the dance floor.

The second this turns weird, I'm out.

"Do you know what happened to your parents?" Jeremy asks, putting his glass down.

"I don't."

"I only met them a couple of times, but they seemed like good people."

I scoff on the inside.

"Yeah, they were okay. I wish I was able to see them before they got cremated."

Their bodies were left unrecognizable. I didn't believe it at first. I thought for sure they were off hiding somewhere. It was something they would do—fake their deaths—but thankfully, it was really them.

I promptly had them cremated.

"I'm sure," he tilts his head, reading me.

I'm in danger, is all I can think.

"I really appreciate you taking me out," I tell him as I stand, teetering on my heels. I launch forward a bit, putting on my best drunk girl act, splashing bourbon all over my front. "Oh my God, I can't believe it. Fuck. I'm so sorry, I have to go clean this up quickly. I'll be right back, handsome."

He nods, smiling a little as I turn my back to him, heading toward the back of the club.

Adam's eyes watch me as I go, knowing not to step in unless I signal for him to.

The second I round the corner, I feel a hand on my arm, dragging me into the corner.

"What the f—"

"Shhh, you're okay, we need to get you away from here," a voice says as they drag me along.

"Who the fuck are you?"

"I think you should have grilled your little friend out there about who he is a little harder."

We walk along a hallway, coming to a large door. The whole place is dark, and I can barely see the man holding me.

"What's happening?"

"He's a cop, princess."

My eyes go round, looking behind us.

"What do you mean"

"The guy was about to take you into custody. They think you have information about your parents."

"I don't, I haven't talked to them in years," I say as he tosses the door open, leading me outside into the dimly lit side street.

He lets go of me, looking from side to side, and I finally catch a glimpse of his face.

He's handsome. His tall frame is tan, and I can't tell whether his hair is black or just a dark brown in the dim light.

He wears a blue Henley and jeans—pure catnip for women like me—and when his deep brown eyes meet mine, I melt.

"Who are you?" I ask again, massaging my wrist.

"Ronan. I'm getting you out of here."

ACKNOWLEDGMENTS

As much as I've thought about writing this series, I haven't really thought about what to put back here. So I'll start simple.

First of all, I want to thank you, the reader, for taking a chance on this book. It was supposed to be a lead magnet book. A short, fast read that just gives you a taste of this new world. I still think it kind of is, considering how long the next ones will be. But I really hope you enjoyed this new world, and I hope you're hungry for more. There are plenty of Easter eggs in here to keep you guessing.

A special thank you to Dotty (@books_with_dott) for the love and support given to me and this book! Thank you to Jules, Maryamm, Lu, Beth, Jennifer (I know you said you don't read these and expect to see yourself there, but you know who you are. Thank you for the love and support!), Bea, Phyllica, Arya, and so many more amazing, wonderful people.

I started writing in eighth grade. Up until then, I didn't have a great English teacher. Someone who really believed in me. That is, until Mrs. Pod. I owe you everything. Without you, I wouldn't be here. The encouragement and love you gave me during a time I didn't really believe in myself, you helped me find my passions, and I'll be forever grateful. I'm hoping we can grab that lunch soon.

I want to thank Ariana Cane, who I also would not be publishing right now if not for. We met randomly on the internet, instantly connecting, and you took a chance on me and trusted me with your books. We've both grown and learned over the last almost TWO YEARS of working together, and I've learned so much from our time together. I would not have the courage and knowledge I do without our time together, even when we drive each other absolutely insane. I hope we're both on top of the world together soon.

Thank you to Darlene, who has been with me since the very beginning YEARS ago now. I'm so happy I've been on this journey with you and that we've stayed friends for so long.

I want to thank my boyfriend Alex, who has been there for me for the last ten-plus years, supporting me as my best friend when I was first writing online. I still smile when you open up a browser and I see my online writing saved in your bookmarks. I haven't posted anything in 8 years or so. I love you endlessly, and your love and support means the most.

A thank you to Stacey R. for being so open about your love for smutty books YEARS ago before they got so big, and before I started reading them. I still constantly go "Oh I wonder if Stacey would love this."

Finally, to the rest of my friends and family for always supporting my writing over the years. I have so many more books coming, and I hope I can make you proud. Even if the books are smutty. Sorry to my grandparents.

Thank you to every single person who is reading this. I hope you can see yourself in one of my characters, and I hope you go easy on yourself.

So much love,

Anna

TERMS

Agent: A person unofficially employed by an intelligence service. They are usually used as a source of information.

Agent-in-place: A government employee who is influenced by a spy to cooperate with a foreign government instead of defecting. These agents work for two employers rather than one.

Agent-of-influence: Someone who works within the government or media of a target country to influence policy.

Asset: A clandestine source or method, usually an agent.

Babysitter: Bodyguard

Bang and Burn: Demolition and sabotage operations.

Black Bag Job: Secret entry into a home of office with the intention of stealing or copying materials.

Black Operations: Covert operations that are not attributable to the organization permitting them.

Black Propaganda: Disinformation that is deniable by its source, and cannot be traced back to them.

Blown: The discovery of an agent's true identity or a clandestine activity's real purpose.

Brush Pass: A brief encounter where something is passed between case officer and agent.

Burned: When a case officer or agent is compromised.

CIA: Central Intelligence Agency; The United States's foreign intelligence gathering service.

Cipher: A system for disguising messages by replacing letters with other letters or numbers. They can also be shuffled.

Clandestine Operation: An intelligence operation designed to remain secret

Cobbler: A spy who creates false passports, visas, diplomas, and other documents.

Code: A system for disguising a message by replacing its words with groups of letters or numbers.

Codebook: A list of plain language words opposite their codeword or number.

Compromised: An operation, asset, or agent uncovered that cannot remain secret.

Controller: Officer in charge of agents (a handler).

Dead Drop: A secret location where materials can be left for another party to retrieve.

Discard: An agent whom a service will permit to be detected and arrested so as to protect more valuable agents

Dry Clean: Actions agents take to determine if they are under surveillance.

Escort: An operations officer assigned to lead a defector along an escape route.

Espionage: The practice of spying or using spies to obtain secret or confidential information about the plans and activities or a foreign government or competing company.

Exfiltration Operation: A clandestine rescue operation designed to bring defector, refugee, or an operative and his or her families out of harm's way.

FBI: Federal Bureau of Investigation; U.S.'s domestic counterintelligence service and federal law enforcement agency.

Ghoul: An agent who searches obituaries and graveyards for names of the deceased for use by agents.

Handler: A case officer who is responsible for handling agents in operations.

Honey Trap: Men or women using sexual situations to intimidate or snare others.

Infiltration: The secret movement of an operative into a target area with the intent that his or her presence will go undetected.

Intelligence Officer: Professionals trained by governments. Most often called case officers, operational officers, or handlers, they run operations and recruit and manage spies.

Legend: A spy's claimed background or biography, usually supported by documents and memorized details.

NSA: National Security Agency; branch of the U.S. Department of Defense responsible for ensuring the security of American communications and for breaking into the communications of other countries.

Pattern: The behavior and daily routine of an operative that makes his or her identity unique

Playback: To provide false information to the enemy while gaining accurate information from him or her.

Spy: In the intelligence world, a spy is strictly defined as someone used to steal secrets for an intelligence organization. Also called an agent or asset, a spy is not a professional intelligence officer, and doesn't usually receive formal training (though may be taught basic tradecraft).

Spymaster: The leader of espionage activities, and an agent handler

Station: Post from where espionage is conducted.

Throwaway: An agent considered expendable

Wet Job: An operation in which blood is shed.

ABOUT THE AUTHOR

Anna Noel is a dark action romance writer based in Upstate New York. Getting her start writing when she was only 11 years old, Anna made it her life's mission to build a career around books.

Anna has been writing and selling plots to authors for over 7 years, and went full-time with her freelance writing career in 2020. Since then, she's worked as a copywriter, plot writer, eulogy writer, and ghostwriter.

Anna has been working on her Project Fallen Angel series for years and is looking forward to finally publishing them!

When she's not writing, Anna can be found watching Star Wars, cheering on the Baltimore Orioles and Ravens, cooking, and hanging out with her two cats and boyfriend.

Her website: https://www.goodreads.com/author/show/29903584.Anna_Noel

Connect with Anna to stay up to date.

Printed in the USA
CPSIA information can be obtained
at www.ICGtesting.com
LVHW101233211223
766988LV00071B/2986